A Duel
to the Death!

Britt and Standing Bear faced one another across the yawning pit. Both men leaned back into the rope, stretching it taut as they nervously awaited Little Buffalo's command.

"Impesa," the *to-yop-ke* shouted.

Unexpectedly, Standing Bear leaped forward, throwing slack into the tight, quivering rope.

The lousy, sneaking sonovabitch, thought Britt. *Mary warned me! Warned me!*

Grasping the rope, Britt hurtled across the pit and charged forward. For a moment in time the men's eyes met in a frozen exchange of understanding. There was no question of asking or granting quarter, for one man must die, and neither would have expected any less from the other. . . .

Books by Matthew Braun

Black Fox
Cimarron Jordan
Mattie Silks
The Savage Land

Published by POCKET BOOKS

Matthew Braun

BLACK FOX

PUBLISHED BY POCKET BOOKS NEW YORK

All characters in this book are fictional, and any resemblance
to persons living or dead is purely coincidental.

 POCKET BOOKS, a Simon & Schuster division of
GULF & WESTERN CORPORATION
1230 Avenue of the Americas, New York, N.Y. 10020

To
Bettiane
The unwavering one

AUTHOR'S NOTE

The saga of Britt Johnson is not a myth. Black men seldom became legends on the frontier, and this former slave proved no exception. Yet the story of his audacity and fearlessness is as real as any to emerge from Western folklore. While his name appears only briefly in the historical chronicles of Young County, Texas, the daring task he undertook ranks high among the boldest deeds recorded in the annals of the West.

Though events depicted in *Black Fox* are historically accurate, certain liberties have been taken regarding time and place. Something over seven hundred Comanches and Kiowas did join forces to raid Young County for the very reasons described in this book. However, the unusual magnitude of this raid has tended to overshadow the awesome courage of a lone black man who risked his life to ransom the women and children taken captive by the hostiles.

Britt Johnson actually made four trips into Indian Territory, each time unaccompanied and with nothing more than his own cunning to protect him from the hazards involved. These daring sorties were not prompted by thought of reward or fame, but rather by the black man's love for his own family and an enduring compassion for the plight of his white neighbors. And the hazards were very real indeed.

Many historians credit the Comanches and Kiowas with killing more settlers, particularly Texans, than any of the southern Plains tribes. They were a proud, fierce people, closely allied for more than a century, and they bitterly resented the white man's encroachment on their ancestral hunting grounds. For any tejano (Texan), black or white, to venture north of the Red River in that day and time was considered both foolhardy and tantamount to suicide. Yet this was exactly what Britt Johnson did *not once but four times*. Had he not been a black man, his name would have undoubtedly become as renowned as the most legendary of frontier scouts.

The saga of Britt Johnson's courage and ultimate death at the hands of the Kiowas actually encompassed seven years. For the purposes of this narrative, his harrowing adventures have been compressed into a single year. While certain aspects of *Black Fox* are pure invention, the story is essentially true and accurate in detail. Possibly even more astounding than the tale itself is the fact that this black man's singular exploits have remained nothing more than a footnote to history for over a century.

MATTHEW BRAUN

BLACK FOX

CHAPTER ONE

1

The wagon lurched along a rutted trail, from a distance its
swaying motion a mere wavering speck in the vastness of
the rolling plains. Stretching to the horizon, the unbroken
terrain shimmered hypnotically in the heat waves from the
sun. Low hills obscured broad valleys beyond, and from
the crest of any given hilltop the viewer observed nothing
more startling than an identical series of stunted elevations.
Three days' journey to the west lay the trackless reaches of
the true Plains, a barren waste devoid of trees or vegetation. Once a man had sampled the inhospitality of that
land, the undulating landscape of north-central Texas
came almost as a relief. Still there was a stark emptiness
to the rolling plains, which made the occasional creek or
shallow-bottomed river all the more appreciated. Here a
man could rest in the shade of the massive oaks and wil-
lowy cottonwoods fringing the prairie tributaries and escape the relentless heat.

2

Braced against the jarring impact of the wagon, Allan and Britt Johnson clung precariously to their seats as the team of sorrels gingerly traversed the pitted track which skirted the Brazos River. Roads were as yet a luxury in the frontier regions of Texas, and when traveling by wagon, the choice between trails or cross-country was determined more by habit then any real sense of convenience. Shifting in their seats as the wagon wheels struck a solid bed of rock, the two men stared wordlessly at the twisting track unraveling before them. Since they had been traveling steadily for two hours, conversation had gradually given way to the resigned silence of those who prefer to endure a jolting wagon without complaint. Occasionally they sighted a house set back away from the river, but the ramshackle dwellings hardly seemed worthy of comment. Neither of the men was especially garrulous, at any rate, sharing a somewhat taciturn disposition. Behind them a distance of some ten miles lay the juncture of Elm Creek and the Brazos, and after an uneventful morning on the trail it seemed apparent that nothing remarkable had happened to the settlers along the way during the winter. Lacking anything of significance to discuss, they both felt more comfortable with the silence; the quiet of strong men whose companionship had withstood the test of time and no longer required the crutch of idle conversation.

Although Allan and Britt bore the same surname and both dressed in the coarse linsey of frontiersmen, the similarity between them ended there. Allan was of medium height and rawhide lean, with the sandy hair and deepset eyes which instantly marked unbroken generations of Anglo-Saxon heritage. When he spoke, his voice betrayed the soft inflections of a native-born Southerner, and something about his manner evoked the cultured gentry of magnolia-studded cotton plantations. While strangers could only surmise, those who knew Allan intimately were well aware that his family had once belonged to the Southern aristocracy. The dissipations of a wastrel father, who subscribed to the theory that gaming rooms and bordellos presented a greater challenge than the pastoral life, ultimately brought the family to ruin. Shortly afterward, the elder

Johnson died from the residual effects of his debauchery, and Allan resolutely determined to seek a new start for the family on the frontier. Enroute, his mother also died, and with her passing an era had ended for the once distinguished family.

Of all the Johnsons, Britt's life was least affected by the sudden change in fortune. For Britt was black, a former slave. And what a man had never possessed could hardly be wrested from him by the caprice of fate. Born to parents who were themselves the children of slaves, his heritage was a curious blend of savage courage fused with docile servitude. As if a predator cat had been crossed with a cream-fed tabby, the mutation that resulted was neither wild nor tame. Much like trained tigers who have surrendered their freedom for a warm cage and full belly, what was once a race of warriors had grown obedient to the lash and humble beyond all understanding.

But unlike his fellow blacks Britt had been graced with a master of enormous compassion. Opposed to slavery solely on the basis of its essential inhumanity, Allan found the degrading of another human being the most repugnant aspect of plantation life. On his twenty-first birthday Allan inherited Britt as a manservant; he immediately renounced the legacy by declaring his newly acquired slave a freedman. But the bond between them remained impervious to a mere declaration of freedom. They had been raised together, separated only by a year in age, and the difference in their color had never proved a deterrent to the closeness they shared. Allan's rashness had marked him as a rebel among the gentry, and those in the slave compounds were equally astounded when word spread that Britt had elected to remain in the service of his former master.

When the Johnson fortune crumbled and Allan turned his eyes to the frontier, Britt once again chose to accompany his lifelong friend. Privately they made a pact that everything acquired on the Texas plains, be it land or wealth, would be held jointly. And in Allan's brassbound strongbox there resided a document of incontrovertible legality which provided Britt and his heirs a full share in all future holdings.

Accompanied by their wives and children, Allan and Britt arrived in Texas only four short years after the battle at San Jacinto. Wandering ever westward, they had searched for land that would lend itself to both farming and cattle raising and had finally homesteaded on Elm Creek a few miles east of the Brazos.

Over the ensuing decade the fertile bottomland proved exceptionally bountiful, and with each passing year their herd of rangy longhorns required more space on the open grazing lands to the west. Prosperity and good fortune had once more returned to the Johnsons, and their decade of toil on the merciless plains had drawn the two men even closer. Seated before the fireplace during the winter of 1860, Allan and Britt had listened to the howling blizzards beating at the door and remarked that the last ten years had indeed been a time of plenty for the Johnsons of Elm Creek.

Spring had come early that year, with the chill winds giving way to warm breezes almost overnight. Where ravaged clumps of brown grass struggled for existence only a fortnight ago, there now flourished a succulent green sea of knee-high graze. Brilliant colors sparkled throughout the gently rolling grasslands, as if nature had robbed from every hue in the spectrum. Absorbed in nature's handiwork as the wagon jolted along the river trail, Britt felt a renewed sense of awe that a stark and ofttimes hostile land could produce such lurid beauty. Bluebonnets spread widely across the plains like deep cerulean pools, and on the hillsides mountain pinks flamed as if the earth had burst forth in molten greeting to the warming rays of spring. Sunflowers reached skyward with tawny, golden delicacy, and like spots of melting snow on the prairie, daisies wove a hoary carpet through the lush green grasses.

Britt was suddenly struck by the deceptive contradictions of the Plains, the awesome spectacle of its vast, serene beauty that, as easily as not, could conceal any number of dreadful fates just over the next rise.

3

While his mind was preoccupied with such thoughts, the wagon crested a slight knoll, and Fort Belknap came into view. A sense of relief swept over him as it had many times in the past; the instinctive waning of tenseness experienced by any man once the ever constant dangers of the Plains are left behind. Although Britt frequently chided himself for this wary attitude, he realized it was a carry-over from a decade of ceaseless raiding by the Indians and would doubtless remain a habit for the rest of his life. Indian Territory lay only a day's ride north of the Elm Creek settlement, and almost from the moment the first homesteader broke ground, the Comanches and Kiowas had retaliated with a prolonged nightmare of bloody raids.

The rolling terrain of north-central Texas had once been the prime hunting grounds of the southern Plains tribes. Until the arrival of the first settlers in the 1830s the prairie lands west of Fort Worth had teemed with game of every description, particularly with immense herds of buffalo. Since the Indians depended on this shaggy-coated beast for their very existence, they were understandably enraged that the white-eyes had violated their sacred hunting preserve. With the appearance of plowed fields and herds of longhorn cattle, the game animals were driven even farther west, and the Indians reacted with savage violence.

Each spring brought a resurgence of the terrible raids, leaving the Plains strewn with scalped settlers and burning homesteads. Only with the first frost and the blinding fury of winter's blizzards did the Comanches and Kiowas halt their bloody depredations. Wintering in the sheltered valleys of the Wichita Mountains, they patiently endured the swirling storms, awaiting only the first signs of spring to resume their war against the hated tejanos.

With characteristic sluggishness the government finally acted to save the settlers of its newest state. Troops poured into Texas at an accelerated pace, establishing a chain of forts across the western Plains. Fort Belknap became a pivital command post for the army, with Fort Richardson located twenty miles to the east and Fort Griffin an equal distance to the southwest. Situated on the Brazos, approximately ten miles below Elm Creek, Fort Belknap's cantonment area rapidly spread across the irregular terrain, eventually housing close to a regiment of troops. As if to compensate for their past indifference, the army took the field with a vengeance and carried the war to the Indians. Striking with unrelenting ferocity, their campaign forced the Plains tribes ever backward. Step by step the Indians retreated, until ultimately they were driven to sanctuary in the vast, unmapped wilderness of Indian Territory. Retaliation was swift and final whenever the Indians dared even a token raid, and by the close of the 1850s the

Comanches and Kiowas seldom ventured below the south
bank of the Red River.

Peace had come at last to the western Plains, and the
unyielding encroachment of the whites now seemed complete. As Allan and Britt rolled through the front gate of
Fort Belknap in their wagon that cloudless spring morning,
there had not been an Indian raid on the Elm Creek settlement in over two years.

4

The fort was a beehive of activity that morning, swarming
with knots of soldiers, freighters, and meat hunters. Spring
had arrived, and every man on the post was eager to shake
the enforced lethargy of winter with a furious burst of energy. Nonetheless, they each paused in their work, nodding
and smirking as the wagon moved onto the road which
skirted the parade ground. Allan Johnson and his freed
slave were well known in and around Fort Belknap. Over
the years, they had become a subject of curiosity, if not
outright envy, due to their rapidly expanding ranch on Elm
Creek. Although few men dared to cross the Johnsons
openly, they looked on Allan with studied contempt for
having so casually freed a black man. For the most part,
soldiers and settlers alike would never accumulate the necessary wealth to invest in slaves. Owning another human
being was a godlike pursuit seldom attempted by any except gentry. And they deeply resented a man who displayed such offhanded indifference to the principal status
symbol of the day.

Envy, of course, was an emotion that no white man
would admit regarding the black half of the Johnson family. Nevertheless, there was undisguised bitterness toward
Britt, often of a more overt nature than that expressed for
Allan. Within the compound and throughout the various
settlements of the area he was known simply as Nigger
Britt, which identified him in terms of both name and rank
in the social order of the white man's newly acquired
Plains kingdom. While the name was rarely used more
than once in Allan's presence, it was in common usage
among the settlers themselves. Circumstances being what
they were, Britt had finally learned to grit his teeth and
hear only that part of the derisive appellation which he

wished to hear. But there were still times when he would have liked to ram the white man's mockery back down his throat with a meaty fist.

Ignoring the stares, Britt jumped lightly to the ground as Allan brought the wagon to a halt before the sutler's store. For a big man he moved with uncommon litheness, betraying a deceptive speed and agility beneath the corded bulk of his shoulders. Although he was raised to be a manservant and never experienced the back-breaking labors of a field hand, Britt had still inherited the towering stance and awesome bulk of his primeval ancestors.

Regardless of their superior attitude and patronizing smirks, no white man had ever risked provoking Britt to the point of physical confrontation. And even in the provincial outcountry of the Plains, it seemed that intolerance and malice had been tempered with equal parts of discretion. The fact that Britt confidently wore a Colt Navy .36 was also a matter of some conjecture among the white community. On more than one occasion he had used it with indisputable results against the Comanches, which doubtless gave pause for thought to those who had been reared in the belief that black men rarely possessed the backbone for a fight to the finish.

Side by side, Allan and Britt mounted the creaky stairs and entered the sutler's store. Stony faced, they ignored the loafers on the front porch, who had stopped talking and were watching their progress with amused winks at one another.

Sutler's stores normally restricted their trade to army personnel. But since the nearest civilian merchant was in Weatherford, some fifty miles distant, the post commander allowed settlers to replenish staples on a limited basis. Colonel Jason McKensie had proven to be a friend to the homesteaders in many ways during his tour of duty, not the least of which was permitting them to purchase necessities whenever weather or events prevented the long trip back to civilization. Passing barrels of dried fruit and an ancient potbellied stove, the two men crossed the dimly lighted store and stopped before the counter.

"Morning, Mr. Phillips," Allan said, leaning across the counter to look down the aisle where the sutler was seated at a makeshift desk.

Turning from his preoccupation with a set of ledgers, the storekeeper smiled broadly and walked toward them.

"Good morning, Mr. Johnson. Haven't seen you since that last big storm." Glancing over the counter at Britt, he nodded. "Britt, see you made it through the winter."

"Nothin' to it, Mr. John," Britt responded with a faint grin. "All you've got to do is breathe in more than you breathe out."

Unsure if the black man's remark wasn't slightly mocking, the merchant ignored him and looked back to Allan. "Well, what can we do for you this fine spring day, Mr. Johnson?"

"Got a list all made out," Allan replied, tossing a battered scrap of paper on the counter. "Hope you can get to it right way. We'd like to make it back to the place before dark."

"Certainly, no problem at all. Just make yourself to home while I start gathering these things."

The sutler began moving from shelf to shelf, selecting items as he glanced at the list. Allan and Britt wandered casually through the store, pausing to inspect goods they had seen many times before. Like most back country people, they never quite lost their fascination for the profusion of items stocked by merchants, almost as if they were overawed by the sheer abundance lining the bins and shelves. Moving quickly from counter to shelf and back again, the sutler began a none-too-subtle probe for the latest gossip as the pile of goods started to accumulate.

"How's everyone over Elm Creek way? Haven't heard much from you folks most of the winter."

"Getting along just fine," Allan said, absorbed in reading the label on a bottle of patent medicine. "Old man Whittiker passed away, and there's two new babies, but nothing of any real consequence, I guess you'd say."

"That's a shame," Phillips commented. Without clarifying whether he meant the death or the births, he resumed without pause. "What do you folks over there think of this new President we've got?"

"Mr. Lincoln?" Allan asked. "Oh, I guess most of our people aren't too happy with a Northern Republican in office. Course, some folks have trouble seeing the good in anything if it's not just according to their own ways." Allan and Britt exchanged glances, and the black man cut his eyes at the sutler, shaking his head in amusement.

"Well, it takes all kinds," the merchant replied cryptically. "On the other hand, though, I hear lots of people saying he's going to split this country right down the middle. And if it comes to that, then we all might as well pack it in."

"Maybe," Allan said. "But it's always been my experience that most fights are started by hot air more than anything else."

"Well, you never know, do you, Mr. Johnson?" Phillips huffed. "You just never know."

Grunting, the sutler began searching through a bin for a spool of thread, and they could hear him mumbling fitfully to himself. Britt smiled fully at Allan, delighted that his friend had gigged the busybody on the prongs of his own shaft. Without further attempt at conversation the merchant toted up the charge and sacked their provisions in burlap bags. The Johnsons hefted their sacks, nodding to Phillips' curt thanks, and strolled unhurriedly through the front door. Both of them were well pleased with the way the morning had started. Crossing the porch they again chose to ignore the loafers' sudden lapse in conversation. Heaving the bags over the side of the wagon, they walked forward and climbed onto the seat.

Suddenly there was a commotion at the front gate, and a sentry's urgent shout carried across the cantonment, "Corporal of the guard!" That instant a mounted courier raced through the gate at a full gallop, sending chunks of turf flying as he bypassed the road and thundered straight across the parade ground. Reining his lathered horse to a halt before headquarters, the trooper dismounted and darted inside, leaving the wind-blown animal heaving and gasping for breath.

5

Allan and Britt remained in their seats for a moment, watching curiously. Then settlers and freighters started streaming toward headquarters from every part of the post, and within minutes a large crowd had assembled in front of the building. Dismounting, the two men hurried across the parade ground and joined the excited crowd. Speculation was rife, and as the murmuring voices swelled in volume, it seemed that each man present had a different opinion as to the courier's dramatic arrival.

At that moment the headquarters' door flew open, and

several regimental officers rushed from the building, moving grim faced and purposefully toward the barracks areas. Close on their heels, Colonel McKensie appeared in the doorway and stepped to the edge of the porch. The crowd grew silent as they noted his foreboding expression, and he observed them closely for a moment, as if collecting his thoughts. Then he seemed to straighten slightly, and the impassive mask of a professional soldier covered his features once more.

"Men, I've got some bad news," McKensie called in a grave voice. "The Southern states have seceded from the Union, and civil war has broken out."

Bedlam swept over the crowd as several men began shouting questions at the officer while others stared at one another with stunned disbelief. Many of those with Southern sympathies were elated beyond words, slapping each other on the back; laughing and yelling like schoolboys who had just been challenged to a snowball fight. Raising his arms for quiet, Colonel McKensie's voice carried over the steady din of the gathering.

"Quiet! Let me have your attention! Now all the details will be posted later, but for the moment you should know that both the North and South are mobilizing armies, and it appears there will be a major battle sometime soon. Since Texas no longer considers itself a member of the Union, we are in effect standing on foreign soil. My command has been ordered east to Fort Leavenworth, and we will depart wthin forty-eight hours. In the meantime, if further information becomes available, I will see that it is passed on to you immediately."

With that McKensie turned to enter the building. The roar of the crowd once more swelled to a fever pitch, and already the two factions which now comprised their severed ranks were eyeing one another with undisguised hostility. Suddenly, like the popper of a bullwhip, the sharp crack of Allan Johnson's voice sliced across the cantonment area.

"Colonel McKensie!"

The crowd fell silent and turned to stare, puzzled by the rage so apparent in Allan's harsh tone. McKensie halted in his tracks as if stung by the command, and then spun about, sweeping the men with a piercing glare in an effort to locate the one who had shouted. Allan separated

from the crowd and moved forward, halting a few paces
from McKensie.

"Colonel, if I understand you right, you and your men
are pulling out, which means the settlement people are
left to fend for themselves. Have you got any idea what'll
happen when the Comanches and Kiowas get wind of
that?"

"Mr. Johnson, soldiers don't make wars, they only fight
them," McKensie snapped, his voice tight and strained.
"This command is under orders, and whether it suits you or
not, that's how it stands."

"Orders be damned!" Allan shouted. "The minute you
ride out that gate the Indian raids will start all over again,
and this country will be knee deep in dead babies and
raped women. Do you want that on your conscience?"

"Lower your voice, sir, unless you want to spend the
night in the guard house. You seem to have forgotten that
the South started this war. Texas is the one that seceded
from the Union, and I suggest you look to Texas for protection!"

Turning on his heels, McKensie marched into the headquarters building and slammed the door with rattling
force. For a moment the crowd stood silent, eyeing Allan
uncertainly. Then the Union men began drifting toward
the sutler's store, declaring raucously that the occasion
called for drinks all around.

Sobered by Allan's brutal statements, the settlers
gathered in a somber knot. Glancing at one another with
apprehension, the men shuffled from foot to foot and pondered the dismal situation. Finally a leathery-faced
homesteader from the Graham settlement spoke what was
in the mind of every man present.

"Johnson, it appears to me you done hit the nail square
on the head. Come summer, this here country's gonna be
crawlin' with Injuns, and a white man won't have no more
chance'n a woodpecker in a rock quarry. I don't know
about you boys, but I'm gonna load up my family and
git the hell back to civilization."

"Mister, if you're bent on running, then you'd best get
started," Allan growled. "Personally I didn't break my
back for ten years just to let a bunch of scraggly-assed
Indians send me down the road."

Glancing around, Allan caught sight of Britt, and
the black man smiled shallowly, nodding his head with

approval. Allan's mind stopped whirling for just a moment, and it occurred to him that with a score of men like Britt he'd take on the whole damn Comanche nation. Suddenly it dawned on him what must be done, and he signaled for Britt to follow as he strode rapidly toward the hitching rack in front of the sutler's store.

6

The horse felt good under Britt. The smooth, rocking motion of the animal's steady lope seemed to stimulate both his mind and his body. Watching the countryside rush by as they pounded north along the Brazos, he realized that since settling in Texas, he had become a real Plainsman. The manner by which a person traveled from one point to another had once been a matter of complete insignificance. But the vast, hostile distances of the Plains quickly reshaped a man's attitudes. After a decade on the frontier he now found himself openly scornful of anything less reliable than a fleet, sure-footed cow pony. The horse he was now astride, while adequate and certainly not a crowbait, was a far cry from the powerful mustangs he and Allan had broken to saddle. But then, under the circumstances, he really had no leeway to be critical of another man's horse.

Allan had stormed into the sutler's store and offered a hundred dollars to the first man who laid the reins of a horse in his hand. That amount of money represented three or four months wages to most men, double the value of an ordinary horse, and when the dust settled, a grizzled meat hunter had led the rush to accept Allan's startling offer. Within moments Britt was mounted and galloping through the front gate. Allan's plan was simple and direct, and unless the situation changed drastically, it was the only way left open to the settlers. A meeting must be called among the Elm Creek homesteaders, and before the night was out, they would have to organize in some manner to protect their settlement.

The army had abandoned them, and with Texas mobilizing troops to fight a civil war, it seemed obvious that the settlers must look to their own defenses. Otherwise, their only alternative was to forsake the land and homes they had struggled so hard to wrest from the wilderness.

Britt was to alert the settlers to the outbreak of war, emphasizing the strong likelihood of renewed Indian raids, and to urge everyone to attend a meeting at the Johnson ranch that night.

Slowing the horse to allow him a breather, Britt's thoughts focused on this unforeseen and now imminent danger to his family and the bountiful life they had found in the West. From the day Allan freed him and their immigration to Texas shortly thereafter, Britt had known a serenity which rarely came to those of 'his race. With Allan's steadfast patronage he was building a secure and substantial future for his children. A legacy bequeathing not only legal freedom but, equally significant, the material independence that would allow them to deal with their white neighbors on a basis of live and let live. Certainly a black man was still a nigger, even in the West, but somehow it was different from the South. Perhaps frontiersmen had all they could do just to stay alive and, as a result, had neither the time nor the energy for preoccupation with fine caste distinctions. Whatever the reason, it was a damn sight more gratifying to be a nigger on the Brazos than it was to have been a liveried manservant back on the plantation.

Not that the frontier didn't have its share of bigots and fiery-eyed racists. Farther south, in the fertile Blacklands of central Texas, there were any number of cotton plantations. And in every sense of the word, a black man's life there was undiluted old South nigger from dawn to dusk. But on the outer reaches of the frontier, where life was an unrelenting struggle for mere survival, there was a tolerant outlook about the time-honored prejudices of civilized men. Certainly the whites of Elm Creek displayed a superior attitude around Britt, and there were many who even evidenced something akin to loathing or hate. But in the main, they were willing to accept him as a freedman and a member of the settlement, albeit one of a peculiar and somewhat ill-defined station.

Of course, he had often mused on the fact that his family comprised the only blacks in Elm Creek, and it was an interesting pastime to speculate on the marked change that would occur should every family suddenly acquire their own resident nigger. Still, it was doubtless more pleasant to remain the community freak, and it had never especially bothered him to be surrounded by a sea of curious, if somewhat aloof, white faces.

Rounding a bend in the river, Britt sighted the juncture with Elm Creek, and his thoughts were once more wrenched back to the more immediate problem. Although he was a long way from gaining the spontaneous acceptance of his white neighbors, there were more pressing concerns on the not-too-distant horizon. For the moment he would have to remain content with the fact that he and his family were allowed to live in peace. Chuckling to himself, Britt momentarily pondered the irony of having won a niche in the white man's world only to find that it was now being threatened by a race for whom he instinctively felt great empathy. The Indians were just beginning to experience the calculated ruthlessness of the white man. His people had trudged through two centuries with that yoke of oppression shackled around their necks, and without probing the thought too deeply, he sensed that the blacks and the Indians were only shortly removed from sharing a bitter repugnance for the white man's callous superiority. Spurring the horse, Britt turned onto the trail bordering Elm Creek and tried to convince himself that the warning he carried was still an alarm against the true enemy.

7

The boundless prairie sky seemed cluttered with a profusion of stars as the men began arriving on horseback. Creaking saddle leather and voices raised in sober greeting shattered the stillness of the night, and within an hour after dusk the yard was filled with settlers. Standing in small groups or squatting down with their backs against the house, they spoke in muted tones, and the intensity of the words laid bare the depth of their concern.

While they would hardly have thought of themselves as frontiersmen, there was a distinct, roughhewn sameness to their appearance. They were dressed in coarse clothing with pants stuffed in cowhide boots and worn pistols strapped around their waists. Their features were windburned and wrinkled beyond their years from constant exposure to the relentless Plains sun. Although the majority had not yet reached forty, their faces seemed leathery, with the grainy surface of poorly tanned rawhide, and the visage of each man reflected the deprivation and hardship they had endured. Their eyes were the eyes of old men, wary and passionless, cold pools mirroring the death and suffering they had outlived to wrench an existence from the hostile plains.

Many were the descendants of men who had once challenged the frontiers of Kentucky and Tennessee, and rather than social position or wealth, their legacy was the irresistible urge to follow the sun and take root where few men dared to linger. They were hard men, accustomed to death in its multiplicity of forms, and in the face of threat they could display the brutal savagery of those who have come to grips with the compromise between conscience and survival. On this still, starlit night, however, their thoughts dwelt not on the danger to themselves, but rather on the unspeakable horrors which awaited their loved ones at the hands of the Comanches and Kiowas.

The conversation ceased, and a silence fell over the men as the rattling sounds of a wagon approached from the darkness. Moments later the wagon came to a halt before the house and Tom Fitzpatrick, the Johnson's closest neighbor, leaped to the ground. Nodding to the curious men, he helped his wife and two children to dismount, and the family walked slowly toward the house. Fitzpatrick was a man of formidable bulk, strapping and husky, with pugnacious features and hands scarred from a lifetime of meaningless brawls. His sandy hair and flashing blue eyes were in keeping with an ungovernable Irish temper, and more than one man in the group had reason to respect the deadliness of his sledgehammer fists.

Fitzpatrick was generally liked and even admired by some, but for the most part men moved cautiously around him, as they would a surly dog or a temperamental stallion. There hovered about him the unpredictability of a wild beast. As he approached the house, the men remained silent, having long since learned that the wisest course was to fathom his mood before testing his humor.

Soft light spilling through the open door created a distorted shadow as Allan stepped into the yard. The men gathered closer, some greeting him by name, and it was readily apparent that the gravity of the meeting had dissipated the jocular manner which they normally enjoyed. Allan glanced around the group, nodding solemnly to the grim faces, quickly satisfying himself that the men of the Elm Creek settlement were present.

Before him stood eighteen men and three boys.

"Glad you could all make it," he announced. "We've got a lot to settle tonight, so why don't you come inside and find a seat while the women serve coffee."

Quietly the men trooped into the house and took seats around the large main room. Sarah Johnson bustled about the kitchen area, busily filling crockery mugs with steaming coffee. Mary, Britt's wife, moved around the room with a tray, serving the men as quickly as they found seats. The Johnson children, Allan's two girls and Britt's two boys and a daughter, stared round-eyed from a corner in the dining area, completely overawed by the presence of so many men. Elizabeth Fitzpatrick quickly seated her own children, a boy and a girl, with the Johnson children and then joined Mary in serving coffee. Within minutes the room was settled, and the somber group sat clutching their mugs, waiting expectantly for Allan to begin. Standing near the fireplace, he stooped to light his pipe with a stick of kindling, then turned to face the men.

"By now you all know the situation. The army is pulling out, and we're faced with the choice of defending ourselves or running. Not a man in this room doubts that the Indians will start raiding as soon as the troops are gone, and I expect everyone here still remembers what that means." Allan paused as the men shifted in their seats and glanced apprehensively at one another, all too clearly aware of what they could expect from the Kiowas and Comanches. "Just so you won't be grasping at straws, I'll tell you now that I spent the afternoon raisin' hell with Colonel McKensie, and there's not even an outside chance he'll give us any help. He's leaving day after tomorrow, and when he goes, every last trooper goes with him. I suppose the first thing we've got to decide is how many of you are going to stay and how many plan on leaving. After we know that, then we can figure out what has to be done next."

Many of the men dropped their heads, wrestling with conflicting emotions as they stared at the floor. Their dreams and years of sacrifice were weighed against the devastation they knew would come. The choice to stand and possibly die or run and start over again now forced each man to search the depths of his own soul. Jonathan Hamby, a thin, ferret-faced man of outspoken views, slowly rose to his feet when it became clear that no one wanted to be the first to speak.

"Seems to me we're losin' sight of the main issue," Hamby said. "Whether your loyalties are North or South, this country's at war, and our first responsibility is to take part in that fight."

"Jonathan, every man has to do what he thinks is right," Allan replied. "If a man feels he has to take part in the war, then that's what he'd best do. Personally I don't feel like I owe the government a thing. North or South. I figure we're going to have all the fight we can handle right here, and if somebody doesn't hold the frontier, then this country will be set back a hundred years by the time the war's over in the East. Britt's staying, and Tom Fitzpatrick is moving his family in with mine for added protection, but it's going to take more than three men to hold the settlement. Right now the only thing I'm interested in is how many of you are going to stay with us."

"Well, I don't know how the rest of you feel, but what Allan says makes sense to me." Grady Bragg spoke from his chair without rising. Somewhat older than the others, normally reserved and slow to take the lead, he was a rotund little man who somehow always managed to look ill at ease on a horse. "We took this country, and the Indians weren't able to drive us off even before the army came. So I reckon it's like Allan says, we don't owe the government a damn thing. But we sure as hell owe it to ourselves and our families to hold onto what we've grubbed and rooted to make out of this country."

There was a murmur of assent from some of the group. Joel Meyer and Bud Williams nodded emphatically and voiced their determination to stand and fight. But others were either skeptical of the settlement's chances against overpowering Indian forces, or else felt that their main obligation was to Texas and the South. Within moments a heated argument broke out amongst the group, and as the acrimony swelled in volume, Tom Fitzpatrick's voice could be heard denouncing the holdouts as a bunch of "chicken-gutted pig farmers." Finally, just as the meeting was on the verge of being transformed into a bareknuckled donnybrook, Allan was able to quiet Fitzpatrick, and an uneasy silence fell over the room. Disgusted by their antics and yet needing their support, Allan stared the men down and waited for their anger to subside.

"It appears to me we've got too many talkers and not enough thinkers in this group," Allan finally informed them. "While you gents have been spewing hot air all over each other, I noticed that one of us has been doing some thinking. And he might just have some answers worth hearing. How about it, Britt, you got any suggestions?"

As a body, they turned to stare at Britt, who was leaning against the back wall and thus far had not uttered a sound during the entire meeting. The expressions on their faces ranged from puzzled amazement to undisguised resentment. The furthest thought from their mind was to seek the advice of a black man, even if he was Allan's pet nigger. But at the same time, their attitude evidenced a faint trace of amused curiosity as to what Britt might say. Watching them, Britt was instinctively aware of their patronizing air, and for a moment he thought to tactfully avoid speaking. Then he glanced at Allan, and as their eyes met, Britt realized that his friend was purposely using him as one would use a hickory switch: stinging the men with their own childishness so as to shock them into rational thought.

"Seems to me you got to decide what comes first," Britt commented frankly, "your families or some war we don't know nothing about. Allan's daddy used to say that wars was made by old men too dried out to fight and all lathered up to get their names down in the history books. I'm not real anxious to fight anybody, but I mean to protect what's mine. So if it was me, I'd let the folks back East fight their war, and I'd look to my own. The only other thing I'd say is that I haven't heard anyone mention asking Austin for help. Even if they don't act like it sometimes, we are part of Texas, and they might just have a few men they could spare."

The simple eloquence of Britt's incisive speech had a stunning effect on the men. With a few words he had cut away the useless gristle and penetrated to the very marrow of their divisive attitudes. Moreover, he had suggested an obvious and yet seemingly elusive solution to the problem of the settlement's defense, one which might easily resolve the threat of Indian attack long before the first raid could even be mounted. But if the men were taken aback by the clarity and directness of Britt's logic, they were also openly affronted that a black would presume to give them a lesson in disciplined thinking. They avoided looking directly at Britt, but sharp, darting glances left no illusion as to the extent of their resentment, and while the solution lay exposed for anyone to grasp, the room grew thick and oppressive with a hostile silence. Somewhat disconcerted himself, Allan finally recovered from the impact of Britt's words and jumped into the breach.

"Something else my daddy always said was that when a man gives you a good idea, you should do something about it. I propose that we form a delegation and send them to Austin with a request that state troops be sent to garrison Fort Belknap. Seems to me they could protect us from the Indians at the same time they're guarding this area for the South."

Allan's assured manner galvanized the men to action. No sooner had he stopped talking than Fitzpatrick and Bragg volunteered to beard the Austin politicians in their own den. Suddenly everyone in the room was shouting, demanding that they also be considered for the honor, and before it was over, Allan was forced to organize an election to choose the delegates. When calm once more settled over the group, Joel Meyer and Grady Bragg had been selected to leave at sunrise for the state capitol. And without actually realizing how it came about, the men of the Elm Creek settlement had elected to stand and fight.

8

As Allan closed the door, after bidding the settlers goodnight, the muffled sounds of their horses began fading in the distance. For a moment he paused, reflecting on the events of the evening, then turned back to the room with a relieved smile. Britt and Tom and the three women were watching him closely, anxious for his reaction to the meeting, and his obvious good spirits quickly eased their minds.

With the first crisis behind them Allan's thoughts shifted to more mundane problems, such as where everyone was going to sleep. Britt had his own cabin less than fifty yards south along the creek, but even with imminent threat of an Indian raid, he knew that Mary would never consider moving. So that aspect of their situation seemed to take care of itself. But the main house had only one bedroom, and the sudden addition of the Fitzpatrick family definitely posed a problem.

"If you're worrying about where everyone is going to sleep," Sarah advised, "don't bother." After twelve years of marriage she had developed an eerie faculty for anticipating his thoughts, and on occasion it had proved downright embarrassing. "Tom and Elizabeth can take the loft, and we'll make pallets for the children in the parlor."

"Good idea," he agreed. Moving to the fireplace, Allan scraped the bowl of his pipe and began tamping in a fresh load of tobacco. "Before we all get off to bed, I want to caution everybody about what we're facing. The Indians might well come raiding before we get any state troops, and I don't have to draw pictures for you women about what they've got in mind." The women glanced at one another, and the fright on their faces made it evident that no further warning was necessary. "The men will never be far enough away that we can't hear a gunshot, and I'll leave my pistol hanging beside the door just in case we do have visitors. And Mary, until things get a bit safer I think it would be a good idea for you and the children to spend your days here in the main house."

Mary looked at Britt, and his quick affirmative nod convinced her that their own home would have to remain neglected until the danger had passed. Allan paused to light his pipe and in that moment of distraction failed to see the frown that crossed Tom's face.

Fitzpatrick had never owned any slaves or even had any dealings with blacks, much less being thrust into a situation where he was forced to live with them. But he was second generation Tennessee, having been raised like his father before him in the foothills of the Smokies, and in his scheme of things there were few creatures lower than a black man. Generations of prejudice and envenomed bigotry had been transfused from father to son, and although there was no rational foundation for his hate, Fitzpatrick was fond of declaring that he'd sooner own a good horse than a lazy nigger. The thought of his children being forced to spend their days playing with

three woolheads was more than he could swallow grace-
fully. Still, he was in Allan's house, and as he glanced
around the room, it occurred to him that it might be best
to take things slow.

"Them goddamn Indians better take care none of 'em
fall into my hands," Tom snarled. The savagery in his
voice brought everyone's head around, and his wife
peered at him quizzically. Hesitant to vent his anger concerning the blacks, Fitzpatrick's wrath had quickly spilled
over onto the Indians. "By Jesus, I'll teach 'em not to
mess around with white women."

If Tom was aware of his insult by omission, he por-
trayed no outward indication. But the others found themselves unable to look at Britt or Mary. The black woman's face blanched perceptibly, and her eyes sought
sanctuary in the floor. The momentary void in the conversation made the slur all the more inescapable, but
before anyone could move to change the subject, Fitzpatrick's rancorous voice again broke the stillness.

"I don't know about the rest of those fainthearts that
was here tonight but if any of them red devils come
raidin' my land, they'll get more than they bargained for."
Gesturing toward Allan, his tone seemed puzzled, as if
he were seeking the answer to some profound riddle.
"Lousy Indians aren't good for nothing anyhow. Why
didn't the army just kill 'em off so they wouldn't come
down here huntin' our women and burnin' our homes?"

"Maybe the Comanches and Kiowas figure this land is
still theirs, even if we are living on it." Britt's sharp reply
startled no one more than himself. Fitzpatrick had obviously intended his remark for Allan, but the black man
found himself unable to hold his peace any longer in the
face of such a crude affront to his wife.

Tom's head jerked around, and he stared at Britt with
open animosity for a moment. Then he relaxed and
glanced at Allan, shaking his head with a patronizing
smirk. "I suppose you couldn't expect anything else from
a nigger. If a man's got any sense at all, he knows we
drove 'em out of this country, and that makes it ours."

"What if they drive us off?" Britt responded mockingly.
"Does that make it theirs again?"

"Boy, you'd best watch that smart mouth while I'm
around here," Tom growled, "or I'll peel a few strips off
your black hide."

"Mr. Tom, you're a good man in lots of ways, and I've always admired the way you work your place, but don't crowd me." A sardonic smile played across the corner of Britt's mouth. "More than one man's tried, and I ain't lost any skin yet."

Fitzpatrick's features contorted with rage as his temper came unhinged, and he shifted as if to move toward Britt. The women stared incredulously at the scene before them, unable to grasp how the situation had become so tense in only a few moments. While Britt was slightly taller than the Irishman, it was clear that the two men were evenly matched, and no one had the slightest doubt that a fight would end with one of them being killed. Suddenly Allan leaped forward, blocking Tom's path, and restrained him with a none-too-gentle shove.

"Tom, let's get something straight right from the start. While you're under my roof, you'll behave accordingly, and in this house Britt is one of the family. If there's any argument on that score, you'd best pack up and move on back to your own place."

Fitzpatrick's anger was replaced with a deep scowl, but his eyes remained on Britt, and the look clearly conveyed the surly emotions he was struggling to control. Allan was the only man in the settlement who had won Tom's respect, and even then it was grudgingly given. Fitzpatrick sensed in Allan the inborn qualities of leadership, integrity, and force of character, all of the traits he secretly longed to possess. And for reasons unfathomable even to himself, he had extended loyalty to another man for the first time in his life. Unable to withstand the force of Allan's stare, Tom's eyes fell to the floor, and then he turned away. Moving to the fireplace, he leaned against the mantle on outstretched arms, stiff and charged with tension, staring sightlessly into the flames.

The room grew hushed and still, as if the others dared not speak for fear of rupturing the fragile truce which Allan's intervention had brought about. Finally Britt broke the spell with a nod to Mary. Gathering the children, she followed him to the front door, where they were joined by Allan. A disquieting influence had entered their lives, and as the men spoke their goodnights, they each felt a strain which had never before existed. When Allan closed the door and threw the bolt for the night, it was as if Britt had been locked out from their home, and he sud-

denly was overcome with a premonition of unalterable
disaster. Some malevolent force was at work, unseen but
not unfelt, driving a wedge between him and Britt. And for
the first time in his life Allan sensed that he was power-
less to forestall what must come.

CHAPTER TWO

1

Seated on a high mesa with sheer red cliffs of sandstone dropping off before him, Little Buffalo stoically kept watch on the distant figures approaching across the plains below. The corners of his eyes wrinkled with concentration, and yet there was a certain impassiveness to his gaze. Broad shouldered and unusually deep chested, with the lithe suppleness of a wary mountain cat, he seemed tensed and poised on the verge of springing at some unseen threat. Still, his sharp, angular features remained frozen in a cryptic mask, and only the slight movement of his eyes betrayed the fact that he was watching the scene below.

Actually his mind was occupied with matters which lay heavily on his shoulders, troublesome thoughts that distracted his senses from the reality unfolding around him. But his eyes beheld the dust trails and the tiny antlike figures moving fatefully across the open grasslands, and in some dim recess of his consciousness there was an awareness that his time had grown short. How could the days have passed so rapidly and without recognition, he pondered. Only yesterday, or so it seemed to him now, he had come to this same spot, alone and somewhat fearful of what he was about to do. Then there had been no distracting movements on the plains below, and he had passed four days and four nights without awareness of anything save the vision which would preserve the tomorrows of his people. Now the Moon of Deer Horns Dropping Off was all but past, and the path over which he would soon lead two nations yawned before him with unsettling finality.

"Little Buffalo greets his warriors in a strange manner." Shaken from his reverie, Little Buffalo turned to find Ten Bears, elder chief of all Comanches, watching him with a concerned expression.

"*Hao,* Ten Bears," he greeted the older man. "Would you have me stand beside the trail and welcome them with the hollow flattery of a Ute dog?" Staring off into the flatlands below, his features grew even grimmer. "Many of those men will not return from the path we are to take, and when a man is rubbed out, his leader must ask himself if the path chosen was one of wisdom and purpose. Have I not seen Ten Bears mourn his brothers and ask himself these same questions when war parties returned with empty horses?"

"Your tongue is sharp," Ten Bears grunted, "and yet it bites to the heart of this thing we do. When there is war, men are rubbed out, and maybe it is the ones who remain behind that suffer the most. And yet a leader must never forget that when a warrior crosses to that other life, he does so willingly. Whether for personal glory or to hold the land for his children's children, he makes that crossing without regret. For are we not men and unlike beasts, who pass over without choice or reason?"

"Yes, that is so. We are the True People, and we decide the fate of our enemies according to our own needs. I have followed you on raids since boyhood and never once questioned your right to lead. Still, now that it is I who am about to become the leader, I cannot shake the thought that no man has the right to decide the fate of his own brother." Looking out over the vast grasslands and the river below, Little Buffalo's eyes narrowed, and he once again fell silent, watching with misgiving as the erratic form of the distant specks drew nearer and took shape.

Stretched across the plains to the south, large bands of Indians moved steadily northward, evoking a spectacle seen by few men on the Western Frontier. On and on they came, weary and trail worn, their scattered columns visible for miles in every direction. Like swirling plumes of discolored smoke, the dust cloud from their horse herds drifted skyward with unbroken symmetry, ending only on the outer rim of the distant horizon. Comprised of countless bands, both Comanche and Kiowa, they came from the barren isolation of the Staked Plains, the craggy slopes of the Wichita Mountains, and from every remote valley and rushing stream in the western reaches of Indian Territory. With the homing instinct of a nomadic race they came onward without deviation or pause, guided solely by the stars and a primitive cunning for recognizing every landmark encountered since childhood. Their destination was the land of Red Bluffs on the Canadian River, and in late September they assembled to hold council. And make war.

Shortly after the snows had melted and the wild flowers bloomed in the Leaf Moon, runners arrived from a band of Kiowas encamped on the Red River with an astounding message. The pony soldiers were deserting the string of forts which for years had desecrated the sacred hunting grounds, and from all that could be learned, they had no intention of returning. Moreover—and this the Indians found all but incomprehensible—word had spread across the Plains that the white-eyes had split into two warring tribes, with one of the tribes disavowing the Great White Father in Washington. Even now the white-eyes were battling each other on the distant side of the Great River to the east, and from the fragments of information available it seemed entirely possible that they might annihilate one another before the fighting was finished.

But greater than all this was a disclosure that made the white-eyes' puzzling war seem pale by comparison. With the pony soldiers gone, the hated tejanos were left defenseless; having grown soft like women, they no longer had the long-knives to cower behind, and now at last their immunity from attack had vanished like a puff weed in a strong wind.

Elation ran rampant through the Indian camps. Warriors fired their muskets into the sky and dashed around the villages lashing their horses to a frenzy; the women sang and cried with joy and prepared great mountains of food in thanksgiving, while the children watched with

growing awe and dreamed of returning to the ancient
tribal lands spoken of so often by their fathers. The pony
soldiers were gone, faded away like the morning mist on
a sunny day, and soon their beloved Plains would grow
fertile from the moldering bones of the helpless tejanos.

After their original excitement had run its course, many
of the warriors spoke of striking the white-eyes while the
pony soldiers were absorbed in preparations for war. Still
others advocated patience, suggesting that it was wiser to
allow the long-knives to weaken themselves fighting one
another and then attack the tejanos. The debates ranged
far into the night, often provoking harsh words and animosity, for within the social order of the Plains tribes each
warrior had an equal voice, and few were noted for any
reluctance to speak their mind in matters concerning war.
According to tribal custom, any warrior could raise a war
party simply by announcing his intention and extending a
ceremonial pipe to anyone willing to listen. Those who
accepted the pipe and smoked with him thereby com-
mitted themselves to the raid, and when an imposing number of braves had been recruited, the *to-yop-ke,* or leader,
was then recognized as the sole authority during the expedition.

In the weeks following the pony soldiers' sudden departure a number of war parties were organized and rode out
to seek vengeance on the hated tejanos. But these were
minor raids, affairs of no consequence, and the great body
of warriors were clearly awaiting some sign; the appearance of a *to-yop-ke* whose wisdom and foresight would
lead them to a victory overshadowing anything previously
known by the Plains tribes. While the preeminent chiefs of
the two tribes, Ten Bears of the Comanches and Santana
of the Kiowas, were as anxious as any to deal a death
blow to the white-eyes, they too felt that an opportunity
of such extraordinary magnitude required a war chief of
invincible character. Thus, as the Leaf Moon drew to a
close, the Comanches and Kiowas girded themselves for a
fight to the death with the tejanos and impassively awaited
the coming of their *to-yop-ke.*

2

Tilted backward in a chair, with his head resting against the wall of the cabin, Britt puffed contentedly on his pipe. Through a haze of blue smoke hanging softly in the still air, he watched the sun merge slowly with the western horizon. He was bone-tired from a grueling day in the saddle, but with Mary's fried steak and milk gravy now on the backside of his belt, the weariness had taken on a pleasant glow. This was his favorite moment of the day; a good pipe, a sense of peace with all around him, and shortly, the soft warmth of Mary snuggled close in the intimacy of their bed. Faintly he heard the children talking inside the house, and as on other nights, it occurred to him again that he had been blessed with about all a man could ask from life.

Frank, his oldest boy, was growing tall and strong, now approaching thirteen, and already there was a quiet steadiness about him which hinted at the man he would become. Young George, on the other hand, was a mischievous hellion, full of fire and spirit even at eight, and it seemed fairly obvious that nothing short of manhood would ever calm his rowdy nature. And then there was Sue Ellen, his favorite simply because she was a tiny replica of her mother. Bright and gay, eternally smiling and asking endless questions, she was the culmination of all his hopes for the new land. Listening now to their distant laughter, Britt was filled with a sense of well-being and fulfillment, if only for a moment.

Then, as frequently happened these days, his mind whipsawed from thoughts of the good life shared by his family to the horrors they would surely face in days to come. Already word had drifted back of sporadic raids on settlements to the northeast; hit-and-run affairs which exacted small toll in lives. But a portent nonetheless of the savage atrocities soon to be inflicted on the entire frontier. Before he had time to become deeply engrossed in worry, however, the thud of hooves sounded on the south trail, and two riders approached the main house. His fears of a moment ago were even further stilled when he noted that the mounted men were Joel Meyer and Grady Bragg, evidently returned from their mission to the state capitol.

Walking toward the main house, Britt saw Allan and Tom rush out the front door. The four men shook hands all around and were excitedly questioning one another as Britt reached them. Meyer and Hamby greeted him with casual nods, but their attention was quickly diverted by Fitzpatrick's bellowed demand.

"Goddammit, boys, are you gonna make us wait all night? What happened in Austin?"

Bragg and Meyer glanced at one another sheepishly, their faces suddenly gone solemn, both of them clearly reluctant to speak. Britt's eyes narrowed as he observed their hesitant manner, and the thought suddenly sped through his mind that the news they carried for the Elm Creek settlement was going to be ominous indeed. Allan and Tom were also watching the two delegates, and their jocular attitude of a moment ago had been replaced by looks of dour apprehension.

Grady Bragg finally broke under the combined weight of their eyes and in a wavering voice confirmed the worst of their fears. "Allan, we did our best. Our dead-level best. But those bastards in Austin don't give a damn for anything right now except fightin' Yankees." Bragg's eyes fell to the ground, and his mumbled tone was barely audible. "They did promise to send us twenty men and an officer."

"Twenty men!" Fitzpatrick roared hoarsely. "Christ, they might as well not send anybody."

"Now wait a minute, Tom," Allan interjected. "Maybe there's more to this than we've heard." The evenness of his tone hardly compensated for the shock written across his face, and the others were only too well aware that their predicament was growing more acute by the moment. Allan's voice remained calm, despite the funereal atmosphere. "Joel, haven't you got anything to add to that?"

Haggard from the long trip and far too little sleep, Meyer's waspish reply inferred that he clearly wasn't about to play whipping-boy for their frustration. "Not much. The governor same as told us to go shit in our hats, and the way I've got it figured, none of you boys could of done any better."

"That's right," Bragg confirmed anxiously. "The governor's got Yankee on his mind, and he just flat out told us that the settlements would have to give ground or else fend for themselves. We finally got to the general in charge of the state militia and damn near had to put a gun on him just to get twenty men."

"Twenty men," Britt repeated dully. "That's like trying to put out a brushfire with spit." The men turned to look at him, slightly startled by his unsolicited remark, and there was a moment of stillness as they digested the full significance of the statement.

"By God, he's right for once," Tom grunted. "Twenty men are worthless as tits on a boar hog. Those Comanches will level this whole settlement, and there won't be a man, woman, or child left alive."

"Don't be too sure," Allan mused aloud. "If we can get everyone to the fort before the attack really gets started, we might just give those Indians more than they bargained for. When you come right down to it, they haven't got much stomach for a head-on fight with forty or fifty well-armed white men." Allan glanced sharply at Britt, suddenly aware of the unconscious slur and sorely embarrassed by the prejudice implicit in his comment. Britt's understanding smile relieved the tension, however, and Allan resumed hurriedly. "There's one thing for certain, though. If any of us start spreading scare talk, we'll end up with half the people on Elm Creek running so fast you won't even see their dust."

Grady Bragg chewed thoughtfully for a moment and then squirted a nearby rock with a juicy stream of amber sputum. "Maybe, maybe not. But if you're looking for a cinch bet, you just wait and see if those same fainthearts don't high-ass it into the fort when word gets around about what happened in Austin."

The other men looked at him quizzically, wondering just how many of the settlers would move into the fort and silently debated the wisdom of such a move for their own families. Shortly afterward, Meyer and Bragg mounted and rode into the dusk toward their own homesteads. Britt discussed the situation briefly with Allan, aware that Fitzpatrick was purposely withholding comment, then walked slowly in the direction of his own cabin. Tom's bigotry had manifested itself in subtle ways since Allan's blunt warning. His latest ploy was to withdraw from any conversation which included the black man: an insidious expression of his bitter contempt for the resident nigger. Approaching the cabin, Britt once again caught the sound of children's laughter, and abruptly he decided that there were far greater dangers afoot than Tom Fitzpatrick's childish prejudice.

3

Among the Comanche there was one warrior who stood out above all others. Since the days of ancient times, when the True People had ridden out to conquer the Plains, there had never been another who fought with such disregard for his own life or struck such fear in the hearts of his enemies. Squatted around their fires during the long months of winter, the Comanches never tired of recounting his deeds in battle. His daring and utter fearlessness in the face of death were known throughout the Plains, and even as a young man his fame spread to the camps of their ancestoral enemies, the Utes and the Crow. Although it shattered centuries of precedent, it was nonetheless understandable when, as a mere boy, he was initiated into the *ko-eet-senko,* the warrior society comprised of the tribe's ten bravest men. And yet, even as a man, recognized as the most formidable warrior on the Plains, he had refused time and again to accept the mantle of war chief. Little Buffalo lived to fight, glorying in the crunch of the ax and the muted thud of an arrow as it struck home, but never once had he sought to lead his brothers to tempt the fate he himself defiantly challenged.

When runners had arrived during the Leaf Moon and word spread that the pony soldiers had retreated from Texas, there was much speculation among the tribe as to who would lead them in a war which was taken for granted. Many names were discussed, among them warriors who had previously displayed remarkable skill in organizing raids on the tejano settlements. But this was to be no mere horse-stealing expedition, one which concerned itself more with adroit theft than with devastation of the settlements. Instead, it would be a full-scale war, a fight to the finish, one last chance to drive the hated whiteeyes from Indian land for all time. And an undertaking of such far-reaching significance demanded the leadership of a master warrior: a tactical genius who would provide the vision and audacity essential to a conquest of such immense proportions. A name frequently heard in these fireside discussions was that of Little Buffalo, but then everyone knew of his aversion to personal power, and they just as quickly passed on to more likely candidates.

Secretly, after it became apparent that the tribe had reached an impasse in selecting a leader, Ten Bears sought out Little Buffalo and urged him to reconsider his lofty views concerning the role of *to-yop-ke*. Far into the night they debated the authority that godlike men arrogated to themselves over other men, but Little Buffalo remained unshakable in his rigid beliefs. Finally, as the last embers of the fire began to dim, Ten Bears lost patience and for the first time in memory spoke harshly to the man he admired above all others.

"We struggle back and forth like two dogs gnawing on the same bone, while our people grow weary seeking a leader. Now you force me to speak of a matter which comes hard to my tongue. You are as my son, and it is not easy to admit that one's son is a coward. But from your own mouth you have condemned yourself, showing the skulking manner of a Crow who fights only women."

Little Buffalo stiffened, his eyes registering both anger and shock at the older man's tongue lashing. Observing him closely, Ten Bears pressed on, elated that he had at last shaken the obdurate warrior. "There are many men who are brave in battle. That is a simple thing, even enjoyable, to risk one's life with the lance or warclub against another man. But there is a higher form of bravery which few men dare to attempt, and so it becomes the test of courage for those who have left all fear behind them. My son, if you learn nothing else this night, then take away the truth that it demands greater courage to send one's brother to his death than it does to count coup on some whining Ute. One is the courage of a man who fights for his people, while the other is the courage of a boy who merely fights for himself. The man who possesses this higher courage and refuses to test it is little better than a coward, for he fears failure as surely as some men fear the knife. Until you have placed the good of your people above yourself and set aside your fears for the cause of your brothers, you must live with the thought that you were found wanting when your courage was brought to the test."

Little Buffalo stared at the chief through a haze of fury, outraged that any man would dare to speak to him in this manner. His hands clenched, and his throat tightened as he fought to control the mounting indignation which swept over him. But the ring of truth had sounded undeniably in Ten Bears words, and even as he smoldered, he knew that for the first time in his life he must come to grips with this haunting fear of leading other men to their doom. Slowly Little Buffalo lowered his head, focusing his eyes in the dull embers of the fire, and within moments his mind cleared. Gradually he became aware of what must be done, and with a fleeting moment of regret for the carefree days now gone forever, he looked once more at the chief.

"My father, you have spoken wisely, and while it is bitter to swallow, I must accept what you have said. In the past I have fought for myself, vainly and without thought to the common good. Now I will set those childish ways aside and attempt to be the man you thought me to be. But I must do it in my own way and without promise as to what might come. With the sun I will go alone to the red cliffs and fast while I await a vision from *Tai-me*. Should He speak to me and open my mind to what lies ahead for the True People, then I will know what must be done. If the vision is a good one, I will seek the honor of *to-yop-ke* and lead the warriors south. Only thus will I dare this higher courage of which you speak and risk lives other than my own. Should the vision be bad or refuse to come at all, then I will ride south alone and fight my last fight in the only way I have known."

Ten Bears nodded solemnly and silently made a prayer to *Tai-me* for a vision of the highest order. Both the life of Little Buffalo and the tomorrows of their children's children clearly demanded a vision which ordained the wholesale slaughter of the miserable tejanos.

4

Britt shifted uneasily in the saddle as they approached Fort Belknap, silently wondering what kind of reception they would be accorded by the new commander. Riding beside Allan and Grady Bragg, he passed through the front gate, nodded casually to the lone sentry, and proceeded toward headquarters.

Only that morning a messenger had arrived with word that the state troops had reached the fort. Captain Buck

Barry, the militia commander, requested a meeting with the Elm Creek leaders just as quickly as practical. Leaving Tom to guard the homestead, Allan sent Britt to fetch Grady Bragg, and within the hour they were riding south along the Brazos.

Britt's presence was something of a ruse on Allan's part; a minor deception to placate Fitzpatrick for having been left behind. Ostensibly Britt was along to serve as a messenger back to the settlement should the need arise. Allan's guile didn't extend to himself, however, and he was distinctly aware that he wanted the black man present during the forthcoming conclave with Captain Barry. After years of observing Britt's instinctive cunning for the right decision in a tight spot, Allan readily admitted to himself that he preferred to have his own judgment supported by the black man's counsel. Not that he would admit it to anyone else, for other people would have scoffed openly at the thought. But both he and Britt were aware of it, and within the very personal bonds of their friendship the fact alone remained sufficient.

Glancing around the cantonment, Britt noticed that a number of settlers had already moved into the fort, occupying buildings recently vacated by the federal army. Most of these were families from the settlements south and northeast of the fort, but here and there he spotted a few familiar faces from Elm Creek. Thinking back to the near panic which followed the governor's haughty dismissal of the settlements, he found himself pleasantly surprised that such a small number had deserted their homes from along the upper Brazos.

Dismounting in front of headquarters, they entered the orderly room and were immediately ushered into the inner office. Captain Barry rose from behind a littered desk and came forward to greet them as they stopped inside the door. Britt smiled inwardly at the puzzled glance the officer darted in his direction and wasn't in the least surprised when Barry failed to extend his hand. Accustomed to being ignored in any white gathering, almost as if he were an inanimate black shadow, Britt studied the new commander and quickly discerned that his extraordinary size had left Allan and Grady somewhat overawed.

Buck Barry was a burly giant of a man, not so much in height as in sheer girth. While an inch or so shorter than Britt, his thick bull's neck stuck atop massive shoulders, and the heavily muscled immensity of his arms more than made up the difference. On first glance he resembled a sour-tempered grizzly bear, and the assured movements of his waddling gait betrayed the enormous power concealed beneath his hulking frame. Lumbering toward the desk, he invited the white men to sit with the wave of a bristling paw, then slowly eased his ponderous weight into a groaning chair.

"Appreciate you men comin' in right away," Barry rumbled amiably. "From all we've heard about you folks at Elm Creek, I sort of expected we'd have to drag you in."

Allan exchanged perplexed glances with Grady and decided to proceed cautiously. "I'm not quite sure we follow you, Captain. Exactly what was it you heard?"

"Why, that you're a bunch of thick-heads," he snorted. Barry's face split in a good-natured grin, and he leaned back in the creaking chair, which threatened to collapse at any moment under the strain. "Some of your friends have already relocated to the fort, and they claimed wild horses couldn't get you to move. I'm glad to see their judgment was misplaced."

Britt observed the heavy frown that appeared over Allan's features and wondered if his friend would see through the officer's rather crude attempt to badger them into relocating within the fort. Allan watched Barry stolidly for a moment, much as a fighter sizing up an unexpected adversary, and a tense stillness settled over the room.

"Captain, do I understand that you intend to order the settlers to leave their homes and occupy the fort?"

"Hell yes, that's what I intend," Barry rejoined. "That's the only way I can keep you people from getting scalped." The wide grin had been replaced with a surly scowl, and all pretense of bonhomie rapidly evaporated. The mercurial transformation in his manner seemed to unsettle Allan and Grady, and they stared at him uncertainly. "You didn't seriously think I was going to ride north and engage the Comanches with twenty men?"

"No, I didn't," Allan said. "But if you expect the people at Elm Creek to just walk away and leave their homes to the Indians, you're in for a shock. Sooner than do that, they'd burn 'em down themselves and move back East."

"No two ways about it," Brady interjected, somewhat recovered from his awe of the officer's intimidating size. "And mister, if you were to go over there and tell them what you just told us, they'd more'n likely laugh you all the way back to Austin."

"By Christ, that's just the kind of stubbornness that gets people killed!" Barry leaned forward, slamming his meaty paw on the desk. Startled, Allan and Grady winced slightly as the desk shuddered from the impact. "Either you move those people over here—every man, woman and child—or goddammit, I won't be responsible for what happens to them."

The room bristled with hostility as Barry finished speaking and glared sullenly at the two settlers. Still standing by the door, removed from the arena itself, Britt suddenly realized that what the captain had failed to obtain with rough cajolery, he now hoped to win through outright bullying. Although Allan didn't turn to look at him, Britt could feel the unspoken convergence of their thoughts, and he willed the white man to hold his ground. The silence lengthened, and just when Britt began to doubt the staunchness of his friend's resolve, Allan spoke.

"Captain Barry, you were sent here to protect the settlements, not to dictate conditions. The people of Elm Creek need your help desperately, and we'll cooperate gladly in organizing a defense. But if your only solution is to try to browbeat us, then we'll just have to look after ourselves. Further than that, I have nothing more to say."

Barry's heavy features reddened at Allan's tone, and he seemed on the verge of lashing out. Then he appeared to gain control of himself, and his rigid tenseness of a moment past settled into a phlegmatic mask of resignation. "So be it, Mr. Johnson. But don't come crying to me when the Comanches get through amusing themselves with your women."

5

Four days after his fateful discussion with Ten Bears, Little Buffalo returned from the standstone cliffs east of the village. Hollow eyed and gaunt, he nevertheless walked with the erect stoicism of a warrior, and his countenance gave no hint as to what he had seen on the mountainside. The vision had been slow in coming, even though he prayed and made repeated offering to *Tai-me*. Only after fasting and denying himself sleep for three full days was he able to summon forth the netherworld images, and what he saw drained his spirit of all power to resist further. The vision prophesied the bloody decimation of the tejanos with stark clarity, and Little Buffalo knew at last that some power greater than himself had decreed that he lead the Plains tribes in their war on the white-eyes. Reconciled, he quickly called a council meeting with Ten Bears and the village elders and related the vision in its entirety. After a moment of stunned silence, the elders confirmed the enormity of the revelation, and Little Buffalo reluctantly became the *to-yop-ke*. Now all that remained was to obtain the sanction of the nomadic bands scattered throughout the wilderness, and the Plains tribes would have at last found their leader.

With the passing of the Leaf Moon, Little Buffalo sent couriers galloping across the Plains in every direction. Lashing their horses to the point of exhaustion, they rode with the determination of fanatics, and within a fortnight word had spread throughout the Wichita Mountains and across the Staked Plains that the famed Comanche warrior was raising a war party. At each village the riders called a hurried meeting and related the vision word for word as he had described it to them. When discussion ceased as to the vision's significance and the full import of its interpretation, the couriers then delivered Little Buffalo's appeal for all True People to join in driving the hated tejanos from their sacred hunting grounds. The message was direct and without adornment: united under one banner, combining both their might and a concerted will to avenge past indignities, the True People could humble the white-eyes for all time. But if the tribes chose to make war with isolated raids, rather than massing for a cohesive assault on the enemy, the Comanches and Kiowas must then resign themselves to the fact that their children's children would forever bear the stigma of defeat at the tejanos' hands.

Over the summer months Little Buffalo also sent a steady stream of scouts riding into Texas, maintaining a close surveillance on both the settlers and the now-abandoned forts. As reports drifted back and a clear picture of the tejanos' defenses began to form, it became aparent to the new *to-yop-ke* that his best chance for an opening blow of crushing impact lay in attacking the remote settlements along the Brazos River. Located on the outer fringe of the white-eyes' westward expansion, as well as being a half-day's journey removed from one another, these settlements were uniquely vulnerable to a sudden, overwhelming assault by mounted warriors. Within the bounds of a two-day march along the Brazos, a fast-moving war party could strike ten or more settlements, leaving in their wake a swath of desolation and carnage unlike anything ever visited on the tejanos in the past.

Fixing in his own mind the most favorable target for th first massive raid, Little Buffalo next sent messengers calling for the True People to assemble at Red Bluffs no later than the passing of the Moon of Deer Horns Dropping Off. But while the objective was firm, his own inner resolution never ceased to waver, and his sleep was haunted with terrifying images of a lone warrior leading the True People into a holocaust of destruction.

Gathering the tribes at one location was a tedious process, at best, and seldom without a host of attending frustrations. Warriors were obliged to hunt far in advance of the gathering, drying thin strips of Buffalo meat into jerky for the lean days ahead. Once the combined villages descended on a given area, the game animals quickly took flight, and a shortsighted man might easily find himself with a ravenous family and no meat in his lodge. Moreover, the Plains tribes were a leisurely people who rarely allowed the future to take precedent over the moment. After all, the white-eyes weren't going anywhere, and if the council should decide to follow Little Buffalo, then the tejanos would still be holed up in those airless, suffocating log huts they used as lodges.

But as the leaves slowly turned from green to hues of gold and the mellow warmth of summer's end gave way to the first crisp nights of autumn, the banks of the Canadian River began to fill with a vast array of brightly decorated tepees. By the time of the Yellow Leaves Moon the prairie west of Red Bluffs was swarming with Comanches and Kiowas from every band on the Plains. While young boys tended a horse herd of six thousand head on the grasslands to the west, the warriors spent their days thrusting jibes at the latest arrivals or whooping with delight at the antics of a small army of children roving mischievously through the village. A medicine lodge was erected in the center of the village to house the sacred gods, and the preparations were at last completed for the council meeting. Observing the comings and goings of so many holy men, the more cynical warriors were prompted to speculate that the war on the white-eyes might easily be waged with nothing more than magic potions and a few well-placed curses.

Finally, as the Yellow Leaves Moon relinquished the night's skies to the Geese Going Moon, the assembled might of the Plains tribes was gathered on the Canadian, and more than three thousand Indians waited for Little Buffalo to speak.

6

"Well, from where I stand, it seems to me that we might— and I stress the word *might*—just be out of danger." Bud William's pronouncement carried across the cantonment as he addressed himself to the crowd of settlers lounging before headquarters.

"Bud, you might not be far wrong at that," Joel Meyer agreed. "If the Indians meant to attack, it seems like they'd have done it before now. I mean, who ever heard of Indians raiding after first frost?"

"By God, he's got a point there, boys." Jonathan Hamby's nasal twang seemed all the more offensive because of the pompous tone he consistently employed. "Anybody that's got anything besides mush between his ears knows that Comanches just don't have a taste for fightin' in cold weather. If they let a whole summer go by without a fullscale raid, you can mark it down that we're not likely to see 'em till spring."

Leaning against a post at the side of the porch, Britt glanced skeptically at Allan and shook his head with a slight, barely perceptible motion. Only last night they had discussed this same subject and concluded that the Indians might very well have delayed a mass raid in the hope that the settlers would grow careless. Second-guessing a Comanche was a hazardous game at best, and it was entirely possible that the Indians had deliberately lulled hem into a false sense of security. The Plains tribes held the element of surprise in high regard, seldom attacking without a distinct advantage. And should the settlers become reckless at this juncture, it might well precipitate the raid they had dreaded throughout the summer.

"You fellows sound like you got it all figured out. But it appears to me you've still got a hell of a lot to learn about Indian fightin'." The crowd turned to find Captain Barry gazing at them from the doorway. Although no one had noticed his silent appearance from the orderly room, it was obvious he had been eavesdropping on their conversation. The mocking grin twisting his features made it even more clear that he felt they were misguided amateurs, if not outright fools.

"Just for openers, you're apt to learn the hard way that a little frost has about as much effect on a Comanche as it does a grizzly bear." Pausing, he looked directly at Hamby, shaking his head ruefully, as if correcting an inept pupil. "Matter of fact, bears and Indians have a lot in common. Neither of 'em quits hunting and goes into hibernation till the first snow flies. Only in this case, what the Comanche is hunting is people."

The settlers' muttered comments were unintelligible for the most part, but they were clearly impressed by the harsh candor of Barry's statement. Each Sunday since the militia's arrival in May, the settlements had alternated in sending crews of men to work on the fortifications. Slowly, week by week, trees were hauled from groves along the river, and a chain of log walls began to interconnect the fort's buildings. When the stockade was at last shored and timbered to Barry's satisfaction, it appeared all but impregnable to the weary settlers. As the summer months passed and the dreaded attack failed to materialize, the men grew increasingly restless and balked at further strengthening the walls. Gradually the Sunday sojourns to the fort deteriorated into brief spurts of work interspersed with lengthy bull sessions, the main topic invariably centering around the Indians' curious disappearance. Toward the latter part of May the hit-and-run raids had ceased abruptly, and for the next four months it was as if the Comanche and Kiowa nations had vanished from the face of the earth. Now on the first Sunday in October, the air was brisk and chill, and the settlers found it extremely difficult to convince themselves that a major raid was still imminent.

Still pondering Barry's remarks and slightly nettled by his partonizing tone, the crowd came alert as Tom Fitzpatrick sardonically voiced their own thoughts.

"Captain, none of us would think of disputing an ol' Injun fighter like yourself, but we just find it damn hard to believe that those redsticks are going to let the summer go by and then start raidin' just as winter sets in." Unable to resist the temptation to show off, Fitzpatrick hitched up his pants in a cocky manner and glanced around the crowd with a smirking grin. "Course, most of us only been fightin' 'em ten years or so, and what with you being the big expert and all that, why I guess we better just go right on sleepin' with one eye open and the hammer cocked."

Buck Barry's features knotted with cold fury and the hair bristled on the back of his massive neck: The settlers were hushed, their faces charged with tension as they waited to see how the officer would handle the Irishman's calculated insolence.

Barry shoved away from the door jamb and a looseness came over his body; the ease of a tested fighter who has steadied himself to meet the likely rush of an antagonist.

"Fitzpatrick, it's thickheaded micks like you that get other people killed. You're so goddamn sure you've got all the answers that you just can't resist flapping your tongue. But when push comes to shove, your kind is always standing around with his thumb up his ass, trying to figure out which way to run."

Tom stiffened and took a step forward, so enraged by the insult that he was blinded to the militiaman's obvious advantage in a rough and tumble encounter. Barry's hand dropped to his side, casually brushing a holstered pistol, and his eyes took on the icy glaze of a seasoned executioner.

"Don't move or, by Christ, I'll dust you on both sides." The rumbling voice had assumed a cold ferocity which jerked Fitzpatrick up short. "I ought to beat the livin' crap out of you, but you're really not worth skinning my knuckles on. Now the rest of you men pay attention. Just so you won't be taken in by this flannelmouth's big talk, I'm going to give you a little lesson in Indian customs. Some of you have probably been wondering why I take such a peculiar pleasure in fighting redskins. Well, I used to be just like Hamby and Meyer and *Mr. Fitzpatrick*— thought I knew all there was to know about Indians. So one day about thirteen years ago, when there was a heavy frost on the ground and I was dead certain the Co-manches were holed up for the winter, I left my wife and three kids at home and went into Fort Worth for sup-plies."

The burly captain paused and looked around the crowd. Later men would tell of having seen his eyes mist over, and when he spoke, his voice cracked. "I'll leave it to your imagination what I found when I got home."

The settlers remained deathly quiet as his words faded, and their faces were etched with shame. Barry stood sightlessly for a moment, seemingly gripped by some in-ner torment, then turned and disappeared through the door. Fitzpatrick was unable to look the other men in the eye, and he was the first to walk away, his head bowed in self-disgust. Slowly the others followed, singly and in small groups, unwillingly to speak of what they had wit-nessed and yet filled with rekindled concern for their own families. Within minutes everyone had returned to work except Allan and Britt.

Allan glanced at the black man and silently jerked his head toward the orderly room. Once inside, Allan knocked on the office door, and they heard the captain's gruff voice bid them enter. When they stepped through the door, Barry was in the process of filling a whiskey tumbler. Without looking in their direction, he downed the drink in one neat gulp.

Turning toward them, his face remained impassive, but Britt was slightly taken aback by the curious twinkle so clearly evident in the officer's eyes.

Allan hardly knew how to start, and his words came in a halting, awkward manner. "Captain, I want to apolo-gize for everyone involved. The people of Elm Creek have always insisted that I act as their spokesman, and I'm sure they would want me to say how very much we regret what happened."

"Well, Mr. Johnson, that's real charitable of you, I'm sure," Barry responded, unable to keep a slight smile from playing across the corners of his mouth. "But as one leader to another I feel obliged to let you in on a little secret. I've never been married, and while I've probably

sired a few kids in my day, I sure as hell never bothered
to keep count." Allan's incredulous expression caused the
officer to falter momentarily, then he rushed on. "Now
don't get your hackles up. Maybe it was sort of a tricky
dodge to pull on those men, but it's a cinch they won't be
so careless from now on. And you'll have to admit, it
was one hell of a lie."

Allan glanced at Britt, and they both started chuckling
at the same moment. Barry's broad face dissolved in a
huge grin, and like three partners in some highly amusing
conspiracy, they shushed one another lest their laughter
be overheard by the humbled settlers. Later that night
Britt awakened by Mary with bed-rocking guffaws as he
recalled the crest-fallen expression on Tom Fitzpatrick's
face.

7

Flickering shadows of light spilled across Little Buffalo's
face from the small fire in his lodge. With a buffalo robe
thrown loosely over his shoulders, he stared vacantly into
the flames, absorbed in reflection on what he was about
to do. Never before had any single warrior united the full
power of the Comanches and Kiowas in a common cause,
and at times the weight of this responsibility seemed all
but unendurable. Dating from the Year of the Stars,
when the sky had filled with flashing meteors, the two
tribes had steadfastly remained allies for seventy winters.
On occasion they had joined ranks in fragmented alli-
ances while fighting the Crows or Utes, but not once had
the scattered bands comprising the tribes come together
as a single, unified force. Little Buffalo's vision had led
him to this moment in time as if he were but the instrument of some greater power, the means by which the
Plains tribes' destiny would be charted on an irreversi-
ble course. And in restrospect, he wasn't at all sure that
Ten Bears had done the right thing in forcing him to seek
a vision.

There was no doubt in his mind that tonight the assembled warriors would proclaim him *to-yop-ke*, war
leader of the combined forces. Already *ko-eet-senko*, the
elite warrior society, had announced their support of his
plan. Now it was a foregone conclusion that the *t'ai-peko*,

the broad spectrum of braves forming the six lesser warrior societies, would unanimously affirm his leadership. Tonight he would be proclaimed the bearer of the sacred pipe: the sign of office of the one chosen both for tactical wisdom and personal bravery to lead the warrior societies into battle. Of these things he was certain, filled with an overwhelming confidence.

He would lead the warriors across the River of Red Waters to the south, and the despicable tejanos would die as if consumed by a relentlessly advancing prairie fire. That much was clear in his vision, and the images revealed on the mountaintop affirmed that his medicine would be strong enough to drive the white-eyes back beyond the eastern perimeter of the Brazos. But what happened afterward remained unclear, shadowed in the mists of his vision, which did not extend past that point in time. And it was the uncertainty of this longer perspective which led to his present ambivalence.

Lost in a maze of introspection, he stared into the fire without seeing the flames, certain beyond doubt of the victory to come and yet apprehensive about the obscure and darkened path which that same victory would set his people upon. Years of slowly retreating before the white-eyes' greedy encroachments had taught him that they were a formidable enemy. Not the least of their strengths being that no matter how many were killed, they seemed to spring anew, performing some miracle of self-regeneration as did the buffalo clover tenaciously clinging to life beneath the wintry snows. Still, his vision had revealed a conquest of overwhelming proportions, one which would leave the tejanos utterly desolate in their defeat. And it was difficult to imagine that a victory of such magnitude could be meant as nothing more than a prelude to the destruction of his own people.

Suddenly a fleeting chill settled over him, and he shivered imperceptibly. Hunching nearer to the flames, he drew the warmth to his body, wondering if this were some further omen of the impending fate which awaited those he was to lead. Slowly his mind surfaced from such ominous thoughts, and he became aware that his *paraibvo*, Morning Star, was standing just inside the lodge entrance. With her presence came the realization that it was a draft of crisp night air through the open flap which had chilled him. And then it flashed through his mind that the fears conjured forth by seemingly grown men are sometimes childlike in their absurdity.

Morning Star watched him silently, her face etched with pride at the honor which was about to be bestowed on her man. Glancing at her, Little Buffalo's eyes softened, remembering both the comforting laughter and selfless love she had brought to his life. For a moment the tenderness in their eyes held, and they shared a wordless communion of all that had passed between them. Then her expression changed to one of somber expectancy, and he knew that the moment for the council meeting had arrived. Standing erect, Little Buffalo filled his lungs and then exhaled deeply, as if to force from his mind all but the significance of what must now be done. With his face frozen in the resolute stoicism befitting a Comanche *to-yop-ke,* he moved forward and stepped confidently through the lodge entrance.

8

Arrayed before the medicine lodge in the center of the village were the warriors who had journeyed vast distances to witness the most momentous event in the recorded history of their people. Crowded behind them, jostling for position, were the women and children. War would be declared on the white-eyes this night, and everyone present intended to carry away an indelible image of what transpired on this occasion. Seated around a fire directly in front of the medicine lodge were the many chiefs who bore responsibility for the nine bands of the two tribes. As befitted their position of preeminence, Ten Bears of the Comanches and Santana of the Kiowas were seated at the head of the chiefs' council.

Excited murmuring arose from the spectators as Little Buffalo strode through the crowd and without hesitation took a seat on the ground between Ten Bears and Santana. Within moments the crowd grew silent, and as was the custom, the assemblage waited patiently for the host to begin the council meeting. After letting the tension build for a few moments longer, Ten Bears rose and swept his arms outward in a dramatic, all-encompassing gesture. Wrinkled beyond his years, the sinew of youth bloated with age, he focused on the crowd and squinted slightly to bring them into sharper focus. Then the wily old politician drew his bent frame erect, and his rasping voice sounded across the deathly stillness of the council grounds.

"Brothers, we come together in this council to decide what must be done about the tejanos, who have taken our lands below the River of Red Waters. When I was young, I walked all over this land and saw none other than the True People. After many winters I walked again and found another people had come to take it away. How is it that we have allowed this to happen?

"The Comanches were once a great nation, but before the white-eyes they have grown as skulking dogs and carry their lives on their fingernails. Should we all put our heads together and cover them with a blanket like squaws and mourn the loss of our lands? *Brothers, are not women and children more timid than men?*"

Ten Bears paused to gauge the effect of his goading challenge, and in that moment of silence a wave of outrage swept through the crowd. They had come to be lauded and cajoled, to be told the manner and variety of ways in which they would strip the tejanos of their manhood. And now this wobbly old man with the croaking voice stood hurling insults at them. Glaring defiantly at the massed warriors, Ten Bears flung his final mandate in their faces.

"Little Buffalo has seen a vision, and his medicine is strong. We have smoked the war pipe. In the days to come, hail him as *to-yop-ke*. When Little Buffalo rides against the white-eyes, the Comanches will ride beside him, and once more the scalp sticks will stand before our lodges as befits a nation of warriors. I have spoken, and my voice is but an echo of the Comanches' will."

The fire held in the old chief's eyes for a moment, and then with a disdainful snort he resumed his seat before the council. An undercurrent of approval moved through the ranks of the Comanches, and it was obvious to the other chiefs that Ten Bears' words had struck a spark which might easily ignite both nations. Now the warriors awaited the voice of Santana, chief of the Kiowas, for Ten Bears' challenge had clearly been directed as much to them as to his own tribe. The Comanches openly referred to themselves as the Lords of the Plains and made no secret of the fact that they looked upon the Kiowas as an inferior people. While the two nations were bound together by ancient tradition, the Comanches nevertheless considered the Kiowas a weaker, somewhat backward tribe and over the generations had eased their adopted brothers into the role of tolerated vassals.

Slowly rising to his feet, Santana glanced at Ten Bears and smiled sardonically, as if amused by an old man's toothless rantings. The Kiowa chief was a man of brutish stature, towering over his brothers; a warrior of enormous gusto, he loved a savage fight or a hearty meal and could never really decide which he enjoyed more. His face was an open reflection of his emotions, hiding nothing, and the jet black hair flowing over thickly muscled shoulders somehow reinforced his evil visage. Arrogantly he waited for the warriors to cease their mumbled conversations, watching them with a churlish expression which was clearly meant to intimidate those still speaking. Finally the crowd grew still and his penetrating gaze briefly crossed the faces of those nearest the council fire. Then he began to speak, the ferocity and hate of his words rolling across the clearing, frightening the children and causing them to clutch at their mother's legs.

"The white-eyes swam across our land as maggots on a rotting buffalo carcass. Before these people ever crossed the great water to come to this land, the plains and rivers belonged to our fathers. But when I cross the river now, I see the lodges of tejanos who turn the soil to the sun. They cut down our timber; they kill the buffalo and drive all game from our sacred lands. And when I see that, my heart feels like bursting.

"When the prairie is on fire and the animals are surrounded by flames, you see them run and hide themselves so that they will not burn. That is the way we are here. The tejanos surround us, destroying the buffalo and our lands, until now we have nothing left except this wilderness to which they have driven us.

"I love to roam the plains; there I feel free and happy. I never wanted to leave that land; all my ancestors are lying there in the ground, and I say to you that when I too fall to pieces, I will fall to pieces there.

"The Kiowas do not cower before a fight, for of the True People none are braver. We too will follow Little Buffalo as *to-yop-ke,* and before the Plains are ours once

more, the Kiowa will match the Comanche blow for blow
in making the land run red with the blood of tejanos."

Santana remained standing as the Kiowa braves
howled and brandished their weapons, excitedly voicing
their delight with the contemptuous tone of his closing
remarks. Satisfied that the honor of his tribe had been
preserved in the face of the Comanche challenge, San
tana eased himself to the ground and cast a mocking
stare at Ten Bears. The old man met his gaze, and a
cryptic smile broke shallowly across the Comanche's face,
almost as if he were congratulating himself on having ensnared the Kiowas in some murky subterfuge. For a fleeting moment it occurred to Santana that the wily old man
had purposely baited him into accepting Little Buffalo as
to-yop-ke, and he returned Ten Bears' amused look with
cold distaste.

This pungent exchange was lost on the crowd, however, for all eyes were quickly drawn to Little Buffalo. As
a warrior and a man of undisputed bravery, he was
known throughout the Plains, and his daring in battle
had long made him the envy of lesser men. But as *to-
yop-ke,* war leader of both nations, there was little on
which to base a judgment. The Kiowas, as well as the
Comanches, had come solely to hear this man speak; to
listen as he revealed his vision so that they might decide
for themselves the wisdom of the one who would lead
them against the tejanos. Although the council had com-
mitted both tribes to war, tribal law decreed that each
warrior remained exempt from obligation, free to deter-
mine for himself whether or not the elected *to-yop-ke* was
a man he chose to follow into battle.

As Little Buffalo came erect, the assembled warriors
edged closer, watching him expectantly. And no man
present was more aware than the *to-yop-ke* himself that
the next few minutes would decide both the size and the
spirit of the war party he was to lead. Revealed by the
bronze glow of the fire, Little Buffalo's face radiated the
determination and force of character which had brought
him unscathed through a hundred separate battles. As if
gathering himself for yet another test of combat, the *to-
yop-ke* stood motionless, appraising the temper of the curious faces before him. Then without any trace of
apprehension, the quiet intensity of his voice spread
throughout the packed ranks of the spectators.

"Two summers ago I rode with many whose faces I see here this night, following the buffalo below the River of Red Waters. I did this as my father had done before me, so that my wives and children might have plump cheeks and warm bodies. But the pony soldiers fired on us and since that time have driven us ever backwards, so that as in a thunderstorm we have not known which way to go.

"The pony soldiers came from out of the night when it was dark and still, and for campfires they lit our lodges. Instead of hunting game, they killed our warriors, and our women cut short their hair for the dead. So it was in the south, and so it will be in this place unless we dare more now than we have dared in times past.

"During the Leaf Moon, I fasted and sought guidance from *Tai-me* as to the path we must take with the white-eyes. And a vision was granted to me, the same vision of which you were informed in the Summer Moon. In this vision I saw the Great White Father fighting for his life against men of his own tribe. White-eyes fighting white-eyes for seasons beyond counting, and all around them the land lay in desolation.

"All that is except the Plains, the land that was once ours. And presently it became clear to me that on that land there were no longer any forts and the land was no longer scarred by the white-eyes' plows. The grass was once again high, and as far as the eye could see, the buffalo browsed undisturbed, waiting as in days past for the True People to feed and clothe themselves as the need arose. And on the edge of the herd, distant farther than three days' sleeps, the white-eyes' women and children wailed into the night, mourning the loss of their men, their lodges, and all that they had once stolen from the True People."

Little Buffalo paused, as much to collect his own thoughts as to await a reaction among his listeners. But the response of the warriors was one of stunned silence, for as a body they recognized the enormity of his vision, instantly grasping the significance of each symbolic revelation in his graphic account. Watching them intently, Little Buffalo instinctively sensed the awe that had been kindled in their minds. Without hesitation he resumed speaking while they were still under the spell of his astounding vision.

"I was born on the Plains, where the wind blew free, and there was nothing to break the light of the sun. I know every stream and woods between the Rio Grande and the Arkansas. I lived happily like my fathers before me, and like them, I will die there. The white-eyes hold that land now, but for those who ride with me, we will roam there once more.

"The tejanos made sorrow come into our camps, and like buffalo bulls when their cows are attacked, we must drive them into retreat. Where we find them, we must kill them, and their scalps will hang in our lodges. The Comanches and Kiowas are not weak and blind, like pups of a dog when seven sleeps' old. They are strong and farsighted like the gray wolf. The white-eyes have led us on the path to war, and as we are not less than men, we must accept it.

"Now it will be the tejano women who cry and cut short their hair, and our lodges will know laughter once more. From this day forward, until the stones melt and the rivers run dry, I live only to kill tejanos. *And this I vow: those who ride with me will once again call themselves warriors.*"

A moment of silence ensued as the beguiled Indians strained for a better look at this man who would lead them back to the old life. Then the warriors went wild as Little Buffalo's seductive promise resounded across the council ground. The tightly packed braves pushed closer, splitting the night with frenzied yelps. Those with muskets thrust them skyward, firing into the darkness, while others brandished axes and war clubs, screaming vile threats of mutilation and death for the cursed white-eyes. Within moments the council ground had been transformed into a scene of insane blood lust, almost as if the earth's creatures had gone berserk and the people in it were running amuck with some virulent madness.

There was a long night of celebration ahead, however, and Ten Bears moved to quell the explosive situation before it got out of hand. Coming erect, he stood beside Little Buffalo, arms swept outward and face raised to the stars in symbolic supplication to the gods. Slowly the nearer ranks of warriors began to calm as they observed his solemn entreaty, and a gradual hush drifted back through the crowd until a reverent quiet at last settled over the council ground. Without lowering his eyes from the heavens, Ten Bears nodded slightly, and an elderly man detached himself from the spectators.

Sky Walker moved with great dignity, as befitted the

foremost *puhaket* of the Comanches. Oblivious to anything save the gravity of his mission, the prophet and holy man strode purposefully to the medicine lodge and entered. Moments later he reappeared with a large rawhide bundle and placed it on the ground before the fire.

Worshipfully Sky Walker removed a smaller bundle from the first and unwrapped it, revealing a large, carefully crafted idol. He then held *Tai-me* aloft for all to see, and at the sight of the Grandfather God a moaning sigh swept over the crowd. Carved from obscure green stone in ancient times, *Tai-me* was fashioned in the image of man and bore a distinct resemblance to the angular-faced warriors. Arrayed in a resplendent robe of white feathers, with a headdress of ermine skin and blue beads around its neck, the idol somehow seemed charged with life. In the flickering shadows of the council fire it was as though Sky Walker held a shrunken, finely garbed old man above his head, and the assembled might of two savage nations bowed their heads in homage. Later they would dance to the beat of throbbing drums and gorge themselves on buffalo hump and boiled dog, but for the moment the fiercest warriors on the plains groveled before their god and prayed that they might acquit themselves as men in the bloody days ahead.

9

As dawn broke over the Plains, a shimmering glaze of frost cloaked the autumn grasses. Shortly the sun eased over the sandstone cliffs to the east, and there was a crisp bite to the chill morning air. A slight breeze carried the discordant strains of barking dogs, and in the village, women stood with their eyes shaded against the sun, anxiously scanning the grasslands for one last glimpse of their men. On the prairie south of the river seven hundred mounted warriors were massed, silently awaiting their leader. The Comanches and their Kiowa brothers were riding to war, and the spectacle of the formidable host presented by their milling ranks was one which even the tribal ancients had never before witnessed.

Suddenly a small party of horsemen rode from the village, and an expectant stir swept through the massed warriors. Little Buffalo led the riders, flanked on either side by Ten Bears and Santana, and in their wake rode the holy man, Sky Walker. Little Buffalo had decorated himself in the garish heraldry favored by the Plains tribes, and he rode astride a barrel-chested *ehkasunaro*, a magnificent, fiery-eyed pinto. Little Buffalo's face was painted the blue of the sky, with an irregular pattern of large red spots, and his war shield was decorated as a brilliant orange sun with showers of flame arching outward. Atop his head was the war bonnet of the *to-yop-ke*, streaming a coveted train of eagle feathers in the brisk wind. The fabled headdress had been a gift from Ten Bears, who had worn it without mishap or defeat for four decades, and its presence on the new *to-yop-ke* was taken as a sign of strong medicine by the superstitious tribesmen. The overall effect of the *to-yop-ke's* appearance was startling and somewhat bizarre; there would be no doubt among friend or foe as to who commanded the war party. And that was exactly what he intended.

Little Buffalo brought his horse to a halt before the vast array of mounted warriors. The *ehkasunaro* pranced sideways, snorting frosty clouds through its nostrils, and the only sound across the wide prairie was the muffled stamping of thousands of hooves. The *to-yop-ke's* wrenching concern for the lifeblood of his nation was now a thing of the past, and as he stared across the sea of painted faces, Little Buffalo realized that from this day forward, the fate of the Plains tribes was sealed beyond the hand of man or God. Before first light he had received Ten Bears' blessing and embraced the aged warrior in final farewell. Now even the thoughts of his tearful wives and the plump children asleep in his lodge departed his mind, and he turned his face to the south. Toward the sacred land. And the tejanos.

Wheeling the skittish pinto to the front, Little Buffalo raised his clenched fist and roared the ancient war cry. *"Ah-ko!"* The stillness of the moment was instantly charged with tension, and the valley suddenly reverberated with the rumbling thunder of the warriors' frenzied reply. *"Ah-ko!"* Little Buffalo kicked the *ehkasunaro* into a scrambling lope, and the warriors parted as he passed through their ranks to the plains below. Santana and Sky Walker fell in behind him, then the warriors closed ranks once more. To a man the Comanche and Kiowa nations had extended an oath of fealty to their reluctant *to-yop-ke.*

Without a backward glance or a thought for the carefree life now left behind, Little Buffalo led the True People to war.

CHAPTER THREE

1

Britt stepped through the cabin door and buckled his gun-belt in place. Tugging at the holster, he settled the Colt over his hip, then glanced automatically at the sky. Methodically scanning the northern horizon, he noted the absence of any darkening clouds, and his brow wrinkled with a slight frown. Glancing at the trees along the creek, his frown deepened as the stillness of their branches confirmed another windless day. Within the past two weeks this had become his morning ritual, hopefully searching the skies and the silent trees for some sign of oncoming winter.

While mid-October was too early for a storm of any consequence, he still awoke each morning hoping to find the ground blanketed with snow. The depth of the snowfall, or the fact that it might melt within a few hours, was incidental. What mattered was some indication that winter had finally arrived; a threat of impending storm, regardless of its intensity. For only then would there be any certainty that the Indians had abandoned all thought of raiding the settlements.

But the skies remained clear and bright, obstinately sunny. Soon great gusts of wind would come sweeping down out of the northern Plains, the temperature would drop with lightning speed, and within a matter of hours a swirling blizzard would have covered the landscape. But prairie storms were capricious, rarely breaking when expected or hoped for. And the nagging thought that left Britt uneasy and even a little frightened was that the first snow might not come soon enough.

Absorbed in his grisly thoughts, Britt was startled by Mary's gentle teasing. "Whatever you're lookin' for must be mighty important to make you forget this."

Turning, he found Mary smiling at him from the doorway, with his rifle cradled across her arm. "Woman, what would I do without you?" Grinning, he jumped to the doorstep and lifted her easily, holding her a few inches off the floor. Playfully jiggling her from side to side, his eyes came alive with laughter. "Keeps my feet warm and my belly full and she's even got time to chase around remindin' me what a forgetful no-account I am!"

"Lordy, just listen to that man talk," she said. Squirming, Mary tried to free herself, but his grip grew firmer with each wiggle. "Now, Britt, you set me down before them big hands of yours pock me all up with bruises."

Suddenly the doorway was filled with dancing, screaming children as the three youngsters crowded around to watch their mother's predicament. Gently Britt eased Mary to the floor and, before anyone could move, scooped George and Sue Ellen up in his arms. Squealing with delight, the children struggled to break loose, their tiny voices shrill with mock terror. Frank, who had only recently grown too serious for such horseplay, watched on with the detached amusement of an elder brother. Releasing the children, Britt snatched the rifle from Mary's arms, kissed her soundly on the mouth, and leaped from the doorstep to the yard before anyone knew what had happened.

"Now that's enough funnin' for one day," he called back, still chuckling. "This man's got work to do. And, woman, when I get back for dinner, I want to find all of you over at the big house just like you're supposed to be."

Mary frowned, still reluctant to spend her days in the main house, even though it had become a routine after so many months. But beneath the humor in Britt's voice there was a stern note which made his statement more a demand than a request. With a saucy shake of her head Mary smiled and nodded just as Britt knew she would, and he walked lightly on toward the corral.

Hearing voices, he looked around and saw Allan and Tom Fitzpatrick leaving the main house, also headed for the corral. Situated west of the cabins, the corral was a crude affair of split logs. Hastily thrown together after the first Indian scare, it formed a rough square with two sides butted against a steep hill which overlooked the homestead. With the Comanches on the loose, herding cattle in the normal manner had become risky as well as time consuming, and the men were fearful of staying away from the house any longer than necessary. After discussing it, they had decided to corral the herd at night and drive them to the grazing lands each morning.

Though nocturnal by nature, the longhorns quickly adapted to the new scheme of things. Famished after a night in the corral, they were content to graze throughout the day, and soon it required only one man to herd them once they reached the grasslands. The log enclosure now held over a hundred head, including Fitzpatrick's small herd. Milling about expectantly, the cantankerous beasts began crowding against the gate as the three men entered an adjoining corral and set about roping their mounts for the day.

As they saddled their horses, Britt noticed that Allan was quieter than usual, seemingly preoccupied with some troublesome thought. Fitzpatrick rarely extended anything more than a perfunctory nod each morning, and his withdrawn attitude was to be expected. But from Allan it was out of character, and therefore, something to think about. Shrugging it off as a passing mood, Britt kneed his horse in the belly, and when the rangy chestnut released a whoosh of air, he jerked the cinch tight. Still bothered by Allan's distant manner, he decided to take a shot at lightening the mood.

"Boss man, I sure could use a good rest today. Don't you think it's about my turn to play drover and catch a few naps?"

Allan's head jerked around, and from the severe expression on his face, it was clear that the black man's humor had missed the mark. "No, I've already asked Tom to herd the cattle. Once we haze 'em out to graze, you and me will come on back here and work on the new well." Britt's smile faded with the sharp tone, and Allan sensed that his dark mood could stand some airing. "Didn't mean to growl at you. I've got a low feeling today and can't seem to shake it. Probably just a touch of the ague."

"Hell, who wouldn't be feeling poorly," Tom cracked, "playin' shit kicker to them steers night and day. What we need is a little excitement around here for a change."

As if the thought left nothing unsaid, the men silently mounted and rode toward the log corral. Once the bars on the gate were dropped, the longhorns made a rush for the creek and began swizzling greedily after a night without water. When the steers' thirst had beeen slaked, the men started popping their backsides with rawhide lariats, hazing them toward the grasslands to the northwest. Within a few minutes the herd disappeared over a slight knoll in the distance, and the gritty dust from their passing settled once more to the ground.

2

Squatted beside the creek, the scout washed his face in the cold rushing water, then paused to scan the open countryside. The brittle stillness of early morning lay unbroken over the land, and except for a crescent-shaped hill to the north, the bleak terrain seemed desolate in its flatness. Satisfied that nothing unusual was afoot, the scout dipped a tin cup full of water and moved back up the bank to a grove of cottonwoods.

Moments later he reached a small clearing in the trees which was littered with blankets, saddles, and assorted gear. Two horses, munching grain, were tied to a picket line, and a second scout was engaged in splashing a rock at the far edge of the clearing. Easing himself to the ground, the first man dug jerky and hardtack from a saddlebag and began eating with an indifference matched only by the stolid chomping of the horses. Chewing a mouthful of stringy meat, he twisted around and watched as the second man finished relieving himself.

"Damn if you ain't the pissingest man I ever seen. You must of woke me up ten times last night splatterin' that rock."

"It's all this infernal waitin'," the second scout grumbled. "Makes me nervous. Besides, there ain't nothin' else to do anyhow, 'cept freeze our asses off waitin' on Injuns that won't never come."

"Yeah. Sorta buggers me too that the cap'n wouldn't let us build no fire out here." The longer he chewed, the larger the wad of jerky became, and he stubbornly ground on it for a few moments. "Do you reckon the cap'n really believes the Comanch is still gonna come raidin', what with cold weather already settin' in?"

"Who the hell knows what Barry's got spinnin' around in his head? That man's the most untalkative bastard I ever run across." Dropping to the ground, he pulled a hunk of jerky from the saddlebag and regarded it with disgust. "I'll tell you one thing, though. When my time's up, they couldn't get me back in the militia if they greased a brass cannon and jammed it straight up my ass."

"Oh, it ain't all that bad. Not near as bad as fightin' Yankees. And anyway, we only got one day to go till the cap'n sends our relief up."

The two men lapsed into silence, occasionally scanning the empty countryside as they finished a cold breakfast. Since assuming command of Fort Belknap, Buck Barry had been sending teams of scouts to guard the upper end of Elm Creek, and the assignment had long since become a grim joke among the militiamen. Barry had speculated that in the event of a raid the scouts could forewarn the settlers, thereby allowing them to reach the fort with a margin of safety. But as autumn passed, and the ground grew hard with morning frost, the militiamen came to resent Barry's undiminished fear of attack. As far as they were concerned, the Indian threat had come and gone, and their surly attitude was evident in the laxness with which they guarded Elm Creek.

The scouts on duty at the outpost that morning were cold and bored and somewhat irritated with themselves for having overslept. But though the sun had risen, there was nothing about to cause alarm, and they leaned back against their saddles, absorbing the warming rays that filtered through the tree tops.

Since chiding the other man about his overactive bladder, the first scout had been resisting a similar urge with gritted teeth. Finally he decided that a bit of teasing was preferable to the discomfort, and he stepped to the edge of the clearing. The second man was about to make a sarcastic comment when he noticed that his partner's back and chest were pierced clean through by an arrow.

Blinking, he stared incredulously as the first scout tottered and began to fall. Still confused, it flashed through his mind that this was either a damn poor joke or one hell of a bad dream. Then as he lurched erect, an arrow ripped through his throat and all doubt was suddenly dispelled. His legs collapsed, and he sank to the ground, vaguely aware that blood was gushing down over his shirt front. His eyes clouded over, and through a haze he saw three Comanche warriors step from the trees behind the clearing. Blackness closed in over him, obscuring all vision, and his last sensation was the tingling sweep of a scalping knife around his hairline.

After mutilating the dead scouts, the three warriors trotted across the creek onto the open plain. Facing north, the Comanches thrust their bows overhead in a rapid up and down motion, then waited passively for some unseen response to their signal.

As they watched, a horseman crested the bald hill and kneed his spotted *ehkasunaro* down the forward slope. Behind him the knoll filled with riders until the skyline was an indistinct blur of war shields and prancing buffalo ponies. Trailing their leader, the loosely massed warriors then advanced down the hill, and the muted rumble of pounding hooves shook the earth as they crossed the open plain.

Little Buffalo reined to a halt at the headwaters of Elm Creek and whirled the pinto to face his followers. Seven hundred strong, they halted before him, holding a tight rein on their ponies as the excited animals reared and tossed their heads in milling confusion. Waiting for the warriors to calm their mounts, Little Buffalo's face settled on Sky Walker, and he nodded firmly.

The elderly prophet kicked his horse forward in a scrambling lope and then spun him about to face the war party. Holding an ornate buckskin bag aloft, he thrust his hand deep inside and groped for something which seemed to resist being caught. With an air of mystery and omnipotence, Sky Walker slowly withdrew his hand to reveal an owl sitting on the end of his arm. The bird ruffled its wings, and its great yellow eyes flashed omniously in the early morning sun. From a distance it looked real, as if it might leap from Sky Walker's arm at any moment and dart into the grove of trees.

The warriors suddenly grew deathly still, waiting with

edgy tenseness for the *puhaket* to invoke a blessing
through the sacred owl. While everyone knew that the
bird was nothing more than a superbly skinned owl, with
Sky Walker's nimble hand providing the lifelike mo-
tions, they nonetheless regarded it as strong medicine.
Even the bravest of warriors feared the ancient prophet's
supernatural powers, and to ride into battle without the
blessing of the owl was considered the act of a *pawsa,* a
crazy man.

Sky Walker thrust the owl even higher in the air,
and the bird cocked its head from side to side as if gazing upon the warriors. Magically the enormous yellowed
eyes blinked with casual disdain and across the stillness of
the plain came the twittering screech of a swooping, predatory owl. Smiling enigmatically, the prophet returned
the sacred owl to its buckskin sack and withdrew his hand
as if it were in no way connected with the godlike creature.

Little Buffalo spun his horse abruptly, reining the *ehkasunaro* with a cruel jerk, so that it reared high as he
thrust his war lance toward the sky. Supremely confident that his orders would be carried out to the last
man, the *to-yop-ke* kicked the pinto into a gallop and led
the Comanches down the north bank of Elm Creek. Without looking back, he knew that Santana was already fording the stream with his Kiowas to attack along the opposite shore.

3

Joel Meyer kicked the stump a solid whack. Off and on
he had been working at this stump for close to a year,
and he had slowly come to feel a very personal animosity
toward its gnarled and battered form. Like some men,
the stump clung tenaciously to life, clutching at the
earth's moist warmth long after hope had vanished.
Shortly after the tree had been struck by lightning, Meyer chopped it down and began hacking at its deeply im-
bedded roots in what now seemed a never-ending contest
of wills.

While he held no firm convictions regarding the soul
of man, it seemed to Meyer that this stump possessed
some power beyond mere bark and life-sustaining juices.

Often he had sat ouside the cabin in the evening, watching it with a burning sense of frustration as he sought to discover some previously undetected weakness. And on this bright, crisp morning it was still there, scarred but unconquered.

Meyer glanced around to find his son eyeing him curiously, and the boy quickly resumed digging with a spade at the twisted roots. Without turning, he knew that his wife was also watching from near the house, and the thought fanned his determination all the more. Hettie derived a perverse sense of amusement from seeing him thwarted by a grubby stump, and he refused to increase her pleasure by acknowledging that he was aware of her scrutiny.

Removing his coat, Meyer dropped it to the ground and shivered slightly as the chill morning air penetrated his shirt. This was a good time of year for stump clearing, he thought. Once a man worked up a good sweat, the cold disappeared, and he could keep chopping all day without tiring. Spitting on his palm, he rubbed his hands together briskly, then hefted the ax and swung it in a high overhead arc.

The glistening blade hung in midair and failed to descend, as if frozen in a moment of time. From the distance came a deepening roar unlike anything Meyer had ever heard, and with the ax poised to strike, he stopped to listen. Puzzled, he slowly lowered the ax and turned toward the northeast, in the direction of the strange noise. For a moment it sounded like the rumble of thunder from a great distance, and then it occurred to him that thunder lasts only briefly, ending as quickly as it has begun. This was a constant drumming roar, and whatever it was, it was rapidly approaching the stunted knoll less than a quarter-mile away.

Suddenly hundreds of mounted warriors spilled over the low hogback, and Meyer gaped in disbelief as they thundered toward him at a full gallop. His first instinct was to run for the cabin, where his guns hung on the wall; to bolt the door and hold off the red savages until help arrived. But within that same instinctual urge came the realization that it was useless to run. He and his family were doomed as surely as hogs in a charnel house, and if a man was to die, it should be attended to with dignity.

Grasping the ax, he stepped forward and swung as a howling Comanche outraced his brothers to count the first coup. Unaware that his son had just been impaled on a lance or that Hettie had been borne to the ground by a horde of yelping braves, Meyer reeled backward as his head was squashed from the impact of a war club. Staggering blindly, he disappeared beneath an avalanche of hooves, and his last thought was to curse the stump that had defeated him after all.

Little Buffalo circled the pinto to the front of his warriors, urging them forward lest the element of surprise be lost. Through the milling swirl of ponies, he saw Hettie Meyer thrashing naked beneath one brave, while another impassively ripped her scalp away. Rising, the warrior vaulted onto his pony and held the thatch of wavy hair aloft, loosing a blood-curdling scream of jubilation. Little Buffalo drove the barrel-chested *ehkasunaro* through the tangled horses, forcing the warriors' attention away from Hettie's gory struggle. Laughing and shouting, offering vile suggestions to the braves who swarmed over the hysterical woman, the mounted warriors finally heeded Little Buffalo's scathing exhortations.

Wheeling their horses, the war party followed their *to-yop-ke* from the carnage that was once the homestead of Joel Meyer.

Within the next ten minutes, striking almost simultaneously, the Comanches attacked the Hambys while the Kiowas besieged the Williams family. The two homesteads were situated on opposite sides of Elm Creek, only a few hundred yards apart, and the war parties stormed the cabins in a fanatic craze, each determined to outdo the other.

Jonathan Hamby had been mending harness when he heard gunfire from the direction of the Meyer homestead. Without bothering to ponder it, he knew exactly what had happened. Racing to the creek, he emptied his pistol into the air as a warning to the Williamses, then turned to the escape of his own family. This moment of selfless concern sealed their doom, however, for as Jonathan was harnessing a team of horses, Comanches appeared along the creek bank a short distance to the east. Escape was now out of the question, and Hamby quickly forted up inside the cabin with his family. Reloading his pistol, he watched with mounting terror as the warriors galloped forward and resolved to make the Indians pay dearly for the lives of his loved ones.

Bud Williams' luck took an even grimmer turn, despite Hamby's warning shots. The fear that gripped his insides was somehow sensed by the horses as he attempted to rope them, and the normally gentle animals fought like cornered wolves. Feverishly chasing the team from one end of the corral to the other, he failed to see the Kiowas until they were pounding into the front yard. And by then it was too late.

Running toward the cabin, blindly determined to reach his trapped family, he went down under the first wave of warriors and was hacked to pieces in a matter of moments. Had he lived, there would have been small consolation in the knowledge that his wife and two children were taken captive even as a screeching Kiowa lifted his scalp.

Across the creek Little Buffalo was infuriated by Hamby's stubborn defense. Already he had lost five braves, and precious time was being wasted on one insignificant cabin. Patience exhausted, the *to-yop-k*e finally ordered a small band of warriors to burn the cabin along with its occupants. While the buffalo medicine men lashed the dead and wounded to their horses, the rest of the war party thundered south beside the winding creek. Little Buffalo whipped the pinto to a faster pace, cursing the reckless, headstrong warriors. Should they persist in treating each cabin as the sole target of the raid, his plan to annihilate the tejanos would surely fail.

4

Alerted by the sounds of distant gunfire, the three women on the Johnson homestead knew immediately what to expect. They were each veterans of countless Indian raids and the sight of a painted Kiowa or a blood-thirsty Comanche was nothing unique in their lives. Still, this was the first time any of them had been confronted with the prospect of facing red savages without their men. Standing in the yard, huddled together with their children, they attempted to sort out the alternatives and decide what must be done.

"We've still got time to hitch up the wagon and make a run for the fort," Elizabeth Fitzpatrick suggested.

Glancing toward a bend in the creek to make sure the Indians hadn't already removed that option, she turned back to Sarah Johnson. "After all, that's what Allan has been talking about all these months. Getting to the fort before those red devils have a chance to trap us in the cabins."

"I know," Sarah replied indecisively. "But what if we left and the men came back? They'd get trapped trying to save us." Hugging her children close, she looked on the verge of tears. "And we wouldn't even be here."

"If the Comanches were already here, the men couldn't get to us anyway." Elizabeth darted another glance up the creek, certain their time was growing short. "Besides, we've got these kids to think about. The men can look after themselves. Leastways, that's what they generally do anyhow."

"Beth, that's not fair," Sarah cried. "You know the men will come back. And even if the Indians are already here, they'll try to fight their way into the house."

Mary had been listening to this exchange without comment. But her eyes were also on the bend in the creek, and she suddenly became aware that the gunfire in the distance had ceased. Survival was an instinct one acquired shortly after weaning in the slave quarters, and she sensed that if the argument went much further, they would likely die where they stood. "Miz Sarah. Miz Beth. I'm takin' my children in that house and boltin' the door. That's what Mr. Allan told us to do, and I don't reckon I'm smart enough to outguess him just cause this raid came along different'n he expected. Whatever you're gonna do, you'd better do it quick, cause them Comanche are headed this way right now."

Startled by Mary's outburst, the two white women stared at her for a moment and then turned to listen. The gunfire had been replaced by a strange rumbling sound, and while they had no way of knowing what it meant, they felt the earth shimmer beneath their feet and realized that something ominous was rapidly approaching.

"Beth, she's right," Sarah announced firmly. "We're going to fort up just like Allan said, and if you've got any sense, you'll do the same thing."

Elizabeth Fitzpatrick regarded Mary with a vexed expression as the black woman moved toward the house, then she gathered her children with a sigh and followed.

Entering the cabin, they bolted the door with three massive cross bars and quickly shuttered the windows. The children were herded into a corner and admonished to remain still. Mary instructed Frank, who was the oldest, to keep the other children quiet and to make sure that no one left the corner, regardless of what might happen. Turning, she saw Sarah pull Allan's pistol from a holster beside the door.

"My God," Sarah moaned. Her lip quivered, and large tears spilled down over her cheeks. "Oh, my God. We forgot to fire the gun, and the men are too far away. They'll never hear the shooting over at the Hamby's." Hysterically she began to tear at the cross bars, obsessed with the urgency of warning her man.

Striding swiftly across the room, Elizabeth jerked her away from the door and slapped her squarely in the face. "Gimme that gun. Right now I'm the best shot in this house anyway." Wrenching the pistol from Sarah's hand, she took the sobbing woman by the shoulders and shook her forcefully. "Now you listen to me. Those boys are going to hear plenty of shooting any minute now, and they'll be headed this way before you can say scat." Glaring around at Mary, her voice took on a harsh edge. "You two talked me into staying here, so by merciful Jesus, you just keep your heads. If any of them red devils come through that door before our men get here, I know just what to do with this popgun."

Only minutes had passed since the women entered the house, and outside, the distant rumble had now given way to the staccato beat of pounding hooves. Little Buffalo rounded the bend at a steady lope and led the Comanches across the plowed-under field bordering the homestead. Within the span of a deep breath the cabin was encircled by howling warriors, and the Johnson *remuda* had been added to the herd of captured horses now trailing the war party.

Still smarting at the delays which threatened to offset his tactical advantage, Little Buffalo merely glanced at the shuttered house and ordered it burned immediately. If the tejanos were to be outgeneraled and outfought, then the red man's war must be conducted according to plan. And if that deprived the warriors of their lusty pleasures, it was unfortunate but no less essential. Little Buffalo fully intended that tribal history would record him as the *to-*

yop-ke who had utterly desolated the white-eyes, and on this raid at least, the braves would have to be content with victory rather than a carnal display of their manhood.

The barn went first. Filled with hay, it became a raging inferno within seconds, and curiously enough, the Comanches' passions seemed momentarily slaked by the roaring flames. The warriors quickly fashioned firebrands, circling the cabin with yipping war cries as they tossed the torches on the roof. The shingles flared instantly, and within minutes of Little Buffalo's order the homestead was wreathed in a cloud of billowing smoke.

Still intent on taking captives, a group of warriors then wrenched a log from the corral fence and converted it into a battering ram against the front door. Granted, the *to-yop-ke* had ordered the buildings fired, they shouted gleefully, but that didn't obstruct men of cunning from collecting a few of the white-eyes' women before they roasted alive.

Inside the house the women huddled in a corner, clutching their children as flames slowly ate through the underside of the roof. The room was filled with acrid smoke, stinging their eyes and throats with a biting rawness. Gasping for a breath of untainted air, their faces streaked with soot and tears, the terror-stricken women watched in horror as the door shuddered from the impact of the battering log. Elizabeth Fitzpatrick slowly cocked the pistol, rising to shield her childrens' bodies with her own. Sarah and Mary also stood, brandishing common butcher knives they had snatched from the kitchen, forming a human barrier before the whimpering youngsters.

Suddenly the door splintered and slowly caved inward with a wrenching groan as the log penetrated the room. Guttural voices filtered into the cabin, and hands began tearing at the shattered door. To the women it sounded as if a pack of wild animals was clawing at the entrance, snarling and slashing with bared fangs as they fought to be the first to reach the helpless prey. With one last blow the sharded door disintegrated completely and collapsed on the floor.

Gouging and kicking, a dozen warriors jammed the breached entryway and tumbled into the smoky cabin. Through the haze the Comanches and the paralyzed women stared at one another for a moment. Then the center beam in the roof cracked with an explosive report,

and Elizabeth Fitzpatrick was jarred into action. Leveling
the pistol, she fired and a brave dropped to the floor
clutching his groin. Before she could cock the hammer
and fire again, a musket belched flame from the doorway,
and the top of her head disappeared in a bloody froth.
As she toppled forward, the gun clattered to the floor.

Without a moments pause young Frank leaped from
behind his mother, scooping the pistol up as he moved
toward the Indians. Thumbing the hammer back, as he
had seen Britt do many times in the past, the boy thrust
the revolver to arm's length and fired into the mass of red
bodies. Another Comanche pitched to the floor. But before the youngster could cock the gun again, a warrior
hurtled across the room and buried a war ax in his forehead. In the same moment an arrow meant for Frank
pinned Tom Fitzpatrick's daughter to the back wall, where
she hung briefly before slumping forward in death.

Screaming, Mary dropped the butcher knife and threw
herself across young Frank's inert form. Howling trium-
phantly, the warriors leaped on their wild-eyed captives
and began dragging them toward the door as a section of
the roof collapsed in a shower of sparks and flame. Struggling with all her might as a paint-smeared Comanche
hauled her through the door, Mary looked back in time to
see a grinning warrior rip away the scalp of her oldest
son.

5

The longhorns ambled along with bovine listlessness, raising a rooster tail of dust in their wake. The herd had
grazed steadily westward throughout the summer, and the
men were now pushing them toward a wide valley en-
closed by a series of low hills. Slightly more than a mile
from the homestead, the bowl-shaped terrain formed a
natural amphitheater which made it easier for one man to
control the intractable animals. Along the way steers occasionally fell behind as they spotted a particularly tempting clump of grass and drifted off to investigate.

Riding drag, Britt had been kept busy hazing the stragglers back into line. He had just finished chasing a stubborn old cow and her knobby-kneed calf when the muffled crack of gunshots sounded from the rear. Reining his

pony about, he stared in disbelief as a thick column of
smoke rose skyward in the east. For a moment his mind
resisted what his eyes beheld, unwilling to comprehend
that the dreaded day had at last arrived. It just wasn't
possible, he raged inwardly, not with winter about to
break. And yet, there was no denying the chilling implications of smoke mixed with gunfire.

Wheeling the chestnut around, he noticed that Allan
and Tom remained unaware of the drastic turn of events.
Riding flank near the front of the herd, they were unable to hear the shots and hadn't the slightest idea that
anything was amiss. Raking the pony with his spurs, Britt
circled the herd at a gallop and overtook Allan. "Indians" he yelled, pointing frantically to the rear. "They're
burning the house!"

With a single backward glance Allan grasped the situation and began motioning to Tom, who had already
turned in the saddle to stare eastward. Looking around,
Allan saw that Britt had spurred his horse back down the
trail, and he viciously kicked his own mount into a
startled lope. Tom was only a moment behind, ramming
his horse through the now-forgotten longhorns. Forcing
their minds away from the certain horror that awaited
them, the three men raced across the prairie, flogging
their horses unmercifully.

Minutes later Britt skidded to a halt in a stand of trees
on the knoll overlooking their homestead. Leaping from
the saddle, he flung himself to the ground and crawled to
the forward edge of the tree line. Allan and Tom followed close on his heels, and the sight they beheld made
each man gasp with terror.

Hundreds of screaming, battle-crazed Comanches were
massed in the clearing that only hours before had represented a decade of labor for the Johnsons of Elm Creek.
The barn had been reduced to glowing ashes, and the
house was a blazing inferno which was slowly collapsing
wall by wall into a fiery rubble. Britt's cabin was also
burning, with flames leaping skyward in great orange
fountains, and even as they watched, the roof caved in
with a molten roar. Billowing clouds of smoke swirled
across the clearing, momentarily obscuring knots of Indians as a hot wind eddied to and fro off the creek.

Suddenly the wind shifted, and the three men strained
forward, their faces gone cold as death itself. Squinting

past the murky haze, they saw a string of captives being dragged through the swarming Comanches, and the horror so long anticipated had now come full circle. Sarah and Mary stumbled forward with their arms cruelly lashed behind their backs, and the wide-eyed children cowered around them in a whimpering huddle. Surrounded by a small band of warriors, the women were being jerked along by rawhide thongs tied around their necks. Abruptly the women were brought to a halt and forced to their knees before a garishly painted Indian on a huge pinto. Even from the hilltop the three men could tell he was a chief, for the eagle war bonnet clearly separated him from the maelstrom of frenzied braves.

Stepping forward, one of the warriors guarding the captives began a loud harangue, gesturing wildly at the women as he addressed the chief. While the three settlers couldn't understand the guttural ranting, the warrior's meaning was all too clear, and their throats went dry with fear. Whether the aroused Comanche was demanding death or the rights of conquest, the ultimate fate of the women was beyond question, and the watchful men stared at the scene below with mounting revulsion. Without warning, Tom Fitzpatrick suddenly leaped to his feet, muttering hoarse curses as his glazed eyes swept madly across the clearing.

"Beth's not down there! Allan, she ain't there. Oh, Jesus, Jesus! Them murderin' sonsabitches have done something to her."

Later he would remember that his daughter was also missing from the nightmarish scene below, but for now his tortured mind could focus only on the hideous, unspeakable things the Comanches might have done to his wife. Crazed with shock and grief, his reaction was that of a wounded animal. Fumbling aside his coat, Tom snatched his pistol from its holster and with trembling hands brought it to bear on the howling savages.

Bounding to his feet, Britt swung with every ounce of strength in his body. His fist landed against Fitzpatrick's jaw with a mushy splat and the Irishman staggered drunkenly, then pitched to the earth with the chalky pallor of a bled-out corpse. For a moment Britt thought he had killed him, but slowly the color returned to Tom's face, and his labored breathing grew more regular. Crouch-

ing beside the unconscious man, Britt's eyes turned once
more to the grisly scene in the clearing.

The chief on the spotted pinto was now speaking, re-
buking the defiant warrior in cold, merciless tones. The
braves surrounding the captives hung their heads, shamed
before their brothers by the scathing attack. The chief's
voice ended with a harsh command, and the crest-
fallen warriors meekly turned their captives about and
marched them toward the rear of the war party. Never
losing sight of the women and children, Britt and Allan
watched closely while they were hoisted aboard ponies
near the prisoners taken earlier in the morning.

Satisfied that the Indians meant no harm to Mary and
the children for the moment, Britt turned back to the
fallen Irishman. As he did so, a searing, white-hot stab of
pain gripped his insides. *Frank wasn't among the captives!* Maybe the boy escaped or is hiding along the creek-
bank, he thought, desperately grasping for some ray of
hope. Then with the fatalism of all black men he knew
that the boy was dead, more than likely buried in the
smoldering ashes of the main house. His face hardened,
and his eyes grew cold with a rage like a wild thing that
has seen its young hunted and killed. Kneeling on the
ground, he savagely drove his fist time after time into the
frost-hardened earth.

Tom Fitzpatrick moaned and rolled over, coming to
his hands and knees as the film of senselessness slowly
retreated from his eyes. Braced against a tree, he hauled
himself erect and stood glaring at the other two men.
Slobber stained his chin a burnt red, and he thoughtlessly
spit a broken tooth out onto the ground. Blinking his eyes,
he fixed Britt with a malevolent expression, but his words
were directed at Allan.

Johnson, you better lock your nigger up and throw
away the key, cause the first time I catch him runnin'
loose, I'm gonna cut his heart out and feed it to the hogs."

Hurtling up from the ground, Britt threw Fitzpatrick
against the tree and rammed his forearm across the Irishman's throat. Tom's eyes bulged, and he gasped for breath
as the pressure on his Adam's apple became excruciating.
In Britt's murderous gaze he saw death staring him in
the face, and he ceased to struggle.

"White man, I'd just as soon kill you as not. But right
now I need you. All three of us has family down there,

and the only chance they've got of stayin' alive is if we
stay alive. If you'd fired that gun, they'd have had their
throats cut like winter shoats." Jerking Fitzpatrick away
from the tree, Britt gave him a violent shove toward the
backside of the hill. "Now get your ass on that horse
and start actin' like a man. We've got things to do."

6

Grady Bragg sucked air into his lungs and ran a little
faster. His short, paunchy frame wasn't suited to quick
movements, especially when the excitement had his heart
beating faster than his stubby legs could run. His face was
flushed, like a plump child choking on a fish bone, and
with each frantic step his breath came in great sobbing
gasps. Staggering under the load, he tossed a huge trunk
into the wagon, then turned for a hurried look at the columns of smoke along the upper creek.

"Maggie, for God's sake, haven't we got enough?"
Leaning against the tailgate of the wagon, Bragg marveled
at the cowlike composure of his wife. Then, patience exhausted, his voice rose in a harried screech. "Woman,
you're gonna get us scalped trying to save this tacky pile
of shit!"

Turning as she was about to enter the cabin, Maggie's
pinched, tight-lipped face was a portrait of righteous indignation. "Grady Bragg, if you insist on using filthy language in front of women and children, then you can just
leave us here, and we'll find our own way to the fort."
Spinning on her heel, she stormed into the cabin and in
calm, measured tones instructed the children to ignore
their father's vile manner.

Bragg was dumbstruck, completely unnerved by a femi-
nine viewpoint which took offense at a man's cursing when
only a mile away the Comanches were probably mounting
everything in skirts. Upon sighting the pillars of smoke less
than an hour ago, he had immediately hitched the team
and saddled his best horse. But Maggie was not about to
be rushed, even by the Comanches. If their home was going to be burned, then she was determined to save the
accumulated treasures of a lifetime, and she methodically
set about loading the wagon. Grady had urged, cajoled,
and finally resorted to curses, all to no avail.

Bragg glanced upstream once more, fully expecting to see the raiders come boiling over the distant hills at any moment. Goddamn women just aren't human, he fumed, worried about saving a wagonload of dodads when we're only a short hair away from gettin' roasted alive. Then his body stiffened, eyes wide with alarm as he sighted riders cresting the stumpy knolls to the northeast. Grabbing his rifle, he ordered Maggie and the children into the wagon, never taking his eyes from the approaching riders. Surprisingly his heartbeat had calmed, and with a touch of pride he realized that his earlier panic had now been replaced with steady coolness.

The horsemen drew nearer, gradually assuming distinct form, and Grady suddenly sensed that they were white men. Squinting, he looked closer. No, two white men and a nigger! By God, it was the Johnsons and Tom Fitzpatrick! Overcome with relief, Bragg waddled forward with a sudden burst of energy, shouting and waving them on.

The three men rode into the yard at a full gallop, reining the horses back on their haunches in a blinding cloud of dust. Without asking, Bragg knew that they would never have come alone unless their women and children were beyond hope. Allan leaned across the saddle, his voice tight and strained, gesturing in the direction they had come.

"Comanches! No more than a mile back. If you want to keep your hair, you'd better get that team movin' now!"

Before the words were out, Maggie cracked her whip with the deftness of a muleskinner, and the team broke into a headlong lope. Grady ran to his horse and mounted clumsily, listing in the saddle like a corpulent bulldog unaccustomed to great heights. The men reined their horses after the wagon and pounded out of the yard.

Glancing back over his shoulder, Britt saw the war party top the rolling hills behind them, and he shouted a warning to the others. Slowed by the pace of the wagon, the four men checked the loads in their pistols and watched the dust cloud to their rear with a growing sense of alarm.

After what seemed a small lifetime they reached the wider banks of the Brazos and thundered south along the river trail. Ahead of them the rutted track was cloaked with the dust of a dozen wagons racing for the fort, and it

suddenly dawned on them that they were the last to escape Elm Creek alive. Turning in the saddle, Britt's eyes
narrowed as he saw two columns of Indians converge
where the stream joined the Brazos. Astounded by what
appeared to be upward of a thousand warriors, he realized for the first time that what had taken place since daylight was something more than a mere raid. The Comanches were bad enough, but if they had joined forces with
the Kiowas, then it might just be that even Fort Belknap
would go up in flames.

Abruptly it flashed through his mind that Mary and
the children now rode with that same war party. Willing himself to live, regardless of the cost to those around
him, Britt rammed the chestnut in the sides and concentrated on reaching the fort in one piece.

7

Earlier that morning, shortly after Jonathan Hamby's
cabin was put to the torch, a sentry at Fort Belknap
spotted a thin wisp of smoke far across the plains. For a
moment he watched it uncertainly, hesitant to sound a
false alarm in the event it was nothing more than an
illusion evoked by the glare of sunrise. Then, even though
he remained skeptical, the sentry decided to play it safe by
calling the corporal of the guard. If he had learned anything after six months in the militia, it was that a smart
soldier always hedged his bet; survival in the army, as
seasoned campaigners had demonstrated, was simply a
matter of passing the buck upward until some hero made
the decision.

Within a quarter-hour the amused sentry was congratulating himself as he watched first a corporal, then a ser-
geant, and finally a grumbling, sleepy-eyed lieutenant
confound themselves staring at his discovery. The lieutenant was also well versed in passing the buck, and with
some misgiving he in turn sent an orderly to fetch Captain
Barry.

Unlike his subordinates, Barry had never lost belief
that the Comanches would ride south before the first snow.
When he lumbered up the stockade ladder to the catwalk
a short time later, the raid was already well under way,
and the distant pall of smoke removed any doubt as to

what was happening on Elm Creek. The prospect of a good scrap instantly aroused him, and with the surly disposition of a grizzly in mating season, he ordered the militia saddled and held ready for a sortie.

Quickly assembling the settlers quartered in the fort, he advised them of the situation and outlined his plan to ride against the Comanches. After informing them that the responsibility for manning the stockade had now fallen on their shoulders, the commander turned and marched brusquely toward headquarters, leaving the gaping civilians to stare after him. Still somewhat incredulous, they watched in numbed silence as Barry led the troop of militiamen through the front gate and galloped north along the river trail.

Less than a half-hour later Barry began meeting settlers as their wagons rumbled toward the fort. Concealing his troops in a shallow depression behind a hill, he stationed himself in a stand of cottonwoods near the trail. With his combative nature at full pitch he relished the idea of ambushing a pack of howling savages, gloating already over the shocked confusion that was sure to result when the trap was sprung. As yet, none of the settlers could actually say they had seen the Indians, and his hurried questioning had yielded nothing firm regarding the war party's size. But Buck Barry was a man of supreme confidence, if not outright arrogance, and he was satisfied that the Texas militia could handle anything the Comanches were able to raise with winter so near.

Shortly afterward Barry saw Grady Bragg's wagon careening down the trail with four horsemen bringing up the rear. Reining his mount out of the cottonwoods, he waved the wagon on and held up his hand to halt the riders. The four men jerked their winded ponies up short and crowded around the burly officer. Exhilarated by the imminence of a fight, Barry greeted them with a huge grin, failing to notice the utter despair written across their faces.

"Boys, here's where you quit running. I've got my troops back over that hill, and we're fixin' to bushwhack ourselves a few redsticks. Care to join us?"

The four men looked at one another with amazement, slowly comprehending that the captain was ignorant of what it was chasing them. Then Tom Fitzpatrick's sardonic voice broke the silence. "Mister, in about five minutes everyone of your soldier boys is gonna be standin' in a puddle full of piss. There's enough Comanches coming down that road to eat your bunch alive and spit out the seeds."

Buck Barry's grin dissolved into a churlish scowl, but before he could reply, Allan confirmed the odds they faced. "Captain Barry, you'd better set aside your personal feelings about Tom and listen. Otherwise, you'll likely lose your whole command before the fight even gets started. There's somewhere around a thousand Indians headed this way, and nothing this side of the swivel guns at the fort is about to stop them. The only reason we got this far is because they couldn't resist burning the cabins along the river trail."

"Johnson, you must have been drinkin' too much pop-skull," Barry growled. "And the rest of you must need spectacles. The Comanches couldn't raise a thousand braves if they had Jesus H. Christ beatin' the drum."

"Cap'n, it's not just Comanches," Britt retorted heatedly. "I've lived through enough raids to know what kind of Indian I'm lookin' at. And about half that war party is Kiowa." The other men looked at him in bewilderment, unaware that he had observed the two tribes regrouping forces on the Brazos. "I'm not real set on losing my hair today either, so I think I'll just get this horse headed in the right direction." Nodding upstream, the black man smiled at Barry. "I got a feelin' you won't be far behind."

Without another word Britt spun the chestnut about and headed toward the fort at a fast lope. Barry and the three settlers glanced north along the trail, and Britt's cryptic remark needed no explanation. Less than a half-mile distant the vanguard of the Comanche and Kiowa nations surged forward at a thundering trot. Barry's features blanched noticeably, and his eyes took on the glassy vagueness of one who has just looked into an open grave and seen his own face. The homesteaders spurred after Britt, and the captain hesitated only briefly before plunging back over the hill.

Gathering the puzzled militiamen, he led them in head-long flight toward the south. Once the soldiers got a look at what was chasing them, they needed no urging. Long before the column reached the fort, Buck Barry found himself overtaken and outdistanced by at least half the troop. When fighting Comanches, stragglers rarely stood to for the next mess call, and among the Fort Belknap complement there was an obvious reluctance to be the last man through the gate.

Toward midmorning Little Buffalo brought the *ehkasunaro* to a halt just out of rifle range on a hill overlooking the fort. Swarmed around him, spilling out over the plains below, the warriors hooted contemptuously as the last rider raced through the stockade gate. Their mocking chant floated eerily across the open ground, filling the air like an ominous hot wind, and those inside the fort knew they were listening to the voice of death.

But their day of judgment was postponed by the wily young *to-yop-ke* who watched from the hill. Little Buffalo had no intention of losing both warriors and precious time by laying siege to a fortified position. Such an attack would be lengthy, as well as costly, and a poor exchange for the lives of a mere forty or fifty white-eyes. Below Fort Belknap lay a multitude of unsuspecting tejanos, and the shrewd tactician always struck first at the weak underbelly of his enemy. Besides, his warriors were interested in scalps and fair-haired captives, and they would quickly grow bored with the childish white-eyes cowering behind wooden walls. Men fought openly, testing their courage face to face, and how was a brave expected to count coup on a race that scampered to their hole like a timorous rabbit?

Reining the pinto downhill, Little Buffalo forded the Brazos and led his warriors south. Death had paid a brief call at Fort Belknap and, finding it wanting, moved on to more receptive company.

8

The brilliant, starlit sky seemed wholly at odds with the mood of the settlers. Ominous black clouds, with an oppressive dirge and tolling bells, would have been more appropriate to their glum silence. Gathered along the stockade catwalk, they solemnly stared at the distant glow which illuminated the southern horizon. Throughout the long afternoon and early hours of darkness they had observed an advancing chain of smoke and flame as one settlement after another was put to the torch. And from the fort it appeared likely that every homestead along the

Brazos had been reduced to ashes. Drained of emotion, they simply stood and watched as the holocaust spread through the night. Remorse for neighbors and loved ones lost in the raid left them overcome with grief, and they could only hope that the families farther south had fared better at the hands of the Comanches. Prayers they reserved for their own dead.

Suddenly the stillness was broken by the sound of a horse being pushed hard, and a rider appeared from the darkness. Rifles came to bear over the stockade wall, and there was the unmistakable click of hammers being thumbed back. Then, as fingers tightened nervously on triggers, a voice from below calmed the jumpy settlers.

"Hold your fire! Scout coming in!"

The gate swung open with a creaking groan, and the rider galloped through on a lathered horse. Clambering down from the walls, settlers and militia alike ran after the scout as he reined to a halt before headquarters and dismounted. Buck Barry filled the doorway in the same moment and stepped forward to greet the man. Observing his haggard appearance, the captain called for whiskey, and the gathering crowd waited tensely as the scout drained a brimming glass with obvious relish. Smacking his lips, the man wiped his mouth with a grimy sleeve and slowly looked around the curious faces.

"Goddammit man, tell us!" Barry roared. "Or are you waitin' for somebody to start pitching coins?"

"No, Cap'n, I ain't. It's just that I don't rightly know where to start. Whatever you expected, it's about ten times worse'n you thought."

"Well, I don't see anybody here crying for a sugar tit, so suppose you just give it to us like we was full-grown."

The scout nodded, glancing around the somber crowd. "It ain't exactly pretty. I done just like you told me and snuck around Elm Creek first. Then I cut cross-country and hung behind the redsticks down the lower Brazos. Cap'n, the easiest way to say it is that there ain't a building left standin' within twenty miles of this fort. What they couldn't burn or carry, they killed. They're trailin' a herd of about a hundred horses, and they slaughtered enough stock to feed an army." Then his eyes wavered, unable to meet the settlers' frozen stares as he voiced their innermost fears. "I couldn't get too close, you understand, but near as I could figure, they've got somewheres around ten women and eighteen kids."

There was a moment of deathly silence, then settlers throughout the crowd began pushing forward to inquire of wives or children missing since the raid. The scout shook his head in response to the anxious shouts, repeating over and over again that he had never gotten close enough to actually see the captives' faces. Suddenly the man noticed Britt among the crowd, and his face took on the look of one who has just recalled a minor but salient detail.

"Say, there's one thing I thought of," he said, quieting the settlers as he nodded directly at Britt. "And it might just interest this man. Even as far away as I was, I could tell there was a black woman and two black young'uns mixed in with them taken prisoner."

The crowd turned to look at Britt, and for an instant in time the separation between black and white became an unbridgeable chasm. Their faces reflected anger and resentment, and about them clung the unspoken thought that a nigger had been singled out over God's own. While each would have given his life for the knowledge that friends and loved ones were at least alive and uninjured, this coveted solace had been granted solely to a black man. And in that they beheld a highly profound injustice.

Watching their faces, Barry sensed the temper of the crowd and quickly diverted their attention back to the scout. "Which way were the Indians heading when you left them?"

"Cap'n, I stuck with 'em till they turned sorta northeast after raidin' Mineral Wells. Appears to me they're gonna circle Fort Richardson and hit the settlements up that way. Ain't nobody chasin' them, but they seemed just a mite anxious to get back across the Red." When the officer failed to respond, apparently digesting what he had just heard, the scout ventured a shrewd judgment. "You know how Injuns is. Once they get enough horses and scalps, there ain't nobody this side of Lucifer himself could talk 'em into more fightin'."

"Why don't you go sample that jug sittin' on my desk?" The man scampered through the door before the unexpected offer could be withdrawn, and Barry turned to the crowd. "You all heard the report, and you know as much as I do at this point. So why don't you turn in and

get some sleep just in case the Comanches decide to surprise us again in the morning."

As the captain turned to the door, the crowd broke up
and began drifting toward the old federal barracks, where
they had been quartered. Their movements were slow and
dispirited, characteristic of those who have seen a lifetime's dreams suddenly go up in smoke. Shoulders
slouched, their features blank and forlorn, they seemed
bereft of hope. And beneath their hollow stares waited
the tears that would come in the solitary night. For while
the dead could be buried and done with, there would be
no end to mourning the women and children now con-
signed to a living death.

Britt walked beside Allan and Tom, seeing in his mind's
eye the picture briefly described by the scout. Hundreds
of leering warriors surrounding an island of white captives.
And within that vast, hostile throng three tiny black faces
searching desperately for some end to their terror. It was
like a grotesque nightmare, clawing its way up from the
slimy depths of a man's secret furies. But it was no dream,
and where death had a finality to it, the thoughts of Mary
and the children being enslaved by the Comanches tor-
mented Britt all the more. Slowly his mind surfaced from
such thoughts, unable to cope with the odious specter
they conjured up, and he became aware of the white men's
strained conversation.

"Tom, I don't give a damn what you say, it was all my
fault," Allan snapped. "I took it upon myself to give the
orders, and if I'd just left one man at the house, none of
this might have happened."

"Hindsight ain't no better than hind tit," Tom replied.
"Even if a man could see every little thing that's going to
happen down the road, he'd still make mistakes, maybe
more." His voice broke, and they walked a few steps farther in silence. "We just got careless. Lazy, goddamn careless! And we're all gonna live with that for a long time."

"You won't get any argument there." Allan's voice was
barely audible, filled with loathing for his own short-
sightedness. "I had a feeling this morning something was
wrong. But I put it off. Just put it out of my mind. And
instead of being concerned with the women and kids, I
was worrying about getting those steers out to graze. By
God, if I had the mangy bastards here, I'd shoot everyone
of 'em right between the eyes!"

"Who gives a shit about cows!" Tom exploded. "You wanna know what sticks in my craw? I lost my whole family and ended up not even killin' *one* of those red sonsabitches!"

"You didn't lose your son," Britt suggested. The two white men glanced around sharply at his unexpected comment. "Leastways, he's not dead. And there's just a chance him and the others might be gotten back."

Fitzpatrick glared at him suspiciously, still rankled by the incident on the hillside that morning. Allan knew the black man well enough to grasp that there was something tangible beneath his matter-of-fact attitude, and a stirring of hope echoed in his insistent demand. "Britt, I'd move heaven and earth if there's even the slighest chance we could get them back. Now don't come at it sideways. Whatever you're scheming on, let's hear it straight out."

The white men halted, facing him, and Britt searched their faces for a moment. When he spoke, his tone was calm and understated, without a trace of bravado. "I'm going to cross the Red River and see if I can find the village where they're being held. Ever since we settled here, I've been hearing stories about people ransomed back from the Comanches. And the way things are, I reckon that's the only chance our women and kids have of not being camp slaves the rest of their lives."

Silence mounted as the two men stared at him incredulously. Many Texans had been ransomed from the Comanches over the years, but always with the army or unscrupulous Indian traders acting as intermediaries. Never had an individual negotiated the release of captives, regardless of the price offered. And for a lone man to cross the Red River was tantamount to suicide. Not as quick, perhaps, for being roasted head down over a slow fire was a prolonged death. But just as final.

"Britt, you're overwrought, or you wouldn't even consider such a plan." Allan's tone was solicitous, slightly indulgent. "Even if you could find where they're being held, the Comanches would more than likely kill you anyway. And what good would it do Mary and the children if you're dead?"

"If you're talking about a white man, I might agree with you," Britt said. "But we both know the Comanches don't feel the same way about blacks. They think we've got good juju, or whatever it is they call their brand of voodoo. I've always heard they're real curious about blacks, and I'm willing to risk it if it means getting our families back."

"Risk is the right word. You'll be staking your life that they won't lift your hair just because it's not straight and blond."

"By God, I hate to say it, Allan, but I think he's got the right idea for a change." Fitzpatrick's support came as a surprise to Britt, and he eyed the Irishman skeptically. "There's only one thing wrong. He needs someone to show him how to outsmart those stinkin' bastards. So, Britt, boy, I just declared myself in on your little expedition."

The black man's cold eyes bored a hole in Fitzpatrick, recalling his hysteria and muddled thinking on the hillside. "Sorry, this is a one-man show. If two of us ride in there, the Comanches will start thinking about scalps instead of how good a deal they can make."

"Slow down, highstepper," Tom cautioned with a patronizing smirk. "Your stride's getting too long for your britches. Maybe it slipped your mind that I got a son up there too. So what the hell gives you the right to say whether or not I come along?"

"Mister, you've got things a little confused," Britt replied stonily. "I didn't say you couldn't go. I just said you couldn't go with me. If you're itching to get killed, do it on your own time."

"You goddamn smart-mouth coon!" Tom flared. "Got your black ass perched up there on some kind of throne and sit around snickering at us dumb white folks!" Heads began appearing in windows and doorways as his strident voice carried throughout the fort. Observing the spectators, Fitzpatrick took courage, ignoring his narrow escape at the black man's hands just that very morning. "You better listen to me good, boy. The day ain't arrived that a uppity nigger can start tellin' white men where to head in! And if you don't want your balls nailed to a tree, you'd best start planning on some company when you ride north."

Britt started forward, determined to still the Irishman once and for all. Their brief encounter on the hillside flashed through his mind and with it came regret that he hadn't killed the bigoted loudmouth when he'd had the chance. But Allan quickly moved to block the black man's path, voicing an unspoken warning as he jerked his head in the direction of the barracks.

Shadowed forms were running across the parade grounds, attracted by an argument that unmistakably involved a white man and the Johnson nigger. More settlers were pouring out of the barracks each moment, and an icy chill suddenly settled over Britt. Earlier their eyes had filled with hate simply because the scout had observed only his family among the captives, and if he read the signs right, they were spoiling for an excuse to vent their anger over the raid—the same anger that had turned to jelly before the Comanches. Black men had died before with even less reason, and Britt had no illusions about his chances now if the crowd suddenly turned ugly.

9

Buck Barry broke off interrogating the scout when he heard angry shouting from outside. Barreling through the orderly room, he reached the porch in time to see men running toward the parade ground. Even in the starlight their forms were indistinct, and it was difficult to make out the exact nature of the commotion. But harsh words were being exchanged, and Barry was in no mood to tolerate dissension among the fort's defenders. Not with the Comanches still ravaging the countryside.

Striding swiftly in the direction of the gathering mob, Barry reflected on the absurdities practiced by seemingly reasonable men once they came under great stress. God knows they've got good cause, he thought, what with their homes being burnt and their women carted off to share some Comanche's blankets. But he had spent most of his life among fighting men, and instinctively he knew that their curious antics after a defeat sprang from a far deeper source. Once he had heard a brimstone preacher rant about a man being a soul concealed in an animal, and after twenty years on the frontier he found it to be a fair judgment. Men could withstand danger and hardship as a matter of course; they could even face death with the civilized veneer intact. But when their manhood was threatened, some strange, atavistic force seized them, and the animal inside was quickly unleashed.

The crowning humiliation, as he had often noticed, was

not that their women were raped or that they themselves
had been forced to run. Rather it was the fact that these
things had happened without any retaliation from them.
Almost anything could be endured, but how could a man
live with himself if he failed to strike back and in the
process lost his own manhood? Curiously this impotent
rage was more often than not turned back on a man's own
comrades, and as Barry approached the crowd, it occurred
to him that a mob of overgrown little boys seeking to regain their virility was no joking matter.

"You men are letting personal feelings get in the way of
your judgment." Shouldering his way through the crowd,
Barry could detect in Allan's voice the urgency of a man
with his back to the wall. "Britt's the one man who has a
chance of crossing the Red and coming back alive. And
that's only because the Indians have always been friendly
toward blacks."

"Johnson, we're sick to death of you and your smart-
aleck nigger." The crowd muttered with approval as a
settler from below the fort lashed out angrily. "Lots of us
here lost women and kids today, and before we'd let some
numbskull coon go up there and get 'em killed, we'd just
as soon cut his throat. Yours too if you don't back off."

The mob edged closer around Allan and Britt as an
undertone of hostility swept through their ranks. Clearly
they were bent on avenging the frustrations of a long,
disastrous day, and an uppity nigger sounded like a good
substitute for the red bastards that had gotten away.
Knocking settlers aside none too gently, Barry sensed the
swelling of their hoarse threats as he reached the center of
the pack. The men were eyeing Britt menacingly, waiting
for someone to make the first grab, and it seemed unlikely
that even the militia commander could stay their wrath.

"Now let's don't go off half-cocked, boys." Tom Fitzpatrick's joshing tone made them hesitate. Surprised,
they turned to look at him with some bewilderment, since
it was his truculent outburst that had started the trouble
in the first place. "I think we got us a coon that's about to
see the light. Aren't you, boy?" Tom grinned crookedly at
the black man, but Britt returned his stare with cold insolence. "See there, he's already learnin' to put a damper
on that smart mouth! And I got an idea him and me will
get along real fine while we're up there talkin' the Comanche out of all them women and kids."

"Fitzpatrick, you're living proof that there are more horses' asses than there are horses!" Buck Barry's malevolent snarl rocked the crowd back on their heels. "You're the one that's got a smart mouth. And the only thing you'd accomplish talkin' to the Comanches is to get yourself *and* Britt staked out on an anthill."

"Soldier boy, I've had about all of you one man can take," Fitzpatrick grated as his face purpled with rage. "This here's civilian business, and we don't need some rumpot muckin' it up. If you're so all-fired concerned, you should of done a little more Injun fightin' this morning, 'stead of running back here like a gelded hog."

Almost before the words were out of his mouth, Fitzpatrick felt something explode in his brain, and the whole left side of his head suddenly went numb. Through a red, star-shot haze he saw Barry standing over him, and as a swirling darkness sucked him under, he faintly realized that he was flat on his back.

Barry gingerly rubbed the knuckles of his bruised fist, staring thoughtfully at the fallen Irishman. The grizzled officer's very appearance was enough to halt most antagonists in their tracks, for no man knew his full strength. And he was always curious about anyone with the audacity to crowd him. Dismissing Fitzpatrick as a reckless hothead, he glowered around at the settlers, amused by their reluctance to meet his eye.

"You men seem to have forgotten who runs this fort. I'd advise you not to listen to blowhards like Fitzpatrick in the future." Pausing, he waited to see if anyone was inclined to pursue the matter, but the men again avoided his gaze. "Now if Britt Johnson wants to cross the river, that's his business, and I don't want to hear any more about it. And just in case any of you are still skeptical, I'll guaran-damn-tee you he's the only man on the Brazos that's got a chance in hell of bringing those women and kids back alive. This meeting stands adjourned. Some of you men drag that thick-headed mick back to the barracks and let him sleep it off." Turning away, he called over his shoulder, "Britt, I want to see you in my office."

10

The three men stood near the front gate, talking quietly in the predawn darkness. Their words hung in the chill air, wreathed in puffs of frost, lingering eerily even after the sound had drifted off. About them there was a sense of grave finality, as if only the moment existed and their tomorrows were obscured by some impenetrable veil. Moments of stillness followed each taciturn flurry of words, and their reluctance to evoke a final parting formed an unspoken bond between them. Finally the larger of the three men shook hands, then turned, and lumbered wearily toward headquarters.

Britt and Allan remained silent for a moment, lost in their own thoughts as they watched Buck Barry trudge slowly across the parade ground. The night had been long and grueling, and their eyes were etched with the tenseness of men embarked on a hazardous undertaking. Less than six hours had passed since their meeting with Barry in the commander's office. After confirming Britt's resolve to ride north, the captain had advised him to leave the fort before dawn. The settlers were in an ugly mood, and if Barry was any judge of men, they wouldn't rest until their own guilt had been absolved in some violent manner. Right now Britt looked to be the most likely prospect for the sacrificial goat, and before the situation worsened, Barry wanted him long gone from the fort's volatile atmosphere. Allan concurred, though not without some misgiving as to the black man's chances north of the Red River.

The rest of the night had been spent in outfitting Britt for the journey. Barry loaned him a sturdy pack horse from the government mounts and opened the fort's storeroom for food and gear. That left only the matter of presents, and Allan quietly roamed the barracks gathering trinkets and household items which might appeal to savage curiosity. When he returned and the three men stood gazing at the assortment of paraphernalia, it became obvious that they lacked anything sufficiently ostentatious with which to honor a proud, and quite probably antagonistic war chief. The problem was one of acute significance, for the chief must be won over before the issue of ransom was ever broached.

Then, in a tone of mock disgust Barry cursed his own weakness and stepped to a gunrack on the wall. From it he jerked a highly prized Belguim Over and Under rifle/ shotgun and handed it to Britt with the awkward stiffness of one who finds selfless acts intensely embarrassing. Gratitude among such men came equally hard, and without a word they began packing the goods and provisions for the long trek northward.

The time to depart had come. The first, diffused rays of light were beginning to break in the east, and the two men could faintly make out one another's features in the dusky glow. Loath to part, they had been avoiding this last moment with idle conversation. But the words seemed forced, hollow of meaning. And they were both aware that Britt had best be gone while the fort still slumbered.

Clasping the black man's hand, Allan's voice was husky and strained. "Britt, we've never been much for words. Seems like there wasn't any need. And I can't think of a hell of a lot to say now, except that I want you back here in one piece. No matter what happens up there. Sleep light and keep your dobber dry."

Britt smiled tightly, sensing the emotion behind his friend's laconic manner. "That's a promise. And I'll stay downwind too, like your daddy taught us." The words came harder now, and he paused. "I'm not plannin' on staying up north, but just in case I don't get back, I want you to know I went under trying to save yours just like I would my own. Even then I reckon I'd still owe you. Watch after yourself, Allan."

Mounting quickly, Britt reined the chestnut around and led the heavily laden pack horse through the front gate. The sentry glanced curiously at him, and he nodded in silent reply, certain that word of his departure would be all over the fort before breakfast. Glancing back, he saw Allan standing just outside the gate, and he waved. Then he put the chestnut into a trot, and the rushing waters of the Brazos were soon left behind.

Presently he crested a knobby hogback and reined to a halt. The sun had now scaled the horizon, casting golden shafts of light across the plains. Far in the distance he could make out the shapeless mass of Fort Belknap, and it occurred to him that the settlers would probably spend the day swilling whiskey and damning his black soul. Then Buck Barry's gruff voice came back to him, and in his mind he again heard the words that had startled him so last night.

"Britt, I wouldn't defend Fitzpatrick if his granddaddy was Jesus H. Christ. He's a loudmouth and a trouble-maker, and if he doesn't force me to kill him, it'll be noth-ing short of a goddamn miracle. But even the devil de-serves his due, and the next time you get to thinkin' about how much fun it'd be to bust him up, you ought to recol-lect a couple of things about Fitzpatrick. For openers, he was the only man in this fort with guts enough to try and join your little expedition. None of the rest of 'em wanted anywhere near it. Now the other part of it has still got me bumfuzzled, and I don't pretend to understand why he did it. But whatever his reasons, he stopped the mob just when they were about to jump you. If he hadn't of spoke up when he did, they'd have left you stone cold faster'n a horse turd draws flies." Then Barry had slowly shaken his head, like a man confronted by some unfathomable rid-dle. "Maybe you can figure it out."

Britt mulled the words around in his head, trying to find some clue to a man who would sic a mob on a lone ad-versary and then call them off just as if they were a pack of bear hounds. Thoroughly at a loss, he pushed the thought from his mind, determined to settle with Fitz-patrick one way or another when he returned. Then his great, booming laugh echoed across the rolling hills. *When I return!* Hell, black boy, you best start worryin' about *if you return!*

Still chuckling, he pointed the chestnut north and gently nudged him in the ribs. Ahead lay the Red River and a wilderness crawling with Comanches. And that, my friend, he chortled, is enough for any smartass nigger to take on at one time.

CHAPTER FOUR

1

Children roamed through the village in small, predatory bands, their chubby coppery faces twisted with mock ferocity. Even the young warriors needed to practice their trade, and the air was filled with squealing howls as they gleefully savaged one another in the never-ending war games. A bountiful summer had left their bellies plumply taut, and their spirited laughter bespoke the sense of well-being which permeated the village. The grove of trees bordering the Canadian was now bare of leaves, making the ground crackly and alive with sound underfoot as they stalked each other through the brush. Gray-barked cottonwoods and amber scrub oaks stood out in bold relief against the bronzed earth and the vermilion bluffs rising to the east. And as the Geese Going Moon approached, the lodges were warm and filled with the happy chatter of women preparing pemmican for the long winter ahead.

The chill wind had fallen away, as it did each evening when the sun retreated westward. Dusk came earlier now, casting dim blue shadows across the sluggish Canadian, and smoke from the cooking fires hung undisturbed in the dry, still air. Later the breeze would come again, crisp and more biting in the clear darkness, and before morning the

trees would moan in creaking anguish as the rising wind
whistled through their stark crowns. But the last rays of
sunlight faded slowly, and old men who squatted before
their lodges watched the prairie to the south with patient,
watery eyes.

Since early morning an air of expectancy had hovered
over the village, causing women to pause in their work and
stare hopefully across the shimmering plains. Somehow,
in ways which they neither understood nor questioned,
they sensed that their men were close, and the long hours
of the day had dragged by with unbearable slowness.
Now as dusk resolutely settled over the village, each
woman stood alone in her mounting concern. The forces
of darkness were evil and pitiless, and for the men to return now might be a bad sign indeed. But it was always
like this when the men returned from a raid. Whether they
rode in with the break of dawn or the shadows of dusk,
fear gnawed at the insides of every woman: the instinctive dread that the face she sought would be missing from
their ranks.

When the war party finally appeared on the plains to
the south, most of the people were in their tepees. The
distant thud of hoofbeats brought their heads around,
making them pause as they cocked their ears to the swelling rumble. Then the lodges emptied, cooking pots forgotten, as lighthearted villagers and a chorus of barking
dogs streamed toward the edge of camp. Far away they
could see a rolling wave of horsemen advancing steadily
across the flaxen grasslands. As they watched, the bobbing
mass slowly separated into distinct forms, and yipping
cries of victory floated in on the south wind. Muttering
among themselves, the toothless elders shook their fists to
the sky, proclaiming deliriously that the tejanos had been
devastated beyond all belief. Clearly it must be so, they
jabbered, for had not Little Buffalo chosen to ignore the
night devils and bring his war party home as the last faint
glow of light slipped over the horizon?

Suddenly the warriors thundered into camp, laughing,
shouting at friends and loved ones, howling the ritual
chants of blooded victors. Reining their ponies tightly,
they never once broke ranks, according their stern-faced
to-yop-ke the honor of leading them on an exultant march
through the village. Little Buffalo stared straight ahead,
closing his mind to the hysterical cries of the villagers who

ran alongside the skittish ponies. His manner was proud and yet filled with humility, somehow above the petty arrogance that such adulation might have exposed in lesser men. As befitted the leader of a conquering nation, he sat the *ehkasunaro* with lordly bearing, aware of nothing save the glory his warriors had brought to the True People.

Before the medicine lodge, he brought the horsemen to a milling halt and spun the pinto around to face them. The villagers fanned out around the war party, jostling and shoving as they sought a better look at the man who had avenged two decades of humiliation and defeat. Little Buffalo thrust his lance to the sky so that all might see the gory, light-haired scalps which festooned its shaft. Then he plunged the lance into the ground, jangling the crusted scalps as they flapped against one another, and raised his voice in savage exultation. *"Ah-ko!"*

Three thousand voices split the night as villagers and warriors alike echoed the war cry with a crazed roar. While the howling braves worked themselves into a frenzy, Little Buffalo cast a searching gaze through their ranks, smiling faintly as Ten Bears stepped forward. Their eyes locked, and for a moment the two men were alone, isolated in a soundless void that excluded all but the force of their own thoughts. The old chief's grizzled features were flushed, buoyant; the face of a man who has lived to see his uttermost prayers answered in full. And the clenched fist he extended in salute came almost as a benediction for the triumphant son. Then the shrill clamor of the spectators broke the momentary spell, and Little Buffalo again became the *to-yop-ke*. The stoic mask fell into place, and his hooded eyes once more swept the crowd. Raising his arm, he commanded silence, and within the space of a heartbeat the screeching voices fell still.

"What was promised has been fulfilled! The tejanos along the Brazos are rubbed out, no more! Their lodges are now ashes in the wind, and behind us comes a herd of horses that will make every man here a person of wealth!" The spectators roared their jubilation, laughing and slapping one another on the back as they congratulated themselves on the good fortune of the True People.

"No more will the white-eyes desecrate our sacred hunting grounds, for they have been left desolate, without the means of food or life in that land. And as their horses and cattle have been sacrificed, so have we taken away the tomorrows of their children. *There before you stand the tomorrows of the tejanos!*"

Little Buffalo's arm slashed in a violent arc, coming to rest on the band of terror-stricken captives. Jerked from their horses, they had been kicked to the ground and huddled there in a filthy, shivering heap. Again the crowd howled with delight, gesturing derisively at the wide-eyed captives as they cowered even closer together. Then the *to-yop-ke's* strident voice sliced across the village, stilling their jeering taunts.

"But we return with more than this! Something that was promised and a thing of far greater meaning to the True People. For what are horses and white-eyed bitches with their pups when stood against the honor of our nations? When we rode from this camp, we were men in name only, cringing in our lodges before the white-eyes' greed. But this night you will hear of the scalps and coup taken from the tejanos. We have come home, brothers, and this time we return as did our fathers and their fathers before them. Once again we rule the Plains, and wherever men gather, they will point to these lands and say, *'There live the warriors!'* "

Little Buffalo kneed the pinto forward, and the spectators' ranks silently opened before him. For a moment they watched in awe as he rode through their midst, and then the warriors' thunderous chant lifted to the sky in acclamation. *"TO-YOP-KE! TO-YOP-KE! TO-YOP-KE!"*

Without a flicker of acknowledgment Little Buffalo rode toward his lodge. *Tai-me* had guided his hand, and only something less than a man would accept credit for what the Grandfather God had ordained. Right now he would settle for the tender rewards that awaited any returning warrior, and they had nothing to do with either immortality or gods. Urging the *ehkasunaro* forward with a lusty kick in the ribs, he briefly wondered if Morning Star was already waiting beneath the robes.

2

Mary staggered under the load of brush wood and braced herself for the blow that was sure to come. When the supple oak switch struck her thigh, she ignored the stinging pain, dimly aware that the squaw behind her had mut-

tered a guttural curse. Gritting her teeth, she straightened
under the load and lurched forward. Whatever happened,
she was determined that these savages wouldn't force as
much as a moan from her lips. Already she had seen
Sarah Johnson and some of the other white women beaten
to the ground simply because the squaws enjoyed hearing
them scream. And it had quickly become apparent that
the only way to survive was to accept their cruelty without
flinching or crying out.

Grasping the rawhide straps holding the branches atop
her back, Mary struggled on toward the medicine lodge.
Great stacks of wood were being gathered there, and it
seemed evident that some sort of ceremonial meeting
would take place later in the night. She had heard of people being burned at the stake, and as the wood pile grew,
she idly wondered if such a fate awaited her bedraggled
group. While it wasn't entirely unlikely, she somehow just
didn't care anymore. Weary and sore from five grueling
days astride a barebacked horse, she only wanted a place
to flop down and submerge her tortured mind in the ref-
uge of sleep. The horror of watching her oldest son killed
had slowly given way to the deeper anguish of knowing
that she would never again see Britt. And with that realization came a numb insensibility that was not unlike death
itself.

Her only other reason to live was to protect George and
Sue Ellen. But they had been taken away from her shortly
after arriving in camp and put out to play with the Indian
children. From the start it was obvious that the two little
blacks were a source of curiosity and amazement to every
Indian in the village, and they had been readily adopted
by their red playmates. As she stumbled back and forth
with loads of wood, Mary glimpsed them shyly but eag-
erly joining in the games around the campfires. At first she
was offended and hurt, almost as if they had forsaken her
when some better diversion presented itself. Then she recalled that little children are all but immune to the sorrow of adults, especially when their grief is shunted aside
by interacting new playmates.

Abruptly she decided she was wallowing in her own
self-pity. Instead of resentment, she should be thankful
that the children were being treated kindly. Whatever
happened to her, they would be cared for, and for the
moment that was all she could ask.

When the chief on the big pinto had ridden away, Mary and the other prisoners had been turned over to the squaws. The captive youngsters were treated with the same gentleness that Indians showed all children, regardless of their race. Within the hour they had been drawn into the games and were soon busily engaged in learning the ways of their new companions. But the women were a different matter entirely, and the squaws were quick to demonstrate that even the slightest hesitation in obeying an order would result in a severe beating. Before the women had time to gather their wits, they were pressed into service packing food and wood to the council grounds, and as the night wore on, their spirits sank lower with each back-breaking load. Children might be revered and coddled, but to the women it seemed abundantly clear that their lot was to be that of slaves, harnessed for life to the drudgery of menial camp chores.

While Mary and the white women had no way of knowing it at that moment, their status was about to undergo an abrupt change.

Trudging wearily toward the medicine lodge with another load of wood, Mary became aware that her gloomy thoughts had been penetrated by a mournful wailing unlike anything she had ever heard. Passing near a tepee, she saw the shrouded body of a warrior being loaded on a travois behind a horse. Earlier she had seen the Indian wounded being carried to their lodges, and quite obviously this one was destined for the burial grounds. But it was the woman seated before the lodge who left Mary gripped with fascinated horror.

Slowing her pace, the black woman watched with growing revulsion as the squaw calmly hefted a knife and slashed deep furrows along her forehead and cheeks. Bright rivulets of blood welled up from the wounds and splashed down over the squaw's face, burying her features beneath a bubbling crimson mask. Then she placed her forefinger on a log near the fire and lifted the heavy skinning knife high overhead. Mary gasped, unable to believe what she was witnessing. With only a moment's hesitation the squaw swung the knife in a downward arc, loping the finger off just below the knuckle. Suddenly another squaw appeared from the shadows, wrapped the grieving woman's hand in a rabbit skin and tossed the severed finger into the fire.

The switch flicked against Mary's legs, warning her that it was time to move on. Perversely she welcomed the pain, for it distracted her mind from her churning stomach. As she passed by, the blood-splattered squaw resumed her wailing chant and followed the burial party toward the plains to the west.

Somehow it had never occurred to Mary that a savage could grieve as deeply as other people, and she was astonished to find her heart reaching out to the mutilated squaw. White people, and blacks too, bottled their grief inside, distilling it into self-pity. Their sorrow was for their own loss, rather than for the soul of the departed. And rarely was there a tear shed or a moan uttered that the dead could rightfully claim as their own. Suddenly Mary's own grief seemed diminished, somehow spent, and as her pace quickened, there was a new awareness for the brutal but strangely tender people among whom she had been cast.

Later that night a huge fire was kindled in front of the medicine lodge, and warriors stepped forth to reenact gallant deeds performed during the raid. While these heroic tales were being related, the women served a feast of buffalo meat and boiled dog, and before long the entire assemblage lay back in a glutted stupor. Afterward, Little Buffalo rose to stand before the towering flames, and in a ringing, impassioned voice honored the most valiant among them with awards of extra horses and captive women. Then four elders seated themselves around a large drum, and the haunting throb of the victor dance floated out over the village.

As the howling warriors began leaping around the fire, the forlorn settler women clutched their children tighter and huddled together in the flickering shadows. Their faces were grim, seemingly destitute of hope, and more than one stared into the night and wondered if the flames might not be a better fate than the one that awaited them.

3

Leaden clouds covered the sky, and a bitter wind gusted across the prairie. Britt hunched forward, pulling the heavy coat up around his neck, and mechanically scanned the bleak countryside. The north fork of the Red crooked

and twisted off to his left, generally paralleling his north-
erly course. Sprawling elms, tupelo, and blackjack lined its
erratic banks, and from a distance the leafless trees rose
from the earth like the towering spine of some ancient
behemoth. Gently rising away from the river, a deep carpet of bluestem and buffalo grass moved constantly beneath the crisp breeze, and for the lone rider there seemed
no respite from the chill bite of the probing cold. With one
last glance at the trees he reluctantly turned the chestnut
northeast and rode toward the faintly ominous mountains.

After fording the Red five days past, Britt had followed
the winding bank in a westerly direction, hoping to cut the
trail of the war party. But the ground remained barren of
sign, and each night as he camped along the shallow waters his spirits had sunk a bit lower. Upon reaching the
juncture of the south and north forks, it became apparent
that the raiders had crossed somewhere far to the east.
Retracing his steps would take days, with no assurance
that a sudden rain squall wouldn't obliterate the already
moldering trail. Suddenly the enormity of the task con-
fronting him seemed all but insurmountable. The vast,
uncharted wilderness beyond the Red was a formidable
and grudging adversary. Desolate plains, broken occasionally by streams and impenetrable tangles of dense under-
growth, stretched endlessly for hundreds of square miles.
And with but a few exceptions, no white man, or black
either, had ever returned to wipe away the mystery
shrouding this hostile and uncompromising land.

Buck Barry had mentioned that the Kiowas were re-
ported to have their camps in the Wichita Mountains,
which weren't especially hard to find if a man was foolish
enough to try. But the whereabouts of the Comanches
within those trackless reaches remained an enigma to all
save a few renegade traders. With Barry's obscure comment as his only lead, Britt decided to follow the north
fork on the off-chance he would encounter a friendly hunting party. Failing that, his only alternative was to enter
the mountains and take his chances with the Kiowas.

Now almost a fortnight after departing Fort Belknap,
he was nearing the foothills bordering the craggy, unex-
plored mountains. Rising abruptly from the prairie, the
sheer granite outcroppings of the Wichitas dominated the
landscape for a hundred miles in every direction. Visible

from the Washita River in the north to the Red in the south, they seemed cloaked in a bluish mist, veiled by an eerie haze which seldom varied from one season to the next. From afar the mountains appeared mottled in tone, but as Britt drew nearer, the soaring palisades broke clear, and he could make out formations of jagged granite boulders delicately splotched with moss. Centuries of erosion had cleaved steep gorges through the massive outcroppings, and the walls of these uninviting corridors were covered with gaunt, drab underbrush.

Viewed from the distant Plains, the Wichitas had only looked faintly ominous. Up close they looked downright deadly.

Slumped in the saddle, weary and somewhat disheartened, Britt passed through the blackjack-studded foothills as the shadows of late afternoon lengthened across the countryside. Though he had crossed the tracks of unshod ponies twice that morning, there had been no sign indicating a village of any size. And the futility of wandering aimlessly over this dismal landscape was slowly beginning to sap his spirit. Reflecting on the turn of events, it occurred to him that while he hadn't found any Indians, there was every likelihood that they would find him once he entered the mountains. But that wasn't quite the same thing. Grimly he recalled once having heard an army scout snort that any man who strayed north of the Red was fool enough to go hunting grizzlies with a switch.

Cresting a small knoll, he suddenly jerked upright in the saddle. Below him stretched a sheltered valley, and grazing contentedly on the wide expanse of grass was a herd of buffalo ponies. But the horses were only of passing interest, for across the way, on the opposite side of the herd were two mounted Indians. Their relaxed, slightly indolent manner confirmed that they were guarding the horses, and Britt's heart quickened at the significance of his blundering discovery. Such a large herd meant there was a substantial village nearby, and if he could somehow befriend these horse guards, there was a fair chance he could enter the camp with his hair still in place. Still somewhat hidden where he had come to a halt in a scrubby stand of blackjack, Britt sensed that he must make some gesture before the braves spotted him and took alarm.

Quickly he tied the packhorse to a tree and kneed the chestnut over the forward slope. Halfway down the hill he saw the Indians snap erect and knew they had sighted him. Holding to a steady trot as he reached the bottom of the hill, he reined the chestnut into a series of tight, jogging circles. He had been told somewhere, by someone long since forgotten, that this was the Plains Indians' signal of peaceful intent, and he could only hope that the custom was still honored.

Alert and cautious, the warriors held their position, scanning the brush-covered hills behind him for any sign of reinforcements. Clearly they were suspicious of a strange black man suddenly appearing from nowhere, and they weren't about to be sucked into a trap. Still they both had rifles and thus far had made no threatening moves, so there was an outside chance they might let him approach closer. With the reins in his left hand and his right thrust outward, Britt circled the herd and rode toward them.

Drawing closer, he saw that they were quite young and growing more apprehensive by the moment. Both were chunky and heavy chested, which was characteristic of most Kiowas, and even from a distance Britt could see that the taller of the braves was watching him with a cold, predatory look. The smaller one seemed curious more than anything else and kept nodding his head with a faint, nervous smile. Britt knew that most Plains tribes spoke a smattering of Mexican, and as he reined to a halt some twenty yards out, the black man offered a silent prayer that his broken Spanish would ring true on a Kiowa ear.

"*Buenos días, amigos.*" Wrapping the reins around the saddle horn, he folded his arms across his chest. "I enter your land in peace for the purpose of speaking with your chief."

The Indians eyed him warily, still unconvinced that this black apparition wasn't in some way dangerous. There was no sign of warmth in the wide, dour face of the taller youth, and the menace in his gaze was clearly noticeable. Pursing his lips, he spat on the ground, jerking his neck forward like a snake striking. "The Kiowa have no business with tejano *Negritos*. Lay down your guns and we will then decide if you are to enter our village with your buffalo wool uncropped."

"Young friend, I come in peace," Britt said, forcing a smile. "But only a fool would set aside his guns when his good will is questioned." His confidence rose as the burly youth mulled the thought over, now somewhat uncertain. "I come offering gifts and ransom. My family was taken in your raid on the Brazos, and I am prepared to pay many horses to buy them back."

"Eeh-yah! This man's words are coated with honey, my brother." The smaller brave spoke for the first time, glancing at his companion with a toothy grin. Horses were the only recognized measure of true wealth among the Plains tribes, and when a man spoke of such matters, he deserved to be taken seriously. The other warrior watched Britt sullenly, obviously thrown offstride by the black man's unexpected proposal. Santana was an ambitious man, and it passed through the boy's mind that the chief wouldn't look kindly on a young upstart who carelessly rubbed out a new source of wealth.

"I can offer horses to match even these you guard, young warriors," Britt said. Alert to the slightest reaction, he caught the flicker of greed growing brighter in their eyes. "Can you tell me if I have come to the right village? Are there women and children taken in the raid being held here?"

The warriors looked quickly at one another, again wary and uncertain as to how much they should reveal. But youthful enthusiasm won out over caution, and the smaller brave couldn't resist a manly boast. "Would you insult the Kiowa, buffalo man? There are many white-eyed slaves in our village. More than you have horses, I would wager." Then he paused, regarding Britt speculatively for a moment. "But now that I think on it, there are none as black as you."

Britt's soaring spirits plummeted back to harsh reality. The Kiowas and Comanches roamed this vast wilderness in many bands, and it surpassed belief that he could have found Mary and the children on the very first try. But the odds were good that he could learn of their whereabouts from these Kiowas, if he could somehow manage to keep from losing his own hair in the process. And that was a damn sight closer than he had been since crossing the Red. Smiling warmly at the two young warriors, he motioned back across the valley.

"Let me catch up my packhorse, for I have many gifts to please your people. Then as you escort me to your village, you can tell me more of these tejanos you have broken to halter."

4

Santana sat alone on the side of a hill overlooking the village. Often he came to this peaceful spot to meditate and thrash out within himself the festering anger which dominated his moods these days. But somehow he hadn't been able to reconcile the malign thoughts crowding his head with the triumphs and good fortune of his people. His gaze shifted down over the village, observing squaws busily engaged in tanning hides for the winter and warriors seated before their lodges gambling with the bones. There was an obvious sense of prosperity about the camp, for each lodge was well stocked with meat and many of the braves had gained added wealth from the recent raid. Their camp was ideally situated in a sung, sheltered valley which would protect them from the blizzards to come. The mountains around them teemed with deer and elk, should their stores dwindle before the snows melted. Being entirely pragmatic about it, as the people themselves generally were, the Kiowa were better off this winter than they had been for many snows past. And that was the thing Santana couldn't bring to light within himself.

Sighing pensively, he lay back under the pines and watched the grass-sweetened wind stir the treetops above him. This thing ate at his bowels like a nest full of worms and, try as he might, he couldn't set it aside. While he hesitated to put a word to it, in the secrecy of his own thoughts he could admit that it was nothing more than simple jealously. He was a proud man, vain and ambitious in his ways, and it was a bitter thing to know that he harbored envy for such dogs as the Comanches. But there it was, and no matter how he skirted around the feeling, there was no way of dodging it.

They were such arrogant scum, those Comanche. Forever scoffing at the Kiowa, ridiculing the ways and customs of a people even more ancient than they themselves. And their audacity knew no bounds, for only a misbegotten Comanche would have claimed that the Kiowa had hung back during the raid on the Brazos. Only with the threat of an open break had Little Buffalo been coerced into awarding horses and captives to the Kiowa braves.

Perhaps respect was too much to hope for from an

ignorant Comanche. Certainly they would never admit it, but their uncivilized behavior regarding the bear was what started the trouble in the first place. They knew that the Kiowa worshiped the bear as a medicine animal; a shaggy reincarnation of ancestors from the unknown of ancient days. Yet they still persisted in killing a bear on the march to the Brazos. But the unforgivable abomination was that they actually *ate the sacred one,* taunting the Kiowas with mocking jeers as the grease dripped down over their chins.

They were barbarians, these Comanches. Backward, ignorant, uncivilized in both manner and speech. For only a barbarian could have eaten the sacred one and laughed at the Kiowas' fears that the raid would be plagued by misfortune. Even to speak the name of the sacred one was bad medicine; to eat one was to invite the wrath of all holy things, who stood united in the face of such vulgarity. Santana's ears still burned when he remembered Little Buffalo's derisive jest on the trail home.

"Brother, your people twist their necks to the rear like a limbful of sick turkeys. Do the Kiowa also hunt for lice behind their wings, or is it that they fear what sniffs at our trail?"

If only he could humble the Comanche in some way. Bring them to their knees and make them cringe with shame at their own ignorance, just as they made the Kiowa slink away like scalded dogs whenever they felt in need of sport. Stretched out under the pines, he looked peaceful and serene, a wise chief musing on the tomorrows of his people. But within him the seed of envy smoldered corrosively, tainting his every thought with the fetid shadow of insults long past.

Shouts from below suddenly snapped him out of his malignant reverie, and he rose to his feet in a quick, fluid motion. Looking out over the valley, he observed a crowd gathering at the far edge of camp. As he peered closer, it became clear that the villagers there thronged around three horsemen. And one of those horsemen wore the garb of a tejano. Galvanized by the thought that a cringing white-eye might just divert his loathsome mood, Santana exuberantly leaped a boulder and bounded down the hill.

Breathing only slightly heavier from the run, Santana cut across the camp and arrived in front of his lodge

moments before the two horseguards rode up with Britt.
Back stiffened, chin outthrust, the chief drew himself into
a dignified pose, determined not to betray his surprise at
the sight of a black man. He had seen *Negritos* before,
of course, and like all of his people, found them objects
of great curiosity. But to have one materialize in your
own camp was another matter entirely, and something to
be considered without haste. Besides, this man had the
look of a warrior about him, and it was just possible
that keeping him alive might be more amusing than killing
him. Watching the black man dismount, Santana was
again struck by the similarity between *Negritos,* with their
woolly-fuzz hair, and the buffalo with their equally curly
topknot.

"*Hao*, Santana," the taller young brave said. "We bring
you a tejano *Negrito* who claims he has come to make
the Kiowa rich with horses."

Santana ignored the boy, having always considered him
a loutish bumbler. Instead, he gazed aloofly at the black
man, his features cold and tight lipped. After a moment
he spoke, resorting to Mexican, even though he found it a
frail, distasteful language. "Only a brave man or a fool
rides alone into a Kiowa camp. Which are you, *Negrito?*"

"Neither," Britt responded, meeting the chief's eyes
with a level stare. "I am a man who seeks his
family and is willing to pay generously to have them returned."

The crowd drew closer, their interest sharpened by this
talk of gifts and wealth. A murmur lapped back over their
ranks as word spread that the tejano *Negrito* was offering
horses for captives.

"Well spoken. A man's affection for his family is a
good thing." Santana casually waved his hand around the
throng of onlookers. "But as you can see, we have no
buffalo people here."

"I have observed as much," Britt agreed reluctantly.
But he had seen something else riding into the village.
Sarah Johnson and her children, along with the Fitzpatrick boy, standing forlornly beside a lodge. He had
nodded in recognition and then hurriedly looked away,
not wanting the Indians to know that he would pay as
dearly for some whites as he would blacks. Now he gently
baited the hook as Santana eyed him speculatively. "But
if the leader of the Kiowa is agreeable, we might still

make a trade. The tejanos have empowered me to bargain for white-eyes also. That is, if they are unharmed and able to travel."

"Hah! The buffalo man sets an inviting snare," Santana snorted. His stony face cracked with a slight smile as he nodded knowingly. "But where are your horses? Are you a *shaman* that you can blink your eyes and a fine herd of ponies will suddenly appear?"

"Hardly that, great chief. But the horses are waiting for those who wish to trade. Before we haggle like tradesmen, though, let me first honor you and your people with a few tokens from those who seek your favor."

Striding to the pack horse, Britt loosened the rawhide thongs and removed a bulky canvas packet. Spreading it on the ground, he threw the flaps back to reveal an assortment of mirrors, knives, cloth goods, and various foodstuffs. As the Indians crowded around to examine the curious treasures, he stepped back to the horse and withdrew a long object wrapped in soft cloth. Unwrapping it, he heard a sharp intake of breath as the nearer warriors caught sight of the rifle/shotgun. Without undue fuss he casually loaded both barrels and checked the caps. Searching the ground for a moment, he selected a fist-sized rock and tossed it high into the air. Throwing the weapon to his shoulder, he triggered the shotgun and saw the rock disintegrate in a cloud of pebbly dust. Instantly he turned, sighted on the lodge pole of a distant tepee, and fired the rifle. As the top of the lodge pole disappeared in a shower of splinters, the crowd began chattering excitedly, overawed by a gun which spoke with two voices.

Britt walked directly to Santana and extended the gun. "This is for the leader of the Kiowa. When it speaks, his enemies will know that wherever they stand, their name has been called."

Santana accepted the gun hungrily, caressing its surfaces tenderly as an old warrior would fondle a nubile young wife. His eyes glowed, and when at last he looked at Britt, there was a spark of undisguised admiration in his gaze. "The buffalo man causes me to think that we have underestimated some of those who walk among the tejanos. My braves will show you a lodge where you can rest and think about how you will make those horses appear. Tonight we will feast and talk of the value you place on white-eyed slaves."

Stroking the gleaming walnut and steel of the gun, the leader of the Kiowas nodded with a crooked, enigmatic grin, then turned and entered his lodge.

5

Santana belched appreciatively and tossed a gnawed rib onto a pile of bones near the fire. Soon the buffalo would disappear for the winter, secreting themselves from the red man as they had for a thousand snows, and fresh meat was a thing to be relished fully. Britt patted his distended stomach and managed a respectable burp. He had eaten till his jaws ached, determined to honor Santana's hospitality with a properly ravenous appetite. Now he felt sated, drowsy from a full belly and the cloyed warmth of the chief's lodge.

Upon entering the tepee, his nostrils had rebelled at the curious stench of an Indian lodge. The odor was a potent blend of sweaty bodies, rank buffalo hides, tobacco, rancid grease, and campfire smoke. Separately the smells might have been acceptable, if not agreeable. But together they formed a pungent, highly seasoned aroma which left his stomach churning and his appetite numb. Nevertheless, diplomacy demanded a hearty eater, and he laid to with gusto, breathing through his mouth whenever possible.

As Santana's wives served them, the chief's reserve lessened with each greasy mouthful, and he steadily grew more talkative. Before the last bone had been sucked clean of marrow, Britt's silence was rewarded with a casual disclosure of his family's whereabout. While Santana couldn't remember the warrior's name, he did recall that the black woman and her two little *Negritos* had become the property of a Comanche. After the victory celebration the Kiowas had returned to their mountains, and presumably the Comanches had split once more into their five nomadic bands. Which band Mary and the children had accompanied and where they would winter on the Plains were matters beyond Santana. And quite obviously one which left him coolly indifferent. The Kiowas had only white-eyes to trade, and these incessant questions about *Negritos* wearied him.

"Enough of this idle chatter." Santana lay back on a

buffalo robe and casually picked his teeth with a grimy fingernail. "Let us talk of horses. Or of more importance, how you intend to make these imaginary horses appear in the Kiowa camp."

Britt eyed the red man cautiously. What he must now attempt was a delicate thing, and unless the words were chosen carefully, there were many white families who would never again see Texas. "Santana is a wise chief, for only the far-sighted man perceives that a horse is of more lasting value than a feeble tejano woman. And in that wisdom he will also see that in order for a man to grow wealthy, he must place a certain trust in those with whom he trades."

"What you say is true. How could I deny my own wisdom?" Santana's bronzed features twisted in a wolfish grin, and his hooded eyes regarded Britt curiously. "But I tire of this game we play. While I wish only to hear of horses, you talk in circles, like a slippery-tongued medicine man."

"Sadly, I must, for it is necessary that you believe what is behind my words." Britt's throat went dry even as his brow grew damp with cold sweat. "I have no horses nearby, nor can I make them appear. What I propose is that your warriors return the captives to the Brazos and exchange them for horses at that time."

Santana's eyes went cold, and there was a deadly chill to his voice. "You are a brave man, and for that I can respect you. But you are a fool. When you rode into camp, I took you to be a warrior, and we may yet test your courage. But even a warrior can be a *pawsa,* a crazy man."

His face remained hard, and a tense stillness settled over the lodge. Clearly he was torn between greed and caution, for his stoic expression couldn't entirely mask the inner conflict. Finally he spoke in a guarded tone, seemingly resolved on which path to explore. "If I am as wise as you say, then how could I trust the white-eyes to honor your word? What is to stop them from killing my warriors instead of handing over the horses?"

"That is a thing to consider, I grant you." The black man's heart quickened as he realized that an opening wedge had been driven into Santana's sullen wariness. Now for the ticklish part, and he had the feeling it would require all the tact he could muster. "While it shames me,

I cannot deny that the tejanos are incapable of trusting even one another. And as wise men know, cynics are rarely a trustworthy breed. But Santana must remember that he holds a mighty club over the tejanos' heads. For if they attempt to betray the trust, your warriors can easily kill the women and children. And that is a threat which even the white-eyes will respect."

"Maybe. Who knows the mind of the white-eyes?" Shaking his head doubtfully, the chief stared into the fire for a moment. "And what is to stop them from killing my warriors after the exchange is made? A herd of horses will slow the march, and they could easily overtake my people."

"There is no need to concern yourself with that," Britt said. "The army no longer patrols the Brazos, and after our exchange the tejanos won't have enough horses left to pull even a wagon. Thus, there will be no one to pursue your warriors when they travel north again."

"That is true," Santana chortled. "After all the horses we took on the raid, such an exchange as this would leave the tejanos afoot like squaws." The thought seemed to please him immensely, and he toyed with it for a moment. "Your words have a certain wisdom, *Negrito*. Still, I'm not sure my warriors would undertake such a hazardous venture. After all, if they had the foresight of which you spoke, then it is they who would sit as chief."

Suddenly Britt sensed that beneath Santana's chiseled mask lurked a vain and ambitious man. The chief had no intention of joining in the exchange himself. He meant to send only the warriors and rely on their wary cunning to make him a wealthy man. Just possibly this deal wasn't as difficult as he had thought. Scenting blood, he decided to strike for the jugular.

"Who is to say that the warriors are not justified in turning their backs on such a risky undertaking? Certainly not I. But from what I have seen, the leader of the Kiowa is not a man whose wishes are treated lightly by his people. When Santana speaks, his warriors listen. This I have witnessed for myself. Of course, like your braves, I am but a common man, and my mind has difficulty in grasping what is right or wrong for the good of all. This is a thing which must be left to the leaders." Britt paused, steadying himself for the final thrust, and then plunged on. "But I have served under many leaders in my life, and there is one thing I have learned above all else. Honor and fame go to the bold, and the meek are left to haggle over the scraps."

Santana blinked owlishly, studying the black man with a puzzled frown. For a moment he couldn't decide whether he had been insulted or praised. But he hadn't survived over forty snows without acquiring some instinct for men's motives, and it slowly dawned on him that he had just been treated to a wily and highly subtle challenge. There was more to this strange tejano than he had thought, and just as he admired a brave man, so did he respect an artful intriguer.

"*Waugh!* My warriors will follow you to the Brazos, *Negrito*. But for the sake of your throat, let us hope that your tongue is not forked." His forehead wrinkled with concentration, and he regarded Britt with a searching gaze for what seemed like a full minute to the anxious black man. "You are a slippery man, not like the white-eyes at all. Just when I think I have hold of what you are, you slide away and show me something else. It pains me to say it of a tejano, but you put me in mind of a fox. For they too are shrewd and crafty, and just as you have done, they employ cunning to see them through."

Suddenly his eyes blazed with amusement, and he leaned across the fire to slap Britt's shoulder. "Hah! I have just decided to rename you, *Negrito*. A good Kiowa name. From this night forward you will be known as Black Fox." Then his voice dropped to a hoarse, conspiratorial whisper. "But if you ever let it be known that you came to this name by outfoxing Santana, I will slice off your manhood and feed it to the dogs."

"And what of the horses, my chief?" Britt inquired with a smile.

"Your white-eyed brothers will pay three horses for each woman and one for each child. That is my final word, so let us hear no more of it."

"Santana makes a just trade, and it is agreed. But do not call the tejanos my brothers. As you have said, they are simply a people who I walk among."

Santana's belly rumbled with laughter, and his great black mane shook with the force of his mirth. "You are a man who bears watching, Black Fox. Your tongue is oily, and it rushes to fill each crevice in a man's doubts. But the Comanches are not wily like the Kiowa. They are blunt and lacking in wit. And it occurs to me that they might mistake your cunning for trickery. Knowing this, I think I might do well to protect the Kiowas' interests by having certain warriors escort you to the Canadian."

"A fine idea, great chief." Britt's teeth flashed in a mocking smile. "For if I am unable to return to the Brazos, how would we obtain your horses?"

"Enough! Your tongue flays me with my own words." Santana rose effortlessly to his feet, and the black man also stood. Glancing through the lodge entrance, the chief lowered his voice and threw an arm around Britt's shoulders. "Come, Black Fox. The warriors await us before the medicine lodge. We will speak to them with solemn words, and for the good of the Kiowa nation I will allow them to convince me that certain of their number should guard your return to the Brazos."

Chuckling like a thief in the night, the leader of the Kiowa led the black man outside and walked with somber dignity toward the expectant warriors.

6

Mary squeezed her eyes tightly and tried to close out the whimpering cries. Then there was a quick, strangled yelp, and she knew it was over. Talking Raven was very good at killing dogs, cutting the throat deeply and fast, so that the animal suffered only a moment's pain. Among themselves the squaws joked that when Talking Raven's cooking pots came out, the wise dogs disappeared in the willows along the river bank. Tonight was a special occasion, and Standing Bear had ordered boiled dog along with the ever-present buffalo meat. Two Moons, his youngest wife, was already in labor with her first child. And since he had paid the *puhaket* a fine roan mare to guarantee a man-child, Standing Bear was preparing to celebrate the arrival of his son.

Talking Raven came around the lodge with the bloody carcass in her hands. Though it was skinned and gutted, she always left it up to Mary to chop it into pot-sized chunks. Mary's throat clogged with bile, but she accepted the still-warm carcass and began cutting it with sickened resignation. All her life she had assisted at slaughter time with pigs and cattle, and she certainly wasn't squeamish.

But a dog that had licked your hand and sidled up to be petted was somehow different. It was almost like eating a member of the family, and Mary's stomach churned as the knife grated against bone.

Still, Talking Raven was a harsh disciplinarian, and she allowed no malingering in her lodge. As Standing Bear's first wife, and therefore the oldest, she ran the lodge with firm, gruff-voiced benevolence. She brooked no nonsense and whipped Mary repeatedly for refusing to kill the dogs. But finally she had conceded to Mary's queasy stomach, and the matter rested there. In all other things the black woman was a strong, willing worker, and Talking Raven had never been one to beat a good horse to the ground.

Little Buffalo had honored Standing Bear's courage in the Brazos raid by sending Mary and the children to his lodge. This was a signal honor, attesting to Standing Bear's ferocity and prowess as a warrior. For of all the captives taken in the raid, the black family had been coveted most by the warriors and their squaws. Many lodges had white-eyed slaves, but the blacks were different, special somehow, and therefore prized above all others. Blacks were believed to possess a strange, mystical kind of medicine, and it seemed reasonable that the power of this medicine would attach itself to the master of their new lodge.

The Comanches also felt some distant kinship with the blacks, the brotherhood of underdogs and outcasts who had fallen before the oppressive cruelty of the white-eyes. Over the weeks of her captivity Mary had noticed that while Talking Raven was rarely hesitant to use the switch, she never struck with the fury that other squaws used on the white women. Slowly she came to realize that because she and the children were black, they had been accorded a dubious honor: they were slaves, but they were treated with a harsh affection which would never be extended to the whites. The children in particular were cuddled and spoiled unmercifully, and it soon became apparent that it was only a matter of time until Standing Bear adopted them as his own.

As she was to discover, Standing Bear had other ideas too. She frequently caught him watching her, and the look was not that of a master inspecting his slave. It was the look of raw, animal lust, the same look she had seen in white men's eyes when Britt wasn't around. But never had she felt so naked or defenseless as when Standing Bear's hungry eyes followed her about the lodge.

She had the feeling he would have bedded her long before this if it hadn't been for Talking Raven. The squaw bullied him just as she did the women, and while he sometimes beat her savagely, her sharp tongue was never still for long. Whenever she caught him watching the black woman, her voice rose in a shrewish screech, and even though Mary didn't understand all of the words, she knew a shamed husband when she saw one.

But these thoughts were far from her mind as she finished butchering the steaming carcass and dropped chunks of meat into a kettle of boiling water. All she could think of was that frisky little brown dog with its waggly tail. Only that morning it had followed her to gather wood, barking and scampering about playfully as she collected branches. And now it was nothing but greasy chunks bubbling away in the smoke-blackened kettle. She grimaced as the odor of stewed dog wafted out from the pot and fought to swallow the sour gorge that flooded her throat. Damning Standing Bear for the inhuman brute he was, she made a mental note to invent some story for the children when they began searching for their curly-tailed playmate. Thank God they had been off in the woods when Talking Raven went to work with her knife.

Suddenly the lodge flap was thrown open, and Standing Bear came through the entrance. Jerking his head back toward the tepee, he uttered a guttural command, then seated himself before the small cooking fire. Mary could understand a few of the simpler Comanche words by now, and she knew from his curt order that Talking Raven wanted her in the lodge. Obviously two Moons' time had come, and the older squaw wanted her inside in case there was trouble with the delivery.

After setting the kettle to one side, Mary rinsed her hands in a water skin and entered the lodge. Two Moons was stretched out on her side near the fire. With the weather so cold and the skies threatening snow, the cooking would normally have been done inside. But Talking Raven didn't want Two Moons sickened by the odors of cooking. Delivering women of their first born was bad enough, but to have a young mother retching and gagging at the same time was more than she could abide.

Two Moons' eyes were glazed with pain, but like all Co-

manche women when their time came, she remained stoic
and silent, never once uttering so much as a moan or a
whimpering cry. Talking Raven was busily applying warm
stones to the girl's stomach and back to relieve the pain.
Though all of her own babies had been stillborn, the
squaw remembered the pains vividly and knew what Two
Moons was going through. Glancing around, she signed to
Mary to heat more stones at the fire. Cooing softly, as one
would gentle a hurt child, she then wiped the girl's fever-
ish brow and combed the matted hair back from her face.

Watching raptly, Mary was again astounded by the conflicting aspects of Indian temperament. Only minutes before, this grim-faced squaw had pitilessly killed a dog
which she had raised from a puppy, and now she was tenderly working over a young mother to bring new life
forth. Shaking her head in dismay, Mary wondered how
long she would have to live among the Comanche to comprehend their savage and yet somehow childlike minds.

The baby was slow and uncooperative. When it finally
began to show, Talking Raven got the girl up on her hands
and knees and coaxed her to strain harder. To Mary the
older woman's insistent tone sounded exactly like the
squaws when they urged the warriors onward in stickball
games. Mary decided that Talking Raven was well named.
Never slackening her demanding chatter, she knelt behind
the straining girl and to all apppearances literally talked
the baby into joining the human race. The lusty squall he
loosed when Talking Raven eased him out onto a doeskin
made it plain that the cold world seemed a bad trade for
the snug womb. His indignant cries seemed to berate her
for having advised him wrongly, and he fought like a little
warrior as she briskly rubbed him dry with the soft skin
and knotted the cord.

Standing Bear would be proud. His man-child had come
into the world like a true Comanche.

Two Moons remained on her knees, panting and arching
her back as if she were about to drop another baby. Mary
watched with breathless fascination, thoroughly bewildered
by the girl's strange behavior. Abruptly Talking Raven
shoved the screaming baby in Mary's arms, snatched up
another doeskin, and knelt once more behind the straining
girl. Suddenly there was a gush of blood and the afterbirth
plopped in a steaming heap on the skin. With a shuddering

sign Two Moons eased forward and dropped in a quivering, exhausted lump.

Talking Raven quickly wrapped the afterbirth, bound it tightly with rawhide thongs, and scuttled from the lodge without a backward glance. Later Mary would learn that the afterbirth was bad medicine, a thing which could bring misfortune and grief to all who came in contact with it. Talking Raven would bury it deep, where even the coyotes couldn't find it, and in a place where no Comanche would ever go near it. Even walking across the spot where it had been buried was bad medicine, which was all right if it happened to a Ute or some dumb Kiowa. But a decent, thoughtful person made very sure that it would never bring disaster down on the head of a brother Comanche.

When Talking Raven returned, she washed the baby, wrapped him in a fresh doeskin, and placed him in Two Moon's arms. Only then did she call Standing Bear. Entering the lodge, he stood for a moment gazing with fierce pride upon his warrior son. Two Moon's face radiated the joy of a mother who has presented her husband with his first male child, and she searched Standing Bear's solemn visage for some sign of praise. But he had eyes only for the boy, and as he knelt, watching the baby suckle greedily, his features softened in a moment of guileless humility.

Then the stern hauteur once more masked his face, and he stalked from the tepee. This was a day for a man to sit in front of his lodge and bask in the adulation of friends and brother warriors.

After the baby had fed, Talking Raven placed him in a bois d'arc cradle lined with velvety rabbit skins. The cradle's deep, rounded hood swallowed the tiny face, and when she hung it on the lodge pole, the bowed frame swung to and fro with a gentle rocking motion.

Watching from her pallet of buffalo robes, Mary was captivated by this blissful scene. For a moment her thoughts drifted back to the births of her own children, and she relived again the intense passion of squeezing a life from one's own body. How proud Two Moons must be, she mused, for every mother dreams of her first born being a son. Glancing at the girl, who was now sleeping peacefully, it occurred to her that all women, black or white, gentle or savage, were really no different beneath the skin. They lived solely for the love they could create, and whatever happiness they found was never far removed from the core of their own family.

Talking Raven's harsh voice shattered her dreamy ruminations. Tenderness had faded from the squaw's narrow features, and she was once more the demanding, sharp-tongued mistress of the lodge. There was dog meat waiting to be stewed, and a ready switch for those who lazed away the day with their head in the clouds. Mary felt herself jolted back to the reality of who she was and, more significantly, where she was. Hauling herself erect, she eased back the lodge flap and stepped outside.

Standing Bear was squatted before the fire, and he regarded her silently as she hung the kettle over the flames. As she stooped to stir the greasy mess, he leaned forward and patted her gently on the stomach. Startled, she found herself unable to move, and his probing fingers kneaded the flesh beneath her dress. Grinning wolfishly, he locked his arms together and rocked them like a cradle, then pointed suggestively back at her stomach. Suddenly his meaning dawned on her, and her mind reeled with visions of his chunky figure mounting her, ramming her legs apart, so that she too might become a good little Comanche mother. Straightening, she stepped back and met his smirking gaze with a level eye. While he couldn't understand her words, their substance was all too clear.

"You red nigger, you come around tryin' to stick that thing in me, and I'll make you wish you'd been born with a sweet potato between your legs."

7

The small column of riders seemed dwarfed by the vast openness of the rolling Plains. The grasslands had now become a gently swaying sea of chilled brown, and as autumn turned to winter, the slumbering landscape appeared more desolate than ever. Behind lay the granite towers of the mountains, and it had taken two days to reach a swirling dog leg of the lower Washita. Running Dog and Britt forded the stream first, then waited on the opposite bank while the women and older children gingerly eased their mounts across the shallow waters. The warriors then whipped their ponies across at a plunging run, spraying themselves and the squealing youngsters mounted behind

them with geysers of icy water. Formed once more in a
strung-out line, the party turned north and resumed their
march. Ahead lay forty miles of barren, wind-swept prairie, and each of the riders had good reason to wish their
journey concluded.

While the distance from Santana's camp to the Comanche village normally took only two days by horseback,
Running Dog had purposely slowed the pace because of
the tejano women and children. Under extreme conditions
the Kiowas had many times crossed this stretch of empty
wilderness without stopping. But the frail white-eyes were
incapable of such a grueling march, and the Indians char-
itably held their ponies to a drowsy, ambling walk.

Altogether, Britt had ransomed four women and nine
children, which accounted for all of the Kiowa captives.
Though they were gaunt and crawling with lice, the captives were beside themselves with joy. Their ordeal was
over, or almost over anyway, and within a fortnight they
would once again be with their loved ones in Texas. Sarah
Johnson had thrown her arms around Britt's neck and
cried like a child when informed of the exchange. Afterward, he had talked with the four women for over an
hour, reassuring them as best he could that they had nothing to fear from their captors.

Santana had been as good as his word, and as the tiny
band thankfully departed the mountain stronghold, he
pointedly reminded Britt that he was expecting twenty-one
of the tejanos' finest horses. The cynical leader of the
Kiowa also made good on his promise to see to it that Britt
was properly escorted, and as the captives rode forth, they
were accompanied by seven of the tribe's most formidable
warriors. Their mission, Santana had declared, was to de-
liver the white-eyes unharmed to the Brazos and return
with a herd of sleek, grain-fattened horses. And if they
stumbled into a trap anywhere along the journey, they
were to make sure that the first man to die was the tejano
now called Black Fox.

Running Dog, foremost warrior of the Kiowa nation as
well as a superlative horse thief, had been selected as
leader of the escort party. Tall and lithely muscled for a
red man, he made an imposing figure. Famed for his
bloodthirsty ruthlessness in a fight, he was fiercely proud of
his people and openly scornful of anything not Kiowa.
Running Dog rarely smiled, and his infrequent bursts of

humor were usually of a grim nature. This fearsome impact was not lessened by the cold intensity of his eyes, the jut of a heavy brow, and the wide, merciless slit of his thin-lipped mouth.

All things considered, he made the perfect choice for the leader of a band which might be called on to slaughter more than a dozen women and children. And the significance of his presence wasn't lost on Britt.

Still, Running Dog had gone out of his way to cultivate the black man, and before the march was a day old, it became obvious that the warrior found Britt to be a matchless, if somewhat puzzling, companion. The Plains Indians revered courage above all other personal attributes, and the black man's lone sortie into the Kiowa nation had made him something of an overnight legend.

Britt's obvious lack of fear, combined with an easy confidence and a natural friendliness, had greatly impressed Running Dog. But there were things about Black Fox that defied understanding, at least for an Indian. Like the jumbled parts of a riddle, these contradictions rattled irritatingly in Running Dog's head, and his normal taciturnity was slowly replaced by an almost childlike curiosity.

Britt, on the other hand, had experienced profound kinship with only one other man in his life, a white man, and as he felt himself being drawn irresistibly to this red savage, he became a confused and sorely perplexed man.

For all the confusion and lack of understanding, it remained a spontaneous admiration of one brave man for another. And from it sprang the genesis of a deep camaraderie that was to develop over the course of their journey together.

The weather was raw and blustery, and as the two men rode along, their words left frosty tentacles dangling in their wake. Running Dog had gradually become more inquisitive, peppering Britt with all manner of questions about the white-eyes' world. But until now he had skirted the thing that puzzled him most, the blacks themselves.

"There is this thing about the *Negritos* that has always eluded me, Black Fox. Maybe you could make it come clear." Running Dog glanced at Britt quizzically, who nodded, wondering exactly what the warrior had in mind. "The Kiowa comes into this life a free man, and until he crosses over to the other life, he is answerable to none save himself and the gods. Whether he chooses to sleep or steal

horses or wander these Plains in search of his enemies,
there are none to deny him. And a Kiowa would die fighting rather than bow before another man's will." Again he
glanced at Britt, somewhat unsure as to how he should
proceed.

Britt smiled soberly, now certain of the question about
to follow. "What you wish to ask is why the *Negrito* has
surrendered his freedom to the white-eyes."

"More than that, Black Fox. Freedom is but the first
loss, and every warrior understands that this can happen
in the defeat of battle. Even Kiowa women have been
taken as slaves by the Ute and the Crow. But never a
Kiowa man." For a moment he stared across the bleak
prairie, attempting to phrase his next thought in a tactful
manner. "And this is what eludes me. Rather than die, the
Negrito has surrendered something beyond mere freedom.
He has renounced his manhood."

Britt was stunned, and for a brief instant his eyes went
cold with fury. Then he got a grip on himself, and reason
slowly asserted itself once more. In his mind arose discarded memories of field hands cringing before a white
overseer, and black women, like brood mares in heat, being mated to the stoutest buck in the slave quarters. The
black man had indeed been emasculated, just as surely as
a colt is gelded or a young bull is thrown to the ground and
cut. The manhood of a people had been torn out, jerked
from the sac as neatly as a rancher clips the balls from his
frisky yearlings. And none knew it better than the black
man himself. It wasn't possible. It was merely true.

"Running Dog sees much for a man who has never lived
among the white-eyes."

"I watch with my mind, Black Fox, and I see that the
white-eyes are not content to defeat a man in battle or
even to kill him. They have this curious urge to strip a
warrior of his manhood and bend him to their will, just as
we would tame a dog or a fine horse." His eyes glazed
over, and for several moments his mind seemed lost in a
distant vision. "They leave a man nothing, neither freedom nor pride, and if they are not soon stopped, they will
be the master of all. Even the Kiowa."

"If you hope to learn their secret from me, you have
chosen a poor teacher." Britt fell silent and shivered from
the icy claw deep in his gut. The moaning wind stung his
face, stripping his thoughts of all pretense and artifice, and

he wondered how long a race of men could hide from themselves. "Those who have been defeated are not always best suited to reveal the inner thoughts of their masters."

"That is true," Running Dog agreed. "But have I asked the question of the defeated ones? Would you have me believe that a *Negrito* who rides alone into the Kiowa nation has been stripped of his manhood?" He turned to look at Britt, and his piercing gaze seemed to search the black man's soul. "Among my people only a warrior would have dared such a thing."

"Perhaps even a man who lives in the white-eyes' shadow can remain a warrior. But that does not mean that he is proud of himself or would presume to advise those who still fight for their freedom."

"Your deeds contradict your words, Black Fox. While he might be a warrior, this person you speak of would only be half a man. Why would he not turn his back on what is past and join those who fight the oppression of the white-eyes?"

Why indeed? Britt silently demanded of himself. "There are some questions to which a man has no ready answers, Running Dog. But this is one I ask myself more and more as I walk among your people."

The Kiowa warrior nodded solemnly, as if the riddle had fallen together and he at last understood the black man who rode beside him. Dusk was approaching, and they would soon have to camp for the night. But they both knew that despite the warmth between them and the campfires they might share in the days to come, they would never broach the matter again.

In the distance Running Dog's keen eyes sighted a pack of wolves snapping and snarling over a lone buffalo carcass. Waiting patiently for the wolves to finish, two coyotes and a badger slowly circled the killing ground. Reining to a halt, the warrior touched Britt's shoulder and pointed to the unfolding tableau of survival on the Plains.

"There are few hunters, Black Fox, but many who want to eat the meat. The warrior must hold himself above the carrion eaters of this life, and when he has done so, then he will never again question his own manhood."

"And if those who wish to eat are his friends?"

"Then he must kill them swiftly and without remorse.

For the scavengers of this earth have no friends other than their own greed."

Watching the wolves tearing at the carcass, Britt pondered the red man's words and felt himself growing more perplexed with each moment he spent in this strange wilderness. Choosing sides was easy, if that were all there was to it, for the Kiowas lived with a dignity that few black men even dared dream about. The trick was in killing the ghosts of those scavengers, especially the ones that haunted a man's past with kindness and love. And brotherhood.

8

Seated around the campfire that night, both men were at great pains to avoid any mention of *Negritos* or white-eyes. Running Dog was well aware that he had led the black man into a bramble patch of conflicting emotions, and he wisely limited the conversation to less troublesome matters. After a cold meal he spent most of the evening with the warriors, gambling and exchanging tales of battle. These stories were crusty with age, familiar to each man gathered around the fire. But they were rarely dull. For the Kiowas were skilled in the art of exaggeration and enjoyed nothing quite so much as giving a tattered and worn tale a fancy new embroidery. Listening with one ear, Running Dog watched the man now thought of as Black Fox out of the corner of his eye. Such men were welcome among the Kiowa, for they brought a fresh infusion of warrior's blood into the tribe, and Running Dog secretly schemed to make this black giant a brother of the True People.

Britt had spent the early part of the evening with the children, making the camp ring with laughter and squeals of terror as he acted out the scary ghost stories that had appealed so much to black youngsters. But his levity was an act and nothing more, for Running Dog's remarks of that afternoon lingered in his mind, suppurating as an open sore would fester and grow putrid with rot. Once the children settled down for the night, he talked with Sarah and the other women at great length, recounting the aftermath of the Brazos raid and what they could expect to find when they returned home. While sobered by the devastation, they had much to be grateful for, and their momentary gloom quickly disappeared beneath the merry chatter of those who have been given a second lease on life.

But the women were exhausted from three days of steady riding, and before long, their lightheartedness gave way to unsuppressed yawns. Finally they decided to call it a night and wearily crawled beneath the buffalo robes with the children. After they were settled, Britt stretched and approached the warriors, who were still trading yarns on the opposite side of the fire.

Glancing up, Running Dog greeted him in the broken Spanish employed by the Kiowas. *"Hao,* brother. Be seated and join us. We were just speaking of the Comanches." Pausing, he flicked a wry smile at the other warriors. "You should listen well to this talk, Black Fox, for sometime tomorrow you will meet our fabled kinsmen."

"Running Dog's voice belies his words," Britt said in a joshing tone. "If I didn't know better, I might believe that the Kiowa mock their Comanche brothers."

"Huh!" snorted Running Dog. "You are well named, Black Fox. Among friends a truthful man might easily say that the Kiowa laughed behind their faces at the Comanche. Sit here by the fire and we will school you in ways to deceive our loutish kinsmen." The warriors crowded closer, vastly intrigued by the idea of conspiring against the detested northerners.

"Black Fox, the thing you must never forget in dealing with the Comanche is that they are thoughtless barbarians, completely untutored in the ways of enlightened people. They think with their gut and lack the vision to see beyond their next meal. They call themselves lords and sing praises to their own ferocity. But as wise men know, it is the dog that seldom barks who will tear your leg away at the roots. Is it not so, brothers?" The other warriors chuckled and murmured their assent, highly amused by this slanderous description of the haughty Comanches.

"I will illustrate for you, Black Fox, why enlightened men ridicule these barbarians." Grinning broadly, Running Dog resumed even though Britt seemed slightly taken aback by the sharp edge to his words. "The Kiowa will consider a matter at length, but when his mind is set, he will act quickly and firmly. The Comanche is like the buffalo, whose brain hangs between his legs. He decides a thing instantly, relying on instinct as does an animal, and then waits and waits some more, before he finally sucks up the courage to act. The Kiowa eats his food slowly and savors the taste fully. The Comanche wolfs his food like a starved beast and then accuses his neighbor of being the one who has broken wind. My words are crude, Black Fox, but from them you will see more clearly how to outwit the Comanche."

Puzzled by the Kiowa's cryptic remarks, Britt stared around the fire as the warriors waited for him to speak. "Running Dog's advice is like a knife that cuts with both edges. The Comanches act hastily, without considering a matter thoroughly, and thus can I hurry them into a stupid trade. But you also say that they are barbarians, who sit on a decision like a duck hatching eggs. This leads me to believe that they would later regret their haste and slit my throat to wipe away an unwise bargain."

The warriors all started talking at once, amazed that the black man could have made so much of such a simple thing. Finally a squatty, flat-nosed brave outshouted the others and spoke directly to Britt in a series of hoarse grunts. "You hear, but you do not see, Black Fox. The Comanches are barbarians, that is true. But there is a higher law that even the Comanches would not dare break. When a stranger comes to their lodges in peace, they are bound to accept him with a spirit of generosity and mercy." Shrugging his shoulders, the warrior made a chopping, dismissive gesture with his hand. "This is a thing that none among the True People would question. It is the law."

"My brother speaks straight," Running Dog interjected. "But there is a thing Black Fox would be wise to remember in the days to come. Among the True People it is known that one never stares at a Comanche. Not even in a peace council. For as a wolf accepts a stare as a sign of hostility, so it is with these barbarians. And Black Fox must never forget that when he rubs shoulders with the Comanches he walks among the wild beasts."

Britt felt the hair bristle on the back of his neck. The men hunkered around this fire were savages, and yet they were warning him against a people that they themselves considered barbarian. Suddenly the chill night wind sent a shiver down his spine, and he sensed an ominous malevolence waiting just beyond the darkness.

9

The terrain had changed markedly just after midday. Running Dog led them through a winding maze of deep sandstone gorges, bounded on either side by sheer, red cliffs. The floor of these formidable, uninviting canyons was studded with trees and generally so narrow that a man had the prickly feeling the earth was about to close its jaws and devour him whole. High overhead, springs gushed from crevices in the rocks, and water gently cascaded down the crimson face of the menacing bluffs. But the abundance of vegetation and water had little effect on the black man's edginess. While the canyons teemed with life, they had about them the stench of death, and Britt's backbone grew stiffer with each plodding mile.

Since breaking camp that morning, he had noticed a distinct change in the Kiowa warriors also. They were quieter, almost guarded, and as the column entered the sandstone canyons, their bantering conversation shriveled to grim grunts. Every now and then Britt would turn to look at the women and children, and it was obvious that they too felt the unseen evil that had stilled the Kiowas. Without knowing why, he began to wish they were back on the Plains. Whatever lurked in these canyons was hidden, a threat of the impending, and it preyed too much on a man's mind. While the prairie was desolate and windswept, at least a man could see his enemy and prepare for the worst. Britt chuckled to himself. What you don't see can't hurt you, people always said. Maybe not, he thought, but it can sure as hell make you touchier than a wet cat.

Later in the day, with the sun a cold ball of light in the overcast skies, they broke out of the canyons and halted on a barren plateau overlooking the Canadian. Along the tree-fringed riverbank they could see tendrils of smoke rising from the Comanche campfires and tiny, antlike figures of people moving about the village.

"There are your Comanche, Black Fox. Let us hope that the woman you seek is in this camp." Running Dog spoke with his eyes fastened on the village, and the other warriors stared glumly in the same direction.

Surprisingly Britt found that being free of the narrow

gorges had done nothing to lessen his sense of dread. The unseen thing shadowing his thoughts waited in that village below, and as he had known all along, it had nothing to do with evil spirits. It was human, and it called itself Comanche.

Staring at the camp, he wondered if Mary and the children were down there right now. A hollow feeling gnawed at his gut, and he swallowed a huge lump lodged in his throat. Silently he called on the Lord God Jehovah to make him man enough and shrewd enough to bring off what must be done. On the spur of the moment he quickly added an entreaty to the gods of darkness—the juju gods that had ruled his grandmam's life to the final moment of her deathbed. When a man's in trouble, she used to say, he needs all the help he can get. And right now, Britt reflected, whatever's waiting down there is trouble enough for any man. Or his god.

"Waugh!" Running Dog's grunt broke the strained silence, and they all turned to look in the direction he was pointing. Far in the distance they sighted a herd of buffalo moving steadily across the plains to the west of the Comanche encampment. Each year, before the first snow, the buffalo migrated south for the winter, and the herd they were now watching numbered in the thousands.

The Kiowa leader gazed at the herd thoughtfully, and a sly glint slowly crept into his eyes. "Black Fox, we are about to make you a brother to the Comanche. Have I not told you they think with their gut? That they never look past their next meal? It follows then that the man who brings them the gift of food is a brother indeed." Observing Britt's quizzical expression, he grinned rakishly. "Have you ever killed a buffalo, brother? Well no matter. Today Black Fox becomes a hunter."

Gesturing toward the buffalo, Running Dog spoke to the warriors in a string of terse, guttural commands. Clearly he had some scheme in mind and was instructing them in their parts. Britt was thoroughly bewildered, particularly when the warriors gigged their ponies and plunged down the incline that dropped off from the plateau. Running Dog watched until they reached the bottom and went thundering across the prairie toward the distant herd. Turning back to Britt, his eyes crackled with excitement, and the black man sensed that whatever he had planned was more than a mere hunt.

"Brother, what you do this day will be discussed in Comanche lodges for many snows to come. My warriors will cut out a plump cow from the herd and drive her toward the camp. You will then ride in and kill this cow in full view of the barbarians. You could offer them no greater honor than to drop a warm, tender cow right in front of Little Buffalo's lodge."

"Little Buffalo?" Britt echoed. "Is this the man who decides if the captives are to be ransomed?"

"No man decides that except the one who owns the white-eyes. But Little Buffalo is their *to-yop-ke*, and he can influence that decision." Glancing around, he noted that the warriors were rapidly approaching the herd. "Now pay attention, Black Fox, for you must learn the ways of the buffalo hunt with only one lesson."

Without wasting so much as a word, the warrior quickly explained the ancient method of dispatching a buffalo from horseback. While it sounded fairly simple, Britt realized that any skill in which the Indians took pride was never as easy as they made it sound. But there was no time to ask questions, for they could see that the braves had now cut a cow from the herd and were hazing her back over the prairie. Running Dog signaled for the women and children to follow, then kneed his pony down the slope. Still somewhat numbed by the rapid turn of events, Britt urged his horse forward, wondering if this wild man was going to get them all killed before they even had a chance to talk with the Comanche chief.

Moments later Britt found himself galloping full out amongst the howling warriors. A blinding cloud of dust enveloped him, coating his throat with a gritty layer of mud. But some ten lengths ahead he could make out the terrified cow lumbering toward the camp. Running Dog rode beside him, yipping like a madman in what Britt assumed to be shouts of encouragement. Spurring the chestnut, Britt pulled ahead of the Kiowas and began closing in on the buffalo. Slowly the gap narrowed, but the animal's ragged gait was deceptive, and it suddenly dawned on him that they were rapidly approaching the village. Raking with his spurs again, he urged the chestnut to a greater effort. But before he quite realized how it happened, he became aware that they were thundering down the main thoroughfare of the village with the cow still out in front.

Scattering dogs, lodges, and cooking pots in every direction, the cow roared through the camp like a shaggy, frothing tornado. Comanches ran from their teepees to gawk in disbelief as the great beast leveled a path through their village. But their stares turned to outright stupefaction when they awoke to the fact that the cow was being chased by a wild-eyed black man and a band of howling Kiowas.

Overtaking the cow at last, Britt kneed the chestnut alongside, matching her stride for stride. Caught up in the thrill of the hunt, he had no thought for anything except the great, humped beast fleeing in terror not a foot away from him. Jerking his Colt, he cocked it and slammed two shots into her chest just behind the foreleg. Tumbling headlong in midstride, the buffalo rolled end over end, cartwheeled high into the air, and dropped with a shuddering crash not ten yards from the medicine lodge.

Britt and the trailing Kiowas skidded to a halt in a roiling upheaval of dust. Whirling their horses, they trotted back to the fallen cow, as hundreds of Comanches began gathering around the medicine lodge. Covered with a mixture of grime and sweat, the black man looked like some onyx centaur emerging from a swirling duststorm. His face split in an enormous grin, glistening with pearly-white teeth, and he seemed to grow taller in the saddle as Running Dog proudly gripped him by the shoulder.

As they reined to a halt before the gaping Comanches, Little Buffalo shoved through the crowd and walked forward. His features were drawn in a tight frown, and he had about him the lordly hauteur of a war chief who can't quite believe that his defenses have just been breached by the enemy. His eyes swept contemptuously over the grinning Kiowas and came to rest on Britt. The black man returned his scowl with a lusty smile, unable to tear his eyes away even though he remembered the warning that one should never stare at a Comanche.

Running Dog nudged his pony forward and signed greeting with an upraised hand. "*Hao*, Little Buffalo. This man is Black Fox, brother of the Kiowa, and the fat cow at your feet is his peace offering to the Comanche. Santana sends greetings and cautions you to treat this man kindly, for his medicine is strong and he walks without hate among the True People. Black Fox has come to trade, and if the *to-yop-ke* is wise, he too may become a rich man." A murmur of excitement swept through the crowd, and out of the corner of his eye Running Dog saw Britt dismount.

Striding forward, the black man handed the still-warm pistol to Little Buffalo. The *to-yop-ke* accepted it solemnly and regarded Britt with a piercing gaze for a moment. Then his features relaxed, and his voice drifted across the council grounds. "Black Fox comes in peace, and he is welcome in the Comanche lodges."

Running Dog chuckled to himself, amazed by the audacity of his strange new brother. Black Fox had strong medicine all right. How else could one explain a man clever enough to disarm the barbarian by disarming himself? *Eeh-yah!* When the fox turns hunter, only his brothers can close their eyes!

CHAPTER FIVE

1

Britt accepted the long-stemmed pipe from Running Dog and puffed on it with grave dignity. It was an old pipe, worn and clogged with slime from years of use, and the pungent smoke left a dirty taste in his mouth. But he pulled on it steadily, ignoring the bitterness, for it was obvious that these Comanches regarded pipe smoking as serious business. Little Buffalo and Ten Bears watched closely, openly curious as to how a *Negrito* would handle a ceremonial pipe. Britt did his best to imitate the mannerisms and solemnity which they had displayed before passing the pipe around the fire. But it still seemed like a terribly clumsy way to get a smoke. With one final puff for good measure he let the smoke curl slowly from his mouth, then passed the pipe on to Little Buffalo.

The four men had been seated around the fire for more than two hours, and Britt began to wonder if these wearisome ceremonies would never end. Little Buffalo's wives had prepared choice hump cuts from the cow he had shot earlier, and throughout the entire meal not one reference had been made to either his mission or the captives. While shelter and food had been made available for the women and children accompanying the Kiowa party, the Comanche chiefs thus far had evidenced not the slightest interest in how they got there or to what purpose. Now the odorous pipe with its dangling feathers and sour taste was being passed around again, and there seemed no end in sight to this sterile formality.

Running Dog had warned him that the Comanches would test his patience by dragging the ceremonies beyond reason, but this was an exquisite form of torture that seemed a cut above mere barbarians. Suddenly it occurred to him that the Comanches might possess more cunning than the Kiowas gave them credit for, and he decided he had better watch his step. But before he could pursue that thought much further, Little Buffalo set the pipe to one side and nodded stonily to Running Dog.

"Brothers, this man comes offering many horses in exchange for the white-eyes taken in the Brazos raid." Running Dog spoke in Comanche, but Britt sensed that the words concerned him and knew the trading session had begun at last. "He is a good man, and unlike the tejanos, his heart bears no ill thoughts for the True People. The Kiowa have dealt with him as one warrior honors another, and we ask only that the Comanche consider his offer in a like manner."

Little Buffalo and Ten Bears stared inscrutably at the black man for a moment. Then the young *to-yop-ke* addressed Britt directly in coarse, broken Spanish. "The Kiowa call you Black Fox, and that warns me you are a sly man. The Comanche have no patience with devious men, but you are here, and we will listen to what you have to say."

"Little Buffalo is known as a just leader, and among such men there is no need for stealth." As he spoke, Britt mustered his thoughts quickly and decided that the man he faced was wholly unlike the vain and crafty Santana. "My mission among your people is stated simply and with nothing hidden in my words. I seek to ransom the captives you hold, and for their freedom I offer many horses."

"You speak plain, and that is good. But you talk to the wrong man. Among the Comanche only the warrior who owns a slave can agree to an exchange."

"This is what I have been told," Britt replied. "Yet I have also been told that among the Comanche there is no voice stronger than that of Little Buffalo. And my hope is that you will speak to the warriors in my behalf."

The *to-yop-ke* frowned, clearly reluctant to take the side of even a black tejano. But before he could speak, Ten Bears hurriedly joined the discussion. "This is a hard thing you do, Black Fox. The Comanche are a rich people and have many horses. They also find it belittling to trade women and children who have been adopted into the tribe." Then he paused, purposely lending weight to his next thought. "Unless, of course, the number of horses offered was so unusual that a man could overlook the grief of parting."

Britt's pulse quickened. This cagey old man was baiting him, and none too subtly either. Still, Santana had advised him that the Comanches were notoriously poor traders, and he might just be able to save the settlers a few horses. "Father, where the tejano's women and children are concerned, he can be generous indeed. I am empowered to offer one fat horse for each captive delivered unharmed to the Brazos."

"That is a madness that only a Kiowa could arrange," Little Buffalo said with biting sarcasm. "Still, a Comanche's courage is greater than a Kiowa's foolishness, and we have no fear of riding again to the Brazos."

"It is done then," Ten Bears pronounced. "Except for one thing, Black Fox. We must have two horses for each white-eye woman."

Britt frowned as the old chief eyed him shrewdly. This was better than he had hoped for, but he had to suffer a little to make it appear that they had ensnared the helpless *Negrito*. "Father, your stick is sharp, but it leaves me no choice. I accept, and though they will moan like squaws, the tejanos will honor my word."

Little Buffalo glanced at Ten Bears, who nodded with a gloating smile, and then back to Britt. "There is a thing you must consider, Black Fox. The white-eye captives are spread throughout our five bands, and it is you who must track each of them down."

"Give me a guide and I will do so gladly," the black man responded. "The only request I have is to be informed immediately of where I might find the *Negrito* woman and her children."

"That is simple enough," Little Buffalo said. "They are in this village. Not ten lodges from where you sit." The Comanche saw Britt's eyes come alive, and his face twisted in a stern warning. "Do not deceive yourself, Black

Fox. You can see none of the captives before I counsel
with the warriors who own them. Until then I caution you
to walk lightly in this village, for the Comanche are not
like the Kiowa. We may trade with the tejanos, but my
warriors would kill any man who oversteps his welcome."

Little Buffalo's cold gaze swept across to Running Dog,
and the message was clear. Both the Kiowas and their
black brother could expect harsh reprisals if they tam-
pered with any of the captives before negotiations were
completed. They had come in peace, and tribal law assured their safety. But only so long as they didn't touch
anything that belonged to a Comanche.

2

The pitch black stillness of a starless sky had settled over
the camp when Britt and Running Dog made their way
back to the Kiowa lodge. Wood smoke hung beneath a
cloudy sky, and there was a hint of snow to come in the
crisp night air. Another week, maybe less, and icy winds
would blast down out of the north, bringing with them the
swirling, snow-choked blizzards. Once started, the storms
would rage unabated throughout the winter, relentlessly
sweeping the plains time and again with blinding ferocity.

Wandering across these snow-swept prairies in the dead
of winter was not a task to be taken lightly. As Britt silently kept pace with Running Dog, he attempted to calculate the time needed to reach the far-flung Comanche
bands, but the variable of the weather was too unpredic-
table. What might take days under normal circumstances
could turn into weeks if a blizzard refused to subside. And
more than one man had left his bones on the Plains because he miscalculated the cussedness of prairie storms.
Besides, there were more immediate matters to be considered just at this moment.

Mary and the children were in this camp somewhere,
and before anyone else got saved, he intended to see to it
that his own family was well out of harm's way.

Near the western edge of the encampment, two lodges
had been erected for the use of the Kiowas and their
captives. The women and children had been quartered in
the one closest to the river, and it occurred to Britt that he
must talk with them sometime during the night. But that

would have to wait. Right now he wanted to think and then talk with Running Dog where they would not be overheard by Comanches.

Entering the men's lodge, they found the warriors lounged around a small fire. Running Dog quickly briefed them on the meeting with Little Buffalo, and their sullen muttering made it clear that they resented having to wait while Black Fox trudged around the countryside collecting more white-eyes. Then one of the warriors made a comment, gesturing toward the black man, and Running Dog began questioning him intensely. While Britt couldn't understand the guttural flow of Kiowa, he knew from Running Dog's sober attitude that something ominous was being discussed. At last the two men fell silent, and Running Dog stared into the fire for a moment before looking around at Britt.

"Black Fox, I have bad news. My warriors went among the Comanche tonight, and they return with word of your woman. She is in the lodge of one called Standing Bear, and talk among the Comanche is that he will not consider trading her."

Britt's eyes widened with disbelief. Such a possibility had never occurred to him, and for an instant he was gripped by sheer panic. "That's impossible! Or else they are lying. The Comanches want horses as much as the Kiowas. And besides, Little Buffalo agreed to the trade!"

"Calm yourself, brother," Running Dog said, "and think with your head instead of your heart. The *to-yop-ke* agreed only to counsel with his warriors. No man is obliged to act against his will. That is the law. And if Standing Bear refuses to trade, then it is out of Little Buffalo's hands."

"Well, it's not out of my hands!" Britt's voice dropped to a savage growl, and his eyes went cold. "I came here to get my woman, and by Christ, I will! Even if I have to steal her back and make a run for the Brazos."

"Your god cannot help you now, Black Fox. You are among the Comanche." There was a moment's stillness, broken only by the crackling fire and the warriors' grunted assent. "Should you steal the woman, the barbarians would run you to earth within a day. And then you would both roast over a slow fire. Besides, what would become of the white-eye women and children if Black Fox abandoned them?"

Britt's gaze remained flinty and remote, but the spark of reason once more entered his eyes. "You are right, of course. If I stole her, many would suffer for my selfishness. But I can't just get on my horse and leave her here. Would a Kiowa do that?"

"No warrior would do such a thing, brother." The Kiowa gave him a cool look of appraisal, almost as if he were sizing him up against some unspoken menace. "Still, there may be a way."

Britt stiffened, his features alert, and Running Dog continued in the same calm, dispassionate tone. "Standing Bear is a member of *ko-eet-senko*, the most highly honored warrior society, and as such, he could not refuse a fight. Since he stole your woman, you could challenge him to combat, and no one would question your right to do so. Should you win, then everything Standing Bear owns would become yours." The Kiowa regarded him silently for a moment, then stared impassively into the flames. "Of course, he might just as easily kill you. Even his own people say that he is more wild beast than Comanche."

Britt's eyes narrowed at the warning implicit in Running Dog's casual manner. Still, he had lived by hunches all his life, and instinct told him that fighting Standing Bear was the only way. But this was different somehow, for while he had killed, he had never before coldly planned another man's death. His eyes lost focus, and his gaze was absorbed in the flickering coals of the fire. Leering from the flames was the face of death, death's ugly, fleshless grin, and an icy hand squeezed down on his heart. He shivered imperceptibly, mesmerized by the specter he saw in the sparkling embers. Then he shook himself, like a dog rousing from a deep sleep, and wrenched his mind away from the grisly apparition. *Wake up. Get hold of yourself. You're one lone nigger in a Comanche village, and if you don't kill this man, your woman and kids ain't never again going to see Elm Creek.*

Tearing his eyes away from the fire, Britt became aware that the warriors were watching him curiously. His face creased in a tight smile, and he glanced at the Kiowa leader. "Running Dog must instruct me in how this thing is to be done."

"When a man has won the fight within himself," Running Dog commented, "all else comes easy. Tonight we will prepare you in the ways of the knife, for this is surely the weapon Standing Bear will choose."

The Kiowa drew a heavy, bone-handled fighting knife, and the other warriors moved back as he rose to demonstrate the surest way of gutting an arrogant Comanche.

3

Talking Raven's rough, bony hands moved with nimble certainty as she wove porcupine quills into a diamond pattern on the buckskin shirt. Mary paused to watch, intrigued by the sight of those calloused, thorny fingers performing a delicate task with such skill and grace. After a moment she returned to pounding the roots and berries which would be converted into bright dyes for staining more quills.

Work in a Comanche lodge was never ending, and there always seemed to be more chores at hand than the three women could possibly finish. Two Moon's new baby, along with George and Sue Ellen, made additional demands on their time, and from the crack of dawn till late at night the women rarely stopped to rest. Still, Mary normally welcomed the grueling workload, for it diverted her mind from her miseries, which in the past week had grown considerable.

But tonight her mind raced with newborn hope, and she was hardly aware of the tasks her nervous hands somehow managed.

Earlier in the day, near the center of the village, there had been a commotion which ended in gunfire. Mary's foremost concern was for the children, for gunshots were almost unknown in the village itself, and she had hurried them inside the lodge. Though it was late in the year for a Crow raiding party, it was better to be cautious, and she stood guard in the entrance while Talking Raven watched from outside. Presently she heard Standing Bear's gruff voice, and she edged closer to the entrance flap. Though he and Talking Raven were speaking in hushed tones, she could still make out snatches of the conversation. Abruptly it dawned on her that they were talking about a tejano *Negrito* who had ridden into camp with a band of Kiowas. Then she heard Standing Bear order the squaw not to let their own *Negrito* out of the lodge until he returned. With that the conversation had ended, and Talking Raven entered the tepee, glancing at her with a curious, hidden look.

Concealing her excitement, Mary had busied herself around the lodge. Her mind flooded with a jumble of thoughts, each more tantalizing and seemingly farfetched than the other. How could a black man have entered the village alive and in one piece? Was he really a Texan or just another renegade trader? And why was he riding with Kiowas? Oh God, could it be? Could Britt have somehow made friends with the Kiowas? Has he come to take us home? Merciful God, please let it be him.

But no matter how she talked to herself, it still didn't seem real or even possible. Texans just didn't ride into Indian lands and live to tell about it. Things like that just didn't happen. But why was Standing Bear holding her in the lodge? What was he afraid she would see? *Or was he afraid someone would see her?*

The day passed, and darkness fell without any resolution to her vexing questions. But as she pondered the situation at greater length, Mary came to the conclusion that if it was Britt, then there was a good chance Standing Bear would let her go. Especially since he had lost face so disastrously in their running battle of wits.

Since the day Two Moons' son was born, Standing Bear had nudged and pinched and leered at her so suggestively that everyone in the lodge became aware of his campaign to bed her. But it was only last week that he had finally managed to corner her alone. Late one morning Talking Raven and Two Moons had gone off on some errand, when the entrance flap suddenly flew open. Standing Bear stepped boldly into the lodge, and from the flushed expression on his face, Mary knew that her time had come. But she didn't intend to whelp any Comanche brats without a struggle.

Moving with the swiftness of a coiled snake, the warrior grabbed her shoulders and forced her toward a bed of buffalo robes. But the black woman was no novice at infighting, and she promptly sank her teeth into the meaty flesh of his forearm. Grunting with pain, Standing Bear cuffed her upside the head, and she dropped on the robes with a hollow ringing in her ears. Grinning like a wolf about to devour a hamstrung cow, the Comanche whipped

his breech clout off, then straddled her, and began forcing
her legs apart.

Dizzy and near passing out, Mary reared up with one
last surge of strength, bucking the warrior's rump high
into the air. Standing Bear laughed good-naturedly at this
delaying tactic, but his humor quickly turned to a roar
of pain and animal rage. For when his rump came down
out of the air, Mary deftly planted her knee in his crotch
and again reared upward with all her might.

Only Talking Raven's timely appearance saved her
life. Between spasms of retching and spewing sour vomit
around the lodge, Standing Bear grabbed a war ax and
was slowly crawling toward her. Just as Mary found herself trapped against the wall, the lodge flap opened and
Talking Raven entered. There was a moment of embarrassed silence as the half-naked warrior gasped for breath
and darted guilty side glances at the squaw. Then Talking Raven found her tongue and began to flay him,
screaming that only a mindless *pawsa* would kill a good
slave just because she refused to grease his pole. Finally
unable to stand her screeching harangue any longer,
Standing Bear struck her in the mouth, snatched up his
breech clout, and fled from the lodge.

Thinking back on the incident as she began dyeing the
porcupine quills, Mary was even more firmly convinced
that Standing Bear would gladly see the last of her. His
pride had been gouged to the quick, and from his sullen
mood over the last week it was clear that he had lost face
among the other warriors. After all, if a man couldn't bed
a frail *Negrito* squaw, how could he call himself a warrior?
Absorbed in these pleasant thoughts, Mary started as the
entrance flap jerked back and Standing Bear stepped into
the lodge. For a moment it seemed like a terrifying repeti-
tion of their last encounter, and she scuttled backward to
where the children were sleeping on their robes.

The warrior glowered around the lodge, then spoke to
the squaw even though his eyes remained fixed on Mary.
"The tejano *Negrito* comes to trade for this black bitch.
She was his woman on the Brazos, and he thinks to take
her from the Comanche."

Mary instinctively rose to her feet, aware only that Britt
had actually come and that the words just spoken meant
freedom. The children had awakened, sensing that something grave was taking place, and clung sleepily to her

skirt. Standing Bear grinned evilly, his features twisted in a cruel smirk.

"Waugh! See how she comes alive with thoughts of rutting once more with her black dog." Snorting, he cast a sardonic glance at Talking Raven, then glared back at Mary. "Calm yourself, woman. This tejano *Negrito* must deal with me, and there will be no talk of trade. When he leaves, he will leave alone, for if you were both dead, you would be nearer to one another than you are at this moment."

Mary blanched and stared without moving, as if she had turned to stone. *This Comanche pig was going to refuse to trade and somehow force Britt to leave camp without us!* Suddenly all her pent-up anxiety exploded in a paroxysm of fury, and she launched herself at the warrior. Clawing and scratching, she screamed every vile name she could dredge up from memory, intent on nothing less than ripping his eyes clean from their sockets.

Standing Bear retreated cautiously before the force of her attack, but her rage was no match for his brute strength. Ducking beneath her blows, his arm swung in a rising arc, and the butt of his hand cracked solidly against her jawbone. Mary hurtled backward and dropped in a limp bundle on the robes. Her eyes blurred, fusing images in a shadowed fog, and a sharp, brassy taste flooded her mouth. Dimly she sensed that little George had leaped past her in vain attempt to halt the warrior. Then the boy fell beside her, his nose bleeding from a vicious backhand. Blindly thrusting the children behind her, Mary cowered before the Comanche, waiting for the death blow to fall.

But Standing Bear had other things in mind for his reluctant black squaw. Wiping the blood from a deep gash on his cheek, his eyes hooded with sinister amusement. "Prepare yourself for mourning, woman. For before the sun sets again, I will show you how a warrior spills blood."

Turning, he pushed through the entrance, and a chill silence fell over the lodge. Mary shuddered, choking back her tears, and the whimpering children clutched her neck. Standing Bear's threat echoed in her head, like a death knell for all she held dear. Filled with sickening dread, she implored her God to strike the heathen Comanche dead or else never let tomorrow come.

4

Later that evening Britt left the warriors and walked toward the women's lodge. In a short time Running Dog had taught him the rudimentary feints and slashes of knife fighting as practiced by the Plains Indians. But this brief lesson left him far short of the lethal skills developed and refined by warriors since childhood, and once his anger had been replaced by reason, the odds seemed to grow worse with each passing minute. From what the Kiowas had said, Standing Bear was clearly a formidable adversary, and the outcome of the duel he intended to provoke tomorrow now seemed far less certain than it had an hour ago. Still, he dreaded talking with the settler women more than he disliked the idea of facing a foot of cold steel.

Most women, as he had learned from bitter experience, were highly unreliable where violence and blood spilling were involved. Their inborn aversion to such things tended to blind them to the harsh necessities sometimes demanded by life. And they failed to comprehend that a man must frequently take the ultimate gamble simply because he could do no less and continue to live with himself. Yet the lady called luck was the most capricious vixen of them all, and tonight even he felt a nagging irritant of doubt as to the aftermath of his scheme to free Mary. But that was a concern which at all costs must remain hidden from the Texan women and their brood.

Entering the lodge, he found the children blissfully asleep, and the four women hovered around a tiny fire. Their open, spontaneous smiles filled the tepee with warmth as they rose to crowd around him. This black man was their savior, and while he may have been an uppity nigger back on the Brazos, he was a lily-pure prince in a Comanche village. With the exception of Sarah Johnson, who had long ago accepted him as a member of the family, these women had not spoken a dozen words to him in the past ten years. But the specter of death has a way of leveling even the most rigid caste system, albeit the man bearing salvation is an untouchable and black as the ace of spades.

"Britt, we were getting worried about you," Sarah said, touching his arm lightly. "You've been gone so long, we were afraid those devils had done something to you."

"Now, Miz Sarah, you know there's nothin' that can touch old Britt." The black man chuckled with a levity that he hardly felt. "Matter of fact, I had supper with the head man of this bunch, and he's agreed to let us trade for their captives."

"Oh, Britt, that's marvelous," Sarah said excitedly. Then her face clouded with anxiety. "But what about Mary? Surely you must have learned something about her and the children."

"Bless me, Miz Sarah, I just plumb forgot to mention it! They're right here in the village, and we'll get them back sometime tomorrow."

The women clapped their hands and exclaimed happily. Then Maggie Williams pounded Britt on the shoulder. "Well, that's grand, just grand. If ever a man deserved to get his woman and little ones back, it's you." Looking around at the other women, she grinned with a sudden thought. "And that means we can start heading home tomorrow too."

"Well, no, not exactly," Britt said slowly. The women's eyes jerked around, and they peered apprehensively at him, like a flock of owls caught in an early sunrise. "Seems that the Comanches have split up into a number of bands, and the women and children have gone off with them. So it appears likely I'll have to hunt them down and bring 'em back here before we can leave."

"Why, that's . . . that's crazy!" Maggie Williams sputtered indignantly. "These red savages might take it in their head to murder us all while you're out galavanting around this god-forsaken wilderness." The other women appeared stunned and for the moment, speechless. "Now you just get it in your head that it's better to save what you've got right now. A bird in the hand is worth two in the bush, and you can always come back for those others later." Then her face split in a sly, mercenary smile. "Besides, my man will pay you real good for bringing us home."

Britt's eyes slitted, and the muscle in his jaw clenched with repressed anger. A moment of strained stillness ensued, and the women shrank before his corrosive stare. "Miz Williams, I'll just pretend like you didn't even say that. If I was after a reward, I'd have made my deals before I left Fort Belknap. And if you want something to think about, just remember it could be you out there prayin' for somebody to come save you from the Comanche."

"That's all well and good," Rachel Ledbetter snapped, "but you'd better start thinkin' what you're gonna say to our menfolks if these Indians decide to . . . well, to do something bad to us women while you're gone."

"That's something I might not have to worry about." Britt paused and glanced around at their fearful faces. "Appears that the only way to save my own family is to fight one of the Comanches tomorrow. And if things don't go just exactly right, it won't much matter what your menfolks think."

Sarah's mouth popped open, and she stared at Britt with mounting terror. The other women appeared equally appalled, and they watched him with unblinking disbelief. Then Maggie Williams found her tongue and lashed out venomously. "You fool nigger! You haven't got the sense God gave a piss ant. What do you think will happen to us if you're killed? We'd be right back where we started!"

"Then I reckon you wouldn't be any worse off than before I got here," he said with chill dignity. "I came here to get the Johnson families, Miz Williams, and whether you know it or not, you're just ridin' on their coattails. If I can't save my own woman and kids, then I'm not going to bother my head too much about anyone else. Especially since I'd be dog meat anyway if I lose that fight."

"Britt's right!" Sarah's harsh tone cracked like a shot. "His first responsibility is to his own family, and if he gets us out along with them, then we can just count ourselves lucky. Instead of cursing him, you should get down on your knees and kiss his feet. And pray to God he wins that fight tomorrow."

Seething, she glared around at the other women. Their eyes dropped to the dirt floor, not in shame but with the manner of those who have been forced to look upon their own shabby corruption. Rather than self-loathing, they were gripped by bitter resentment and the abiding fear that their lives hung by a thread on the fighting skills of this fool nigger.

"Well, I'm sure as Christ not about to kiss his feet." Maggie Williams glanced around with a dour, unrepentant expression. "But you're right about one thing. We'd better ask the good Lord to make him strong as an ox, come daylight."

The black man regarded them stonily for a moment, then turned without a word, and walked from the lodge. Somehow life had become confusing, a frustrating riddle that threatened to penetrate his aloof shell with its barbed uncertainty. The Indians looked upon' him as a man, nothing more and nothing less. And they accepted him for what he was, rather than what he had been born. Yet tomorrow he would kill one of their number and, in so doing, save the very people who hated him for not being white. If there was a God, he had a strange sense of humor. A white man's humor.

5

The council ground was thronged with warriors, curious elders and a scattering of squaws. Little Buffalo and Ten Bears stood before the medicine lodge, waiting patiently for the crowd to assemble so that the trading session could begin. The *to-yop-ke* had called the council for midday, and the dull glow of the autumn sun was now almost directly overhead. Presently Running Dog and Britt shouldered their way through the swarm of Indians and came to a halt beside the Comanche chiefs. After a brief exchange with the Kiowa and his black brother, Little Buffalo stepped forward and the assembled warriors fell silent.

"Brothers, the tejano called Black Fox has come to trade for those captured in the Brazos raid. He is a man of honor and speaks straight. Both Ten Bears and I have accepted him as a fair man, one who deals justly with the True People. He offers two horses for each Tejano woman and one horse for each child. We feel this to be a worthy offer and have agreed to speak to you in Black Fox's behalf. There is to be no haggling. This is the offer, and it is a good one. Now who will be the first to trade with Black Fox?"

An undertone of muttering swept through the spectator's ranks, and Britt sensed something vaguely ominous in the sharp, disgruntled jabbering. There was unmistakable hostility in the warriors' glances, and he suddenly realized that something had inflamed them to the point of open belligerence. Then a stout, barrel-chested brave stepped forward, and when Running Dog nudged Britt with an elbow, he knew beyond question that this was Standing Bear. The black man eyed him closely, silently gauging his adversary. What he saw was a chunky man with a broad, spongy face, whose heavily muscled figure betrayed no sign of weakness. Standing Bear's glaring eyes slanted upward, hollow and cruel, and when he spoke, his words were riddled through with cold sarcasm.

"I, Standing Bear, will not trade with the *Negrito* dog! Like all *tejanos*, he thinks the Comanche are children who will fall before words of honey and shallow trickery. His words flow from both sides of his mouth, and as a *ko-eet-senko,* I am not bound to trade with a white-eyed liar."

Little Buffalo's eyes darted suspiciously at Britt as the warrior finished speaking. Something was afoot that surpassed understanding, and the *to-yop-ke* intended to have it out in the open. "You are within your rights, brother. As a Comanche you are bound by nothing but your own will. But you leave me wondering. Do you refuse because you wish to have Black Fox's family for your own? Or is there some greater thing that you back away from speaking?"

"The *to-yop-ke* forces words that I would have left unsaid," Standing Bear replied. "For they dishonor you and thereby make fools of all Comanches. The black dog laughs behind his face at us and would ridicule us before our southern brothers. For he has offered us less horses than those given to the Kiowa. I have this from the mouths of the Kiowas themselves."

Little Buffalo's head snapped around, and his smoldering gaze came to rest on Britt and Running Dog. The Kiowa leader cast a piercing glance at his warriors who stood in a knot to one side, and from their crestfallen expressions he knew that they had bragged prematurely and unwisely to their Comanche brothers. Running Dog quickly translated for Britt what had occurred, and the black man's features stiffened under the impact of this new crisis.

Britt instinctively sensed that all was lost unless he moved quickly to regain the Comanches' confidence. Mustering his most candid tone, he spoke in broken Spanish to the *to-yop-ke*. "Great chief, hear my words. Do not the

Comanche seek the best terms when they trade? Is it not so with all people? I sought not to cheat the Comanche and certainly not to dishonor them, but only to obtain the best bargain for my own people. This is the accepted way of trade since our fathers and their fathers before them. But if the Comanches doubt my good will, then I will offer the same as given to the Kiowa. Three horses for each woman and one for each child. Petty scheming to save a few horses is for children, not men. So let us trade as friends and have no more talk of such things."

Little Buffalo stood motionless, unblinking, like some great horned owl passing judgment on a nest full of fat mice. He regarded Britt with disgust for a moment longer, then turned back to the assembled warriors. "The trade has been set, and the Comanches do not step away from a promise. Those of you who would trade will be given the same as the Kiowa. And as your *to-yop-ke,* I say give this *Negrito* your slaves and let us be done with the white-eye filth."

"*No!*" roared Standing Bear. "I refuse. You are the *to-yop-ke,* but you have no right to make us do this thing." Malevolence twisted his features, insidious and creeping like some cankerous growth, distilling the rage within him. Whirling on the black man, he shouted in bastard Spanish, "*Negrito,* your woman is mine to do with as I choose. From this day forward, she will labor like a horse, and her legs will spread for any Comanche who wishes to ram his pole in black meat!"

Britt's mind seethed and boiled with blind fury, searing out all thought. He started toward the warrior, determined to still that rancorous voice once and for all. But Running Dog grabbed his arm, restraining him, and after a moment his outrage gave way to calculated cold-bloodedness. Turning back to Little Buffalo, his words were spat out in a low, savage snarl. "I demand the right of combat with this coward who makes his fight on women. If he refuses, I will ride throughout the Comanche nation telling how he crawled before me like a whimpering dog."

"Show me your knife, *Negrito!*" Standing Bear shouted. "Step forward with steel in your hand instead of brave words and we will see who leaves his guts in the dirt."

"Hold your tongues," Little Buffalo growled. "Since you have both seen fit to involve me in this thing, it is I who will decide how this fight is to be made." His harsh glare shifted from one to the other as a startled murmur swept through the crowd, and the malice in his eyes was only partially obscured by a glaze of autocratic hauteur. "When the sun drops below the earth, it is then you will fight. And as you are each filled with your own courage, I order it to be the Dance of Snakes. Now a warning: should either of you attempt to back away from this thing, I will gladly cut your throat with my own hand."

The *to-yop-ke* spun on his heel and stalked off, followed closely by Ten Bears. Within moments the council grounds was deserted of Comanches, and the Kiowas stood in a sober knot around their black brother. Running Dog had difficulty meeting Britt's eyes, and when he spoke, his words were halting, shamed.

"Black Fox, the Kiowa are to blame for what has happened, and rightfully it is I who should fight Standing Bear." He shifted uncomfortably under the black man's quizzical look and rushed on. "Before we left the mountains, Santana ordered me to guide you in tricking the barbarians into a poor trade. After you had gone, he planned to taunt them with the thought that a *Negrito* had made fools of the arrogant Comanches."

Britt shook his head with a wry, distant smile, finding it difficult to be angry with the Kiowas and their childish games. Right now his thoughts centered on sundown and what he would face with the first shadows of darkness. "Do not flay yourself needlessly, my friend. What is done is done, and it is of no consequence. Instead, tell me of the manner in which I am to fight Standing Bear. For the *to-yop-ke's* words made clear only that it would not be with knives."

"No, not with knives," Running Dog said with a strange, hollow voice. "You are to face Standing Bear over a pit filled with the evil ones, rattlesnakes. The fight will end only when one of you has thrown the other amongst the crawling death." He faltered as the black man's face dissolved into an incredulous mask. "Little Buffalo chose the Dance of Snakes because he was displeased with you both. He felt you tricked him in the trade, and Standing Bear was fool enough to make this known in front of the other warriors. The *to-yop-ke* has lost face, and he means to regain it in the cruelest way known to the True People."

"I see," said Britt, somewhat shaken by the diabolic

twist his simple scheme had taken. "But why must we wait until tonight? If this thing is to be done, why not do it now?"

"Black Fox, winter is near," Running Dog explained quietly. "The evil ones have already retreated to their dens. Little Buffalo made the fight for the hour of darkness because it will take many warriors the rest of the day to build fires and smoke them from their caves." The Kiowa glanced eastward and nodded toward the distant sandstone cliffs. "Bear in mind that with their winter sleep disturbed, the *to-yop-ke* knows the evil ones will be enraged beyond all belief."

Britt shuddered as the icy hand of death again clutched his heart. The fleshless specter he had seen in the fire last night took shape before his eyes, and for a brief moment he stared into a vision of writhing horror that seemed cleaved straight from the hell of a madman's demented ravings.

6

Britt sat alone before the small fire. Running Dog and the Kiowa braves had fanned out through the village to arrange bets with the Comanches. Indians were inveterate gamblers, willing to risk everything they possessed on a toss of the bones or a fast horse, and the extraordinary fight to take place that evening had created a furor of betting within the camp. Moreover, the Kiowas had considerately absented themselves because they wanted Britt to have the lodge to himself. Black Fox had become one of them, and when a brother was to be reunited with his family, he deserved at the very least to be left alone.

Shortly after the discordant meeting that morning, Running Dog had approached Little Buffalo as an intermediary in Britt's behalf. There was every likelihood, he said, that Black Fox would never see another sunrise. And while bitterness now existed toward the *Negrito,* tribal law still dictated that the Comanche were his hosts. Therefore, it was not too much to ask that a man facing certain death be allowed to see his family one last time. After all, the Comanches were not heartless dogs like the Ute or the Crow, he had concluded, and even a condemned man had the right to make one final request of his accuser.

Little Buffalo wasn't for a moment deceived by Running Dog's deference, but he found the Kiowa's obsequious manner highly appealing and in some perverse way was immensely gratified by the life or death power he held over the black man. While he was not a vain man, he found himself curiously intrigued with the idea of manipulating the lives of lesser men, particularly those who had incurred his displeasure. But a great leader must be magnanimous as well as stern, and after deliberating for a few moments he had granted the request.

Standing Bear was summoned, and in no uncertain terms the *to-yop-ke* ordered that the tejano *Negrito* be allowed a brief visit with his family. The warrior's eyes crackled with resentment and indignation, but he had offended Little Buffalo enough for one day, and he reluctantly yielded to the demand. With a withering glance at Running Dog, he turned and stormed from the chief's lodge.

Now Britt waited tensely in the strangely silent Kiowa tepee. Needing some distraction to curb his impatience, he methodically cracked branches and fed them slowly into the fire one at a time. Almost a month had passed since he last saw Mary and the children, and the thought weighed heavily on his mind. What could happen to a woman in an Indian camp in a month's time wasn't pleasant to dwell on, and the treatment to which his family had been subjected might easily have affected them in some gruesome, unthinkable manner.

For that matter, he himself was hardly the same man who had ridden into the Wichita Mountains only a fortnight past. So much had happened to reshape his perspective of the world around him, and more significantly, the simple, unvarnished birthright that all men should reasonably expect from their short tenure on earth. The Kiowas had shown him a way of life where each man was his own master, beholden to none save his conscience and his god. Moreover, it was a federation of men based not on ancestry or race or the color of a man's skin, but rather upon the intrinsic qualities of one's manhood and the courage with which he faced life's uncompromising trials. It was a wild, exhilarating freedom unlike any he had ever known, and the thought coursed through his mind that he might never again be content to trod the nigger's path in the white man's shadow.

Suddenly the lodge flap whipped aside, and before he could move, Mary and the children swarmed over him with great wrenching sobs of joy. His eyes brimmed with tears, and a sodden, moist lump lodged in his throat. Wordlessly he swept them into his arms and hugged them fiercely, burying his face in the familiar scent of Mary's hair. Moments passed in silent physical communion, broken only by their sniffling cries and whispered words of endearment. Then as they gulped back their tears and dried their eyes, they began to see each other clearly for the first time, and it was a sobering experience.

"God a'mighty, it's good to see you, woman!" Britt hugged her again, trying to hide his shock at her greasy buckskin dress and worn features. "And would you just look at these two little Injuns!" Chuckling warmly, he scooped Sue Ellen and George up against his chest, and they clutched at his neck, smearing his face with wet, sticky kisses.

"Papa, have you come to take us home?" Sue Ellen said between hugs and kisses. "We been waitin' an awful long time."

Britt swallowed hard and felt his throat tightening. Thinner now, with her hair in braids, she had the cameo perfection of her mother's features, and her round, child's eyes stared trustingly into his face. The black man looked away, unable to stand her searching eyes, only to find his son watching him with the same unspoken question formed silently on his lips. Then the boy smiled bravely, choking back a fresh burst of tears. "It's not so bad, Pa. We can wait some more if you say so."

"Son, your waitin' is just about done with. This time tomorrow we'll all be back together again. That's a promise." Glancing at Mary, he saw fear kindle in her eyes, and he quickly looked back at the children. "Now you two just sit down here and be real quiet for a minute. Your mama and me has a lot to talk about, and we've only got a little time. Bet you never expected this old horned toad to come chasin' you down?" he said, forcing his voice to sound light and carefree.

Mary's eyes remained troubled, but she smiled and shook her head. "Lord, when I heard it was you, I just couldn't hardly believe it. How in the name of heaven did you keep 'em from killin' you? And how did you know

where to find us? They said you was ridin' with the
Kiowas, but I just don't—"

"Whoa! One question at a time, woman." Quickly Britt
explained his curious alliance with the Kiowas and how
he had come to the Comanche camp. Once or twice Mary
interrupted with questions, expressing ámazement at the
sheer audacity of his scheme. When he came to the part
about killing the buffalo cow, the black woman's jaw
dropped open in utter astonishment.

"Gal, it wasn't nothin' but pure nigger luck. Just like a
blind old boar hog stumblin' across an acorn." Then he
smiled broadly and took her hand between his two meaty
paws. "But that's all over and done with now. Come tomorrow we'll be together, and there's nothin' ever again
going to come between us."

Mary smiled shallowly, finding it difficult to meet his
gaze. Then she glanced up and her eyes were rimmed with
terror. "Don't try hidin' it from me, Britt. I know all about
what's happening tonight. Standing Bear came back from
the meetin' this morning and like to tore the lodge apart.
He means to kill you, and you just haven't got any idea of
what he's like when he's mad."

"Woman, don't you beat all!" he chortled. "When did
you ever know ol' Britt to lose a fight? Why, if he's even
twice as tough as some of those nigger studs I stomped
back on the plantation, he still won't even get me breathin'
hard. Or maybe you forgot how many I had to whip till
they'ed stay clear of you."

"No, I haven't forgot," she said grimly. "It was me that
sewed you up and nursed you more times than I like to
remember. But you was fightin' with knives and fists
then."

"Ummm," he grunted with a wry smile. "Appears
you've already heard how it's to be."

"Couldn't help but hear. It's all over the village. This is
the first time they've had a fight like this in more'n six
years."

"Little mama, don't get yourself all heated up." Britt
lifted her chin gently in his hand. "I've been killin' snakes
since I was old enough to spit. And I don't reckon it's
botherin' me much to face some half-assed Comanche
over a pit full of rattlers."

"Oh, Britt, how can you be funnin' at a time like this?"

she cried. "That man's a devil, and he's gonna trick you somehow. I just know he is!"

"C'mon now! Have you forgot all that good juju my grandmam taught me? You think I'm not going to peel his red hide with some of that hoodoo double whammy come nightfall?" Britt laughed deeply and gathered the children in closely. "What do you say we quit borrowing trouble before it even happens and start thinkin' about what we're going to do with ourselves when all this is over?"

The black man's light manner eased Mary's strained face somewhat, but beneath his casual cockiness there lingered the icy dread he had foreseen earlier. And within the guileless crypts of his inner self there was far less certainty of the night's outcome than he pretended. Shunting these grisly thoughts aside, he laughed and joked, clowning with the children, and in an engaging flow of anecdotes revealed to them the warm, selfless humanism he had found among the men he now called brothers.

All too soon the time would come to face Standing Bear, and before that moment arrived, he wanted this woman he loved so dearly to know of the burgeoning dream that had taken form during his days with the wild and fiercely proud Kiowas.

7

The entire Comanche camp was gathered near a large, roaring fire as Britt, Running Dog, and the Kiowa braves approached. The flames shot high in the air, casting golden shadows across the hushed crowd, and Britt noticed a deep pit off to one side of the fire. The Comanche warriors and their squaws eyed the black man speculatively, still somewhat awed by his enormous size and yet curious as to how a *Negrito* would fare in the most deadly of all tests known to the True-People. Rarely had warriors been subjected to the Dance of Snakes, and in the memory of the tribe no Comanche had ever refused this ultimate test of courage after being challenged. But the tejano *Negrito* was not a Comanche, much less a blooded warrior, and there was much concern that he might spoil this grand event by backing off at the last moment.

The fight was to be held on a flat stretch of ground near the riverbank, and the peaceful, rushing waters of the

Canadian somehow seemed out of place with this eerie scene. A cavernous hole had been dug in the ground a few paces from the fire, and as Britt glanced quickly at the gaping pit, it appeared to be something more than six feet in length and breadth and quite deep. Strangely the darkened silence of its depths lent an added sense of evil and unseen menace to the pit, and Britt once again felt the cold, fleshless hand of death clutching at his spine.

Little Buffalo and Standing Bear stood alone before the fire, regarding the Kiowa party impassively as they drew nearer. As the Kiowa braves moved off to one side, Britt and Running Dog came to a halt before the two Comanches. Little Buffalo nodded solemnly and, without any attempt at ceremony, launched into the rules governing the fight.

"You men have sworn to kill one another, and that is a good thing, for a warrior is obligated to defend his manhood. But this thing tonight will be done with honor, so that the one who lives can justly lay claim to the possessions of the other." His stoic features betrayed no sign of compassion or mercy as he paused for a moment to gaze coldly into their faces. "Should either of you shame yourself before the fight is finished, my warriors have been instructed to kill you without hesitation.

"You will both be placed on opposite sides of the hole, and your purpose is to throw your opponent into the pit. How you do this is a matter of your own choosing. You can use no weapons, and you must never move past the outer edges of the pit. Should you break either of these rules or shame yourself with cowardice, you will be clubbed and thrown alive into the hole. If you do not understand what I say, then you must speak now."

"I have no questions my *to-yop-ke*." Standing Bear's words were laced with sardonic brittleness, and he regarded the black man with a brash, amused impudence. "When a Comanche warrior lowers himself to fight a *Negrito* dog, then he asks only to have it done with."

Britt chuckled contemptuously, hoping to unsettle the warrior, and was rewarded with a brief flicker of uncertainty in the other man's eyes. Then he looked back to Little Buffalo. "What you have said is clear, but there is one thing that bothers me. We are not allowed to step past the outer edge of the hole, and this I understand. But is it also forbidden to cross over the pit itself? I would understand this thoroughly, for I have no desire to be killed by your warriors."

Standing Bear snorted as if confronted with the babblings of the village idiot, and Little Buffalo stared at the black man in some astonishment before speaking. "Black Fox, if a man is foolish enough to cross that pit, then his fate is such that he need not fear the Comanche." Turning, the *to-yop-ke* selected a stout branch from the pile of wood near the fire and tossed it into the hole. From within the pit the night was filled with a terrifying maelstrom of angry, buzzing whirs, and no man present doubted that a coiled, beady-eyed death waited just beneath the lip of that ominous trench.

Britt darted a glance at Running Dog, and the Kiowa's face was set in a grim frown. Clearly the floor of that deadly chamber was ankle deep in a writhing, twisting carpet of prairie vipers, and the man who tumbled into their midst would thrash out his life in an unimaginable hell.

Little Buffalo signaled a warrior at the edge of the crowd, and the man stepped forward with a lengthy rope of plaited rawhide. Quickly he secured one end of the rope to Britt's right wrist, and then bound Standing Bear in a similar manner with the other end. The *to-yop-ke* then grabbed the middle of the rope and strode forward, forcing the antagonists to trail along like two yoked bulls. When he reached the center of the pit, Little Buffalo dropped the rope and returned to the sidelines. As he did so, a dozen or more warriors carrying heavy war clubs stepped from the crowd and formed a rough square around the two contestants.

This was to be a fight to the death, and Little Buffalo clearly intended that neither of the men would escape, should their bowels suddenly grow tight with fear.

Britt and Standing Bear faced one another across the yawning pit. The Comanche glared murderously at the black man and took a firm grip on the rope. Britt twisted the rawhide around his left hand, priming himself for the deadly tug-of-war that was about to ensue. The lives of his children and Mary hung in the balance as surely as his own, and the fate that awaited them, should he fail, seared his brain with the urgency to kill this man swiftly and without mercy. Both men leaned back into the rope, stretching it taut as they nervously awaited Little Buffalo's command.

"Impesa," the *to-yop-ke* shouted.

Without warning, Standing Bear leaped *forward,* throwing slack into the tight, quivering rope. Straining against the braided lariat, expecting the Comanche to pull in the opposite direction, Britt was taken totally unawares and tumbled backward to the ground. Raging at himself for having been maneuvered into such a childishly simple trap, the black frantically attempted to scramble to his feet.

The lousy, sneaking sonovabitch! Mary warned me! Warned me! Cursing himself, he suddenly realized that the rope had been jerked taut once more and he was being dragged like a bleating calf toward the open trench. Standing Bear had now thrown the rope over his shoulder, leaning into the dragging weight, digging furiously with the corded muscles of his legs to gain momentum. Skidding helplessly along the ground, Britt fought like a madman to regain his feet, but he was being dragged head first, and there seemed no way to halt the Comanche's relentless surge forward. Then, like some recurring nightmare come to life, the black man sensed that he was only a few yards from the gaping darkness of the pit.

For a moment he was paralyzed, unable to breathe or think, aware only that he was about to be buried in a seething, writhing hell. Then abruptly, his mind cleared, and his one hope dawned with the clarity that comes only to those who find themselves staring eyeball to eyeball with the specter of death.

Leaning into the rope with all the power of his massive shoulders, he jerked backward, twisting his legs forward and stiffening his body into a rigid slab in the same moment. Propelled forward by Standing Bear's violent heaving, he managed to gain a purchase on the ground with one foot and awkwardly launched himself into the air and over the pit.

Straining into the lariat with all his might, Standing Bear was caught completely by surprise as the slack now whipped in his direction, and he pitched to the ground like a felled ox. Dumbstruck but still game, the warrior rolled with the fall and came to his knees. But his recovery was short lived, for as he attempted to rise, the black man stepped forward and kneed him squarely in the face.

There was a mushy sound, like a pumpkin being squashed on a sharp rock, and the mangled Comanche dropped in a gory, sodden heap.

Grasping the rope, Britt instantly hurtled back across the pit and charged forward, hauling Standing Bear closer to death with each quickening step. Instinctively he glanced back over his shoulder and saw the stunned warrior struggling to rise as his head cleared the edge of the trench. Standing Bear's face was etched with mortal terror as he clawed hopelessly at the crumbling earth, and for a moment in time the two men's eyes met in a frozen exchange of understanding. There was no question of asking or granting quarter, for one man must die, and neither would have expected any less from the other.

Setting himself, Britt jerked the rope, and the Comanche brave tumbled into the pit.

Suddenly the night was split with a shrill animal cry, and Standing Bear leaped erect, desperately trying to claw his way from the hole. His face and body were covered with a score of rattlesnakes, clutching and gouging, biting again and again as they sank their fangs into his defenseless flesh. Screaming with the fury of the damned, he tore at the snakes with both hands, his body oozing venom and blood as the flickering shadows of the fire played across the grotesque mask that had once been a face. Then as the venomed death sped through his system, constricting his heart, the warrior weakened, and his thrashing arms ceased to struggle. The silent gaze of the dead spread over his eyes, and without a sound he toppled backward into the pit. There was a brief flurry of angry rattles as the reptiles ravaged his lifeless form; then all was still.

The spectators were breathlessly silent, awed and more than a little frightened by the inhuman terror of a brave man's death. Running Dog strode forward and slashed the rawhide that bound the black man's wrist. Their eyes met, and the Kiowa clasped his shoulder compassionately. Black Fox had met the test, and while some killings would haunt a man even to his death bed, it was simply the price a warrior must pay if he chose to walk among the True People.

Britt suddenly felt very wary, as if the essential matter of his soul had shriveled into a hard, tight knot deep within his gut. Glancing about, he became aware of the curious, hollow stares of the hushed warriors. Then he looked at Little Buffalo and was momentarily startled by the Comanche's stern nod of approval. Silently he removed the rawhide loop from around his wrist and tossed it at the *to-yop-ke's* feet. Turning, he walked slowly into the darkness, wanting only to be gone from this place and what lay at the bottom of that pit.

It had been a long night, and while the fleshless grin of death had passed him by for another, he felt small comfort in the fact.

8

The children were asleep, snuggled beneath the furry warmth of their buffalo robes. Britt and Mary sat close to the small fire, talking quietly. His arm encircled her waist protectively, and her head rested on his shoulder. For long moments they hardly spoke, cuddling close as they stared into the flames, grateful merely to be alive and together. Only that morning their chances of ever becoming a family again had appeared slim indeed, and now their lifetime stretched once more before them.

Shortly after the fight that evening, Britt had sent word to Little Buffalo that all he wanted from the lodge of Standing Bear was his own family. Moreover, he was awarding to the dead man's family the five horses that were rightfully theirs if the exchange had come off as originally planned. In effect, this made Talking Raven and Two Moons the richest squaws in the village. And while Standing Bear's body was barely cold, few doubted that any number of warriors would soon be extending offers of marriage to the two widows.

Struck by the black man's magnanimous gesture, Little Buffalo had ordered a lodge erected for Britt and his family. Further, he assigned a small party of warriors to lead the tejano *Negrito* to the outlying Comanche villages. The True People respected generosity second only to courage, and Black Fox had amply demonstrated that his character was that of a brother in heart, if not by birth. While this did not wholly erase the stigma of his bonds with the white-eyes, he was nonetheless elevated to a position of honor in the camp, and was to be accorded every courtesy.

Watching the flickering tongues of flame dance hungrily in the fire, Britt felt at peace for the first time in close to a month. His own family was now safe, and soon he would have arranged the trade of every captive taken in the Brazos raid. Looking back, he was more than a little amazed that he had been able to pull it off. Maybe it was like the white folks said after all, that God had a special way of watching over fools and dumb niggers. Whatever the variety of spirits that had protected him, he had done what he set out to do, and that was all that counted in the long haul. Nuzzling his head against Mary's cheek, he squeezed her tightly, reassuring himself that she was actually there and all his once more.

"Suppose I'll be ridin' out tomorrow." He felt her stiffen as she glanced up from his shoulder. "Snow's not going to hold off much longer, and if I'm going to get them women and kids out of the other villages, I'd best be about it."

"I guess it's not like you have any real choice." She relaxed, snuggling closer again. "But God knows one night's not much to up and lose you again."

"You're not losin' me, woman," Britt chuckled. "Why, I'll be back here before you even know I'm gone. Way I got it figured, it won't take me more than three, maybe four weeks at the most."

"And if winter sets in?" She queried anxiously.

"Well, maybe a little longer," he admitted reluctantly. "But these Comanches guiding me know their way around, and don't forget, they'll be wantin' to get back here just as fast as I do. You know, it's not like they was headin' out on this little jaunt just because they like ridin' around in the snow."

"No, I guess that's right enough." She pressed closer to his shoulder and watched the flames silently. Moments passed as her mind drifted back over the day and everything that had happened. She shuddered slightly as she recalled Talking Raven and Two Moons mutilating themselves as they wailed over Standing Bear's body, already bloated and turning black from the massive injections of venom it has absorbed. That foul, chewed-over horror could just as easily have been Britt, and the sickening thought made her stomach churn. Then something half-forgotten flashed through her mind, and she looked up, regarding the black man solemnly for a moment.

"You know what Talking Raven said to me when I was leaving her lodge? She said, 'Make your man a coward so that he will not die fighting. Teach him to lower his head and turn from trouble. Sap his manhood, let him grow fat and afraid, for then at least your bed will never be empty.'"

Mary paused, watching his face. "After today it makes me wonder if she's not right. Maybe we ought to go back where we come from. Even if they do treat you like dirt on them plantations, at least you know you're gonna live long enough to die peaceful."

Britt glanced at her and then stared back into the flames. The silence grew, and she began to wonder if he would speak or just ignore her comment. Then he drew a long breath and exhaled it slowly. "Once a long time ago that might have been enough for me too. But I've seen something livin' with the Kiowas that I never knew anybody could have 'cepting a white man. They're free, woman! Free as the wind or the trees, just like God meant for all natural things to be free." Then his voice lowered, impassioned with the vision that had slowly formed and taken root in his mind over the past month. "It's not just the South I'm talking about. I don't even know if I can ever go back to Texas again."

"Lord God, Britt, are you talkin' about livin' with these heathens?" Her eyes widened with fear, and she drew back from him. "They've already killed one of our boys. Or did you forget that? *Do you want Sue Ellen and Little George to grow up to be savages too?*"

"I haven't forgot nothin'." He sighed, rubbing his forehead with a gnarled hand. "I only know a black man's not free in a white man's world. Maybe never will be. The Kiowas accept you and me and these children for what we are. Not black or white, but just people. Human beings! And that's a hell of a lot more than we ever got in Texas, even with Allan's help."

"So you're just gonna throw all that over and be a red nigger instead of a black nigger?" Mary hesitated as tears welled up in her eyes, somewhat shaken by her own vehemence. "And what about Allan? All these years he's spent protectin' you from the white folks and helpin' us to make a decent life for ourselves. Don't you owe him anything?"

"Goddammit, don't crowd me, Mary!" He rose and jerked the lodge flap back, peering out into the night. The chill air swept gently over his flushed features, and after a moment his temper subsided. Finally he spoke, his voice weary and filled with uncertainty. "I don't know what to do. I'm not even sure I know what's right. I only know that with the Kiowas we'd be free and nobody would ever again be able to put his foot on our necks and grind us down into the dirt."

"And what happens when the whites kill all the Kiowas? Cause they will just as sure as there's a God in heaven."

Glumly he stared into the bleak darkness. What was it Running Dog had said about a man not being a man unless he held himself above the scavengers? Maybe it would be better to die fighting alongside the Kiowas. *At least you'd die free*, he thought, *like a man*. Not like some spineless, jelly-gutted thing always backing off from looking a white man straight in the eye. *But did he have the right to play God with the kids' lives?* Maybe if they lived to come of age, they'd rather be a live nigger than a dead free man. Sorely perplexed, he shook his head and turned back into the lodge.

"Let's go to bed, woman. I've got a long way to ride, and we've got plenty of time to decide what's best to do." Forcing a smile, he leered at her suggestively. "Besides, if you haven't forgot all them games we used to play, you might be able to whip me down just like that old squaw told you to do."

Her eyes hooded seductively, and a knowing smile played over her mouth. Stretching her hand to meet his, she followed him to their bed of buffalo robes. Curiously there was some strange new excitement which manifested itself at the thought of making love to the warrior that the True People now honored as the Black Fox.

CHAPTER SIX

1

Christmas had come and gone, and a new year lay over the land. For the True People it was the time of the Snow Moon. But for Britt it was merely January, 1861, and a damned cold one at that.

Snow fell silently in the false dawn as they crested a hill east of Fort Belknap. Behind them the shivering band brought their mounts to a halt. Long moments passed as Britt and Running Dog sat gazing through the snow flurries at the fort below. The white stillness seemed deafening, broken only by the stamping hooves and frosty snorts of their horses. And somehow, for warriors and captives alike, there was a sense of the unreal about the dim outlines of the distant stockade.

Britt drew the buffalo cape tighter, burying himself deeper in its furry warmth, and stared at the fort with hollow, spent eyes. Three months had passed since he rode north from the Brazos, and in all that time he hadn't once slept the night through with any certainty of what the morrow would bring. The task of ransoming only the Johnson families had somehow gotten out of hand. Once in the Indian camps he was unable to resist the pitiful stares of the Texan women and their children, and more

by circumstance than design, he had found himself cast in
the role of their savior. While this wholesale ransoming
had been undertaken without any great reluctance on his
part, the burdens it entailed had multiplied out of all
proportion to anything he could have foreseen.

Somewhere along the line he became aware that each
word he uttered, his every action, could affect the lives of
more than twenty women and children. If it were the
wrong word or some thoughtless gesture which offended the
Comanche, then the effect could very well be permanent
and deadly. The fight with Standing Bear had served to
clarify this role even more in his own mind, and with it
the responsibility he had assumed so lightly came crashing
down on his shoulders. Whether the captives lived or died,
remained slaves or returned to the Brazos, rested squarely
on his head. And whatever the outcome, there was no one
to blame but himself.

Upon leaving the Canadian in search of the far-flung
Comanche bands, the dangers seemed very real, and the
future never more uncertain. Then the howling blizzards
broke across the Plains, and what began as a quick sortie
into the other villages gradually evolved into a prolonged
odyssey throughout a frigid, snowbound wasteland. With
the Comanche guides to lead the way and Little Buffalo's
prestige backing him, the black man had eventually located each of the camps and was able to ransom the
captives without any great difficulty. But it had required
almost six weeks, and the burden of that many lives, along
with the grueling journey itself, had taken its toll.

Silently watching the fort through the predawn gloom,
Britt wondered what, if anything, he had actually accomplished. Certainly he had saved twenty-three women and
children from a miserable existence, and that was something. But in the process he had the very distinct feeling
that he had lost his own soul. And he wasn't at all sure
that the settlers would evidence the same gratitude as
shared by those he had rescued. Especially when they
heard how many horses it was going to cost them.

Snow settled gently over his buffalo robe, spotting his
matted beard with flecks of white. Three months without
shaving had changed his appearance sharply, and as drop-
lets of frost formed on his moustache, it occurred to the
black man that his insides were no longer the same either.
While a nigger had ridden forth from the Brazos, a

blooded warrior had returned. North of the Red River he was known by another name, a respected name, and welcomed as a man of courage in the camps of both Comanche and Kiowa. Below in that fort he must once again resume the identity of Nigger Britt, Allan Johnson's pet darkey. Assuming, of course, that he wished to remain on the Brazos and live in peace among the white man. And this was the gut-wrenching decision he hadn't yet reconciled within himself.

"Black Fox has the look of a man who sniffs rancid meat." Running Dog's voice shattered the early morning stillness, and the black man started as if an icy finger had probed beneath his furry robe. The Kiowa's grave look of concern rested only briefly on Britt before sliding back to the fort. "Sometimes it is wiser for a man to go on instead of returning to what he has left behind."

"There is truth in that, brother. More than you know." Britt glanced wearily at the warrior, but his gaze was drawn once more to the distant walls. "My grandmother used to say that any man born of woman is few of days and full of trouble. It seems I have only begun to understand the wisdom of her words."

"Among the True People there are also women *puhakets*," Running Dog commented pointedly. "Perhaps we would all be better off if we heeded their counsel. But then even wise men have been known to ignore the counsel of those who offer it freely. Is it not so, Black Fox?"

Britt's head swiveled around, and he peered quizzically at the Kiowa's inscrutable features. With the dark, snow flecked robe pulled up around his ears, the black man resembled a grizzled buffalo bull, but his hide wasn't nearly so thick. Running Dog's words stung, making him forget the bitter cold for a moment. They were the words of a friend, the counsel of one brother for another, and this significance was not lost on Britt. But still, they hurt.

"Your words have a bite to them, like the morning chill. Had I not heard Running Dog speak to his Kiowa brothers in the same manner, I would think he was addressing a white-eye."

"I do not talk to white-eyes, Black Fox. I kill them. The only reasonable discussion with a tejano is at the end of a gun."

"And if the tejano happens to be a brother in spirit? What then?"

"You speak of half-way things, my friend. And in this life that is not to be found." The warrior looked at him steadily, searching his face. "Now that I think on it, your words have about them the sound of parting. It makes me wonder whether I speak with Black Fox or the tejano *Negrito?*"

"Can you not speak with both?" Britt asked, aware even before the words were out that he was still dealing in half-way measures.

But the question hung between them, for the Kiowa never had a chance to answer. From the fort came the sharp, rolling crack of a rifle. Their heads snapped around, and as they watched, they could see activity along the stockade walls. Their arrival had been timed to coincide with dawn, so that Britt could approach the fort without alarming its occupants. That possibility no longer existed, however, for it was clear that a sentry had spotted them, and the alarm had been sounded. Cautioning Running Dog to hold his position, the black man spurred his horse and rode through the swirling flurries toward Fort Belknap.

2

Buck Barry came awake slowly. These mornings he never had to worry about the orderly awakening him. Along toward dawn his room in headquarters would become so cold that no amount of blankets could hold off the chill. Somehow it seemed that his toes always came awake first, growing frigid and brittle just as the biting darkness surrendered to the faint rays of dawn. Then the cold would slowly creep up his legs and across his body until he was full awake, shivering and cursing the lot of a civilian soldier.

Drawing his feet up below his rump, Barry snuggled deeper in the blankets, dreading that final moment when he must whip the covers back and jump from bed. Again he silently cursed the state militia and the deadwood that enlisted in order to avoid fighting Yankees. If this were the regular army, his orderly would already have a cheery fire blazing and a pot of coffee brewed long before he opened his eyes. But it wasn't the regular army or, for that matter, anything that even remotely resembled an army.

It was a collection of misfits, sharpers, and outright cowards who had yet to fire a shot at an enemy, red or white. They had joined the militia to escape the hazards of a greater war, and so long as they had three squares and a warm bed, they couldn't have cared less about the fortunes of the South.

Such thoughts set his blood to boiling and warmed him for a moment. But the piercing cold quickly returned, and only with great concentration could he keep his teeth from chattering.

Lying there, shivering and still unwilling to forsake what warmth the blankets afforded, the nagging thought returned that some people might even consider him a coward. After all, if he was so brave, why wasn't he off fighting the Yankees with Lee and Beauregard? Damned good question, he answered himself. Thinking back, he cursed the day he had allowed the smooth-talking governor to convince him that he should head up a company of militia. The frontier needs defending just as badly from Indians, the governor had announced, just as the Northern borders need to be held against the Yankees!

Remembering the words, his temper flared briefly as he reflected on the inequities of life. *Hell yes, the frontier needs defending! Except that we muffed our one chance for a real fight. So now we sit on our ass and wait for spring, until they're ready to raid again. And while we freeze our butts off here, Stuart and Jackson and Lee are makin' heroes out of themselves fighting Yankees. What a way to fight a war! Waiting on a bunch of bare-assed Comanches to come raidin' instead of moving up there in force and attacking their winter camps.*

Thoroughly galled by the thought, he ripped the covers back and bounded from bed. Shivering violently now, he threw a blanket around his shoulders and padded across the icy floor to the fireplace. Forcing his numb fingers to remain steady, he quickly stacked a handful of kindling and lighted it, then fed a load of dried branches into the greedy flames. Soon he had a roaring blaze going and the galvanized coffee pot perking merrily. Adding a log for good measure, he stood with his back to the flames, luxuriating in the crackling warmth, and slowly began dressing.

Thoughts of the distant war and the Indian raid last October set Barry's mind off on a tangent all too familiar

these days. While destiny passed him by, robbing him of
the glory that would surely have been his fighting with the
Confederacy, he was saddled with playing nursemaid to
a pack of bellyaching settlers. After the debacle in October they had moved into the fort lock, stock, and barrel.
Ever since, they had sat around swilling corn liquor and
bemoaning the fact that the government hadn't sent
enough troops to protect them from the red savages. Of
course, that didn't hold true for everybody.

There were some, like Johnson and Fitzpatrick, who
rumbled out each morning in their wagons, come rain,
sleet, or snow. Determined to rebuild what the Indians
had burned to the ground, they hacked at frost-hardened
trees with brittle axes and slowly snaked the logs back to
their homesteads. Come spring they would be ready to
start erecting cabins again, and unless the raids came
earlier than expected, they would have crops planted and
their cattle gathered before the Comanche struck. But
there wasn't many like that. Most just sat around and
slopped whiskey, declaring that when the winter storms
finally broke, there would be plenty of time to start rebuilding. Goddamned fools, Barry fumed. All they want
to do is piss and moan and feed off the governent till good
weather forces them back to work.

Thinking of the settlers brought the officer's mind
around, as it invariably did, to Tom Fitzpatrick. While he
admired the Irishman's gumption and his willingness to
pitch in wherever help was needed, Fitzpatrick's constant
presence in the fort was a grating irritant that chafed him
raw. Generally they avoided each other, for it was clear
that Tom would never forgive Barry for the way he had
humiliated him the night Britt Johnson went away. But
whenever they chanced to meet or found themselves in the
same room, there was an astringent, smoldering expression
to Fitzpatrick's face. And if he did speak it was through
clenched teeth.

Clearly he harbored bitter resentment, if not outright
hatred, toward the captain, and it was this unspoken animosity that continued to rankle Barry. Any man who
carried a grudge couldn't be trusted, at least in Buck
Barry's scheme of things. And lately he had grown increasingly suspicious of Fitzpatrick, convinced that the
Irishman was only waiting to catch him off guard in order
to exact some backhanded kind of revenge.

Buttoning his shirt, Barry next thought of Britt Johnson, for if anyone shared his dislike of Fitzpatrick, it was the black man. Idly he wondered what had happened to Britt. Probably skinned alive, he mused, and staked out for the Comanche squaws to torture till he begged for death! Still, you never knew. Some of those niggers had God's own luck, and he might just have pulled through after all. Of course, the settlers had their own theories about what had become of Allan's uppity nigger. Most believed that he was long dead, scalped and hacked to pieces not too many days after he had crossed the Red River. Otherwise, why hadn't he come back, they demanded, for as sure as a horse fart draws flies, no man in his right mind would willingly spend the winter in a Comanche camp. Not even a smart-ass nigger like Johnson's boy!

Others were of a different mind entirely. They knew niggers, by God, and this one wasn't no different than the rest of his breed. Sure as Christ was nailed to a cross, that black bastard lit out for parts unknown! Probably struck out for California to work in the gold fields or went north to join the Union Army. But you can bet your sweet ass on one thing, they chorused, that black sonovabitch never went anywhere near the Red!

While many a jug had been emptied in speculation as to Nigger Britt's fate, the settlers were unanimously undivided on the most chilling conclusion of all. Whether he had crossed the Red or simply kept on running, the women and children taken captive had long since been given up as dead. Perhaps some of them were still alive, they agreed, but by merciful Jesus, they'd be better off dead!

Barry rammed his foot in a boot and dismissed the subject from his mind. There were more important things to worry about than some fool nigger. Food was growing short with this many people drawing down on government provisions, and unless the settlers wanted real trouble before spring, they sure as Christ better start cinching their belts a little tighter. While there was plenty of meat available, what with so many cattle running loose, the supply of vegetables and tinned goods in the storehouse was running drastically low. And he sure as hell didn't intend to see the whole fort come down with scurvy or some other strange disease before the roads opened up that spring. Making a mental note to call a meeting that evening, he

poured a cup of scalding coffee and gratefully let its
warmth spread through his chilled innards.

Suddenly a rifle shot cracked from the direction of the
front gate, and he froze with the cup half raised to his
lips. *Goddamned fool probably shot his toe off. If those
sonsabitches are shootin' at rabbits again, I'll peel their
asses clear down to the backbone!* Slamming the coffee
cup down on the mantle, he bolted through the orderly
room and took off running across the parade ground.

3

Buck Barry reached the catwalk along the stockade wall
just as a horseman appeared on the forward slope of a
hill to the east. Alerted by the sentry's rifle shot, settlers
and the small contingent of militia poured from the barracks and went streaming across the parade ground toward
the front gate. While the drifting snow partially obscured
Barry's vision, there was something vaguely familiar about
the way the approaching rider sat on his horse, and a wild
thought suddenly raced through the officer's mind. Abruptly he grabbed the small telescope which sentries were
required to carry and jammed it to his eye. As Barry
peered into the distance, Allan Johnson scrambled up the
ladder, half-dressed and squint-eyed from sleep, followed
closely by Tom Fitzpatrick.

"Well, I'll be double goddamned!" Barry snorted.

"What is it, Captain?" Allan demanded. "Is it an Indian?"

The advancing rider certainly looked like an Indian,
except for his wide-brimmed hat, but before answering,
Barry elevated the telescope and scanned the distant hilltop. "Johnson, it appears that nigger of yours was as good
as his word. That's him comin' across the flats, and unless
my eyes are going bad, there's a bunch of Injuns holding
our women and kids up on that far rise."

Leaping forward, Fitzpatrick snatched the telescope
from Barry's hand and thrust it to his eye. His hand trem-
bled with excitement but finally he steadied the glass on
the group of riders crowding the hilltop. Suddenly his
head jerked forward, and he studied the distant band
even more intently for a moment. Then he slowly lowered
the telescope, his face flushed with a stunned expression.

"Allan, it's them. All of 'em," he said in a hushed tone. "And my boy's with 'em!" Turning to the settlers jammed around the bottom of the ladder, his voice tremored with emotion. "Goddammit, men, he did it! That black devil has brought every one of them women and kids back with him."

There was a shocked, disbelieving murmur from the crowd, almost as if they were afraid to risk having their hopes dashed again. Then Captain Barry ordered the gates thrown open, and Britt Johnson trotted into the compound. Even before he could bring the chestnut to a halt, the settlers swarmed around him, laughing and shouting, each one trying to touch him in their mad unrestrained joy. Allan and Tom jumped from the catwalk and tore their way through the crowd. Barry chose the more dignified route down the ladder, but he was not far behind.

"Britt, you old war-horse!" Allan shouted. Physically dragging the black man from the saddle, he embraced him in a crushing bear hug. "Godalmighty, we gave you up for dead months ago! Where in the billy-blue hell have you been?"

"Allan, even if I told you, you wouldn't believe it. Sometimes I'm not real certain I believe it myself."

Suddenly Tom Fitzpatrick pushed forward, clasping the black man's hand and shaking it profusely. "I don't even have to ask you. I saw 'em up there. My boy and Allan's family too." For a moment the two men stared into each others eyes, then the Irishman gave his hand another crunching squeeze. "Mister, I don't know how you did it but from now on you're ace high in my book. Anything I said in the past, you just mark it off as a damned fool with his tongue unhinged."

Before Britt could answer, Buck Barry shouldered his way through the packed mob and gave the black man a jarring whallop across the back. "By Christ, it's good to see you, Britt. I don't mind admittin' I'd wrote you off a long time ago. Figured that topknot of yours was decorating some Comanche scalp stick."

"Cap'n, you don't know how close you are to bein' right." Britt smiled and glanced around the grinning crowd. "There was more'n once I thought they were gonna cash me in, but I guess I just got lucky somewhere along the line."

"Luck, my ass!" Barry boomed. "It takes more than

luck to cross the Red and come back to tell about it." The settlers laughed in agreement and pushed closer, not wanting to miss a word. "Now level with us, Britt. How in Christ's name did you get them women and kids away from the Comanches?"

The black man looked around the anxious, curious faces and slowly shook his head. "Well, it wasn't just the Comanches, Cap'n. First I made friends with Santana. He's chief of the Kiowa. Then with his help I was able to get in good with Little Buffalo. He's the head-dog Comanche. The one that led the raid last fall." An angry muttering swept over the crowd at this last disclosure, and Britt glanced around in surprise. "I reckon you've all got reason enough to hate him, but I'm here to tell you that if it weren't for Little Buffalo, there wouldn't be any women and kids waitin' on that hill back yonder."

"By God, he's right, men," Allan announced forcefully. "Let's quit talking about Indians and start thinking of our families!"

"That's the ticket!" Fitzpatrick bellowed. "How many are there, Britt, and what'a we have to do to get 'em back?"

"Well, there's eight women and fifteen kids. I got 'em all back, but Miz Wilson. Way I heard the story from the Kiowas, she grabbed a knife and killed herself before they even got her across the Red."

The crowd grew silent, glancing at one another with undisguised skepticism. Then Buck Barry spoke up in a subdued voice. "Maybe it's just as well. We found Hank Wilson and their three kids butchered in some willows down by the creek. Looked like he went under tryin' to save the children."

The silence grew, and a few of the women wiped tears from their eyes. But the settlers were more interested in the living than the dead, and they quickly began peppering the black man with questions about their own families.

"Now if I was you, I wouldn't get my hopes up too high." Britt's sober tone stilled their anxious queries. "They're all alive, but they've been through a rough time. And you're liable to be a mite shocked when you see 'em."

"What about the women?" Lester Thomas asked quietly. "Did the Injuns . . . you know, did they . . . ?" His voice faltered, and he was unable to go on.

"Mr. Thomas, I reckon that's something you'll have to

find out for yourself," Britt responded gently. "I didn't ask no questions. I just made the deal and got 'em out of there as fast as I could."

"That's good enough for me." Tom Fitzpatrick said. "But you still haven't told us why the redsticks are holdin' them up on that hill."

The Irishman's question brought an alert look to the settler's faces, and silence again fell over the crowd as they watched the black man curiously. Britt glanced around, aware that their stares demanded an answer. Determined that he wouldn't be intimidated by the throng of white faces, he drew a deep breath and let them have it squarely between the eyes.

"Now I know that none of you gave me leeway to make deals for you. But once I got up there and saw I was able to save 'em. I just sorta figured you wouldn't think the price was too high." The stillness thickened, like a murky fog settling to the earth, and he saw them stiffen with apprehension. "The deal I made was three horses for each woman and one horse for each child. And if I've calculated right, that means we've got to scare up thirty-nine horses to make the exchange."

The settlers stared at him incredulously, hardly able to believe their own ears. Then the storm broke. Their faces twisted with dismay and consternation, and all started shouting at once. Watching them, the black man somehow felt removed from the vortex of their anger, almost as if he had gone stone deaf and was aware of nothing but the movement of their lips. As their faces purpled and their abusive voices swelled in pitch, a tight smile played at the corners of Britt's mouth. No doubt about it, none at all. He was back in the land of the white-eyes. And things hadn't changed, not even by the width of a gnat's ass.

4

"I don't give a goddamn what you say, this black scutter has sold us out to the Indians." Sam Ledbetter's eyes glistened with anger as he stared at Britt. Shifting his gaze, he glared at Buck Barry in baffled fury. "I say if you lie down with dogs, you get up with fleas. Only in his case he's probably crawlin' with Comanche lice."

"Ledbetter, offhand I'd say you weigh in at about

twelve ounces of bullshit to the pound!" Barry's harsh growl momentarily stilled the rabid settlers. "Near as I recollect, your woman is waitin' up on that hill for you to come and get her, and all this yellin' about a few horses sorta leaves a man to ponder where your stick floats."

Still crowded around Britt, the settlers' eyes darted back to Ledbetter, tensely awaiting his reaction to the charge implicit in Barry's insult. Ledbetter's face went florid, and his eyes popped out of his head with rage. But only a fool tangled with Buck Barry, and when he spoke, his voice shook with restrained hostility.

"Cap'n, that's a low thing to say to any man. And you got no call to whipsaw me." Seeking support, he glanced around the watchful crowd, somewhat like a forlorn badger cornered by a sour-tempered grizzly. "I want my woman back as much as anyone here, but that don't change the fact that Johnson's nigger went out of his way to make the Indians rich at our expense."

"By God, he's right, Cap'n," Ike Claiborne snapped. "All them coons is tarred with the same brush, and whether he did it on purpose or just out of plain ignorance don't make no difference. The fact of the matter is that every man on the Brazos is gonna be left without a horse to his name."

"Well, I'm damned if I'd go along with that." Eli Thompson's grating voice jerked the settler's heads around. Short and fat, with a mushy face, he quivered with rage like a lumpy bowl of oatmeal. "For my money, the nigger sonovabitch did it just out of pure spite. He was still carrying a grudge 'cause of what happened the night he left here, and he just flat went out of his way to break every man jack of us."

"Mister, I'm surely gettin' tired of all the horseshit you people are slinging around. *You especially!*" Tom Fitzpatrick jabbed the corpulent, heavily-jowled settler in the chest with a thorny finger. "And if you ain't real careful, I'm gonna strop up my skinnin' knife and make me two little fat men out of one big one."

Thompson's pudge features dissolved like a pail of lard in a hot sun, and he attempted to back away from the belligerent Irishman. But the settlers' packed ranks brought him up short, and for a moment it looked as if Fitzpatrick was actually going to jump him. Then Allan stepped forward, clasping Tom's arm firmly, and began speaking in calm, measured tones.

"Now hold on, Tom. There's no call to start fighting among ourselves." Looking around, he regarded the crowd with a benign expression for a moment, then resumed in a placating manner. "You men seem to have lost sight of what's at stake here. Whether Britt paid too high a price is no longer the issue. The fact is that the women and children are waiting up on that hill, and if we want them back, we're going to have to come up with enough horses to make the exchange. Personally I'm willing to throw in all the horses I own, and I'd think that every man with a family would feel the same way."

"Not by a damnsight!" Ike Claiborne snarled. "We got enough men and guns to go up there and make dog meat out of those red bastards. Why the hell should we give 'em good horses for women they stole from us in the first place?"

"Now you're talkin'," Sam Ledbetter whooped. "We could all mount up and be on 'em before they ever knew what hit 'em!"

A murmur of assent swept through the crowd, and they looked at one another as if this were the first sane idea they had heard all morning. Britt darted glances at Allan and Buck Barry, his face etched with a mixture of rage and disbelief. Clearly the situation was about to get out of hand, and if someone didn't act quickly, that distant hilltop would run red with blood before the sun was hardly over the horizon.

"Shut your goddammed mouths!" Britt commanded in a hoarse bellow. Backing a few paces away from the crowd, he let his hand come to rest on the Colt at his side. "Before you heroes get any fancy ideas, you'd better listen to what *I've* got to say. My family's waitin' on that hill too, and there's a Kiowa warrior up there with orders to cut the throat of every woman and kid if we even look like we're gonna pull a doublecross. So before you get through that gate, you'd better figure you gonna have to come over me."

Without warning, Tom Fitzpatrick suddenly leaped forward. Jerking a shotgun from the scabbard on Britt's horse, he backed up beside the black man. Slowly he cocked both hammers and glared at the settlers with a malevolent smile. "I stand with Britt. And the first sonovabitch that makes a move toward that gate is gonna get a quart of buckshot up his gizzard!"

The crowd wilted before the scatter gun. But a low rumble of sudden outrage spread virulently from man to man. While being backed down by Fitzpatrick was bad enough, the black man's contemptuous manner was almost more than they could swallow. But the sheer audacity of a nigger threatening white men with a gun was so shocking that for the moment they stood rooted in astonishment and confusion.

Then Tom's voice again split the compound, grating and wracked with emotion. "Just so there won't be any doubt as to where I stand, you boys better listen close. This man saved my little boy, the only family I got left. So as far as I'm concerned, from now on, Britt Johnson's name might as well be Fitzpatrick, 'cause me and him are gonna be just about that thick. And any man ever again calls him *nigger* is gonna get the crap beat out of him by me personal."

Buck Barry regarded Fitzpatrick with an astounded expression, and the fleeting thought passed through his mind that he might just have misjudged this thick-headed Irishman. Glancing about the crowd, he saw that the settlers were equally bewildered and decided it was time to put a halt to this slack-jawed lunacy. Striding to a point directly between the two factions, he turned on the settlers with bristling anger.

"Gents, it's like the buzzard said when he dumped his load two miles up . . . a little of this shit goes a long way. And I've had about all I'm gonna take for one mornin'. Just between us *good neighbors,* I don't think the whole friggin' lot of you is worth the powder it'd take to blow you off a johnny pot. But that's neither here nor there." Jerking a thumb in Britt's direction, he glowered at the crowd with a shaggy, upraised brow. "That man risked his life to save your women and kids! But like a bunch of simple-minded turds, all you can do is moan about how much it's gonna cost you. Well, by Christ, I've had it! Either you rustle up them horses pronto, or I'm gonna send Britt back up there and tell them Injuns they can just keep your goddamned women. Now make up your minds fast and not another word from any of you!"

The settlers suddenly found themselves unable to look at one another, shamed to the marrow by Barry's stinging rebuff. With hang-dog expressions they slowly separated and silently drifted one by one toward the stables where their horses were quartered. Within minutes they rode through the front gate, led by Allan and Tom. Hunched against the blinding snow flurries, they thundered along the river trail toward their homesteads, intent now on collecting every loose horse in the Brazos valley.

5

Britt walked the chestnut across the parade ground and dismounted before headquarters. Since it would take the homesteaders at least two hours to gather a horse herd and return, he had ridden back to the hilltop to reassure Running Dog that plans for the exchange were well underway. While the Kiowa was growing increasingly wary of remaining in such an exposed position, he was willing to honor Black Fox's word, even though the *Negrito's* manner clearly indicated that something sinister had taken place within the fort. Running Dog had already sent warriors to fetch wood from a grove along the river, and when Britt arrived, he found the hostages huddled around a small fire. Though they had eaten and were relatively warm, their faces were taut with strain, and their eyes beseeched him to bring this miserable waiting to an end.

When Britt had mounted after talking with the captives, Running Dog cautioned him that time was growing short. While he could control the Kiowa braves easily enough, he had no real authority over the Comanches, and he sensed that they were growing more edgy with each passing moment. Wondering how in God's name he would ever pull this exchange off without bloodshed of some sort, the black man spurred his horse and headed back across the flats.

Entering headquarters, Britt found Captain Barry seated before the fireplace, sipping a mug of coffee laced with whiskey. Noting the grave concern written across Britt's face, the officer rose wordlessly and fixed a similar concoction for the black man. Only when they were seated before the fire, with Britt staring vacantly into the flames, did the burly Texan speak.

"You look like a man that's carrying a heavy load.

And I reckon I don't have to ask what's botherin' you."
Barry took a long swig from the mug, letting the liquid
fire sear its way down his gullet. Thinking, he watched the
spitting logs for a moment. "You know, Britt, it's not easy
for these rockheads to live with the idea that a colored
man has suddenly become the community hero. It sorta
goes against the grain for a white man to think that a
nig— What I mean to say is that a black has got more
balls than they ever thought about havin'. Something like
that sorta knocks the pins out from under their high and
mighty attitudes, and it's a mite hard to swallow grace-
fully."

"Why don't you just come right out and say it, Cap'n?"
Britt's flashing eyes reflected the white heat from the fire.
"If it had been anybody but a *nigger,* they'd have pinned
a medal on him and started shoutin' hallelujah the minute
he rode through the gate."

Barry hunched forward in his chair and sighed heavily.
"That's about the size of it, for a fact. Instead of being
grateful they resent what you've done. It's not the horses
they worried about, mind you. Hell, a man can always get
more horses. They're just downright jealous 'cause you
showed 'em up where guts count, and there's no gettin'
around it."

"So I'm just supposed to bow my head like a good little
darkey and let 'em sit around cackling about how Allan's
fool nigger let himself get flimflammed by the Comanche."

"Well, I reckon you could clean house, if it'd make you
feel any better. Looks like that thick-headed mick has
already come over to your side. And I suppose with you
and Allan and Fitzpatrick standin' back to back, you
could probably whip the whole goddamned bunch." Barry
leaned back in his chair, and a malicious gleam flickered
in his eyes. "Just between you and me, most of these
homesteaders are a pack of conniving little mouse farts.
There's not a man among 'em with strength of character
enough to pull his pecker out of a pail of lard."

Britt chuckled in spite of himself. Glancing around, he
saw Barry's face twist in a cynical, wolfish grin. "And
where do you stand, Cap'n? With the big, bad nigger or
agin' him?"

"Son, I gave up on the human race a long time ago,
black or white. You could fit the brains of mankind in a
thimble and still have room left over for a team of mules."

Stretching, he took the jug from a nearby table and sloshed a healthy portion into his mug. "I figure every man is entitled to fight his own fights, and so long as he don't crowd me, I'm willin' to let him kick whosever ass seems most handy."

"But what if he don't want to fight, Cap'n? What if he just wants to be left in peace and allowed to live his life with the little bit of dignity every man has comin'?"

"Britt, assumin' there is a good Lord, he didn't put man on this earth to live in peace. Whatever anybody ever got out of life worth havin', they had to fight for. And more'n likely kill too. Leastways, that's been my experience." Sipping at the whiskey, he regarded the black man with a curious gaze for a moment. "Course, it might just be that you haven't got as big a fight on your hands as you think. Offhand, I'd say that sooner or later most of the folks hereabouts will come around to thinkin' you're a pretty good man to have as a neighbor. Might be they'll never invite you to break bread at their table or ask you to join their church. Maybe they'll never even work up the guts to thank you for savin' their women and kids. But I've got an idea they'll eventually get around to admitting among themselves that you've got more balls than a billygoat."

Britt shook his head with disgust and looked back into the fire. "What you're saying is to bite my tongue and act humble and maybe someday—*just maybe*—they'll treat me and my family with the respect we're due."

"No, that's not what I'm sayin'," Barry growled. Leaning forward, he spit in the fire and studied his thoughts as the flames consumed the juicy wad in an angry hiss. "You're a colored man livin' in a white man's world, and no matter how hard you try to change it, you're gonna have to live according to his rules. You can kiss white ass and scrub your hide with lye soap the rest of your life, but when it comes time to plant you in a box, you'll still be as black as the day you were born. I'm not sayin' it's right, mind you. I'm only sayin' it's the nature of the beast, and there's not a goddamned thing you can do to change it."

"So what it comes down to is that the meek don't inherit the earth after all."

"Only six feet of it," Barry snorted cynically.

"The strong fight the strong for the right to harness the meek to the plow." Britt's eyes glazed over with the fiery glow of the flames centered in his gaze. There was a long pause, and his next thought was spoken absently, as if to himself alone. "And if one of the strong just happens to be black, then the best he can hope for is to get killed clean, without sufferin' too much."

The grizzly officer studied his face for a still moment in time, searching the black man's stoic mask for some deeper meaning behind the enigmatic words. Finally he drew a long breath and drained the mug.

"Britt, if I was a bettin' man, I'd say right about now you're entertaining some notion of joinin' up with the Comanches or maybe the Kiowas." The black man flinched imperceptibly, and Barry saw that his shrewd guess had struck home. "Thought so. Now let me tell you something, son. I don't care no more for you than I do the next man. Just happens that I've got a bigger distaste for these turdheads that call themselves settlers. But I'm gonna give you some advice, and you'd better think on it real careful."

Tilting back in his chair, he paused for a moment and gazed at the ceiling, as if some distant vision was unfolding on its beamed surface. "Long before the maker meant for you to die, this land is gonna be knee-deep in dead Injuns. 'Cause the whites mean to own this country, even if they have to kill everything that walks, crawls, or slithers on its belly. And even if some of the redsticks do come out of it alive, they're gonna be herded onto reservations just like so many cattle, 'cept theys won't be fed nearly so well. It happened back East, and in the South, and it's gonna happen out here. No two ways about it. And if I was a man with a family, I'd think real careful before I put 'em in that kind of fix." Again he hesitated, watching Britt steadily. "You know, sometimes dying is the easiest part of all. Mostly it's the livin' that forces a man to find out what kind of grit he's got in his craw."

"Cap'n, you're a real soothing kinda man." Britt smiled shallowly, regarding the officer with a shake of his head. "Fellow could listen to you for a little while and discover his problems were really only beginning."

"Son, you just haven't got enough faith, that's your problem." Barry's booming laugh shook the room, and his chair slammed to the floor as he leaned forward to shake Britt by the shoulder. "Listen, you're not some broken-down sodbuster with a couple of mangy cows and a boil on your ass. You and Johnson have got a good thing going for you, and if I *was* a bettin' man, I'd just be willing to wager you two will outlast that whole goddamned bunch of bellyachin' shitkickers."

"Hallelujah!" the black man chortled sardonically. "The great day is comin', and all the black folks has got to do is shuffle along and wait till it's our turn at the trough. Cap'n, you may not think much of mankind, but I'm damned if you wouldn't of made one hell of a preacher."

Buck Barry grinned like a shaggy dog trailing a butcher's gut wagon and refilled their mugs with his own special brand of liquid fire.

6

Some two hours later Allan and Tom led the settlers back through the main gate, driving before them a herd of forty-one horses. With the exception of the mounts they themselves rode, this pathetically small *remuda* represented every remaining horse from Elm Creek in the north to the scattered homesteads on the South Brazos. While the men no longer appeared openly hostile, they continued to grumble sullenly among themselves. For it was apparent to everyone concerned that the settlement would be sadly lacking in mounts for many months to come. Leaving the other men to hold the horses bunched on the parade ground, Allan, Tom, and Grady Bragg rode on to headquarters and were dismounting just as Britt and Captain Barry stepped onto the porch.

"Well, I'm glad to see you boys didn't have any trouble," Barry said heartily. "For a while there I was beginning to think I'd have to pony up some of the government mounts."

"I wouldn't exactly say we didn't have any trouble, Captain." Allan's voice sounded cheerless and somewhat pensive, like a minister who had just discovered that his congregation was composed primarily of agnostics and fornicators. "Some of the men took a bit of persuading after we left the fort. They're still of a mind that we could surprise the Indians or else ambush them after the exchange has been made."

Barry shook his head derisively and stared across the compound at the settlers. "Don't surprise me none. Like

I've said before, most of 'em don't have sense enough to pour piss out of a boot."

"Cap'n, for once you and me agree about somethin'," Fitzpatrick said. "If I had my way, we'd knock a few heads together and let 'em worry about loose teeth instead of that sorry bunch of broomtails. But Allan's got some fool notion we've gotta convince 'em polite like, so that everyone can live peaceful when this thing's over."

"Well, it's not all that cut and dried, you know." Grady Bragg's tone was skeptical, edged with a faint trace of ambivalence. "These men have lost everything they owned, and it's only natural they'd think Britt sold 'em down the river."

Bragg glanced apologetically at Britt, and the others watched silently, waiting for the black man's reaction. But Britt merely regarded the pudgy settler with an indifferent look, as if he were weary of jousting with dim-witted fools. After a moment of strained silence the tension passed.

"Horseshit!" Buck Barry's explosive growl shattered the stillness. "Grady, the only thing wrong with your friends is that they can't work up any courage except what they get suckin' on a bottle. Not one of those weak-kneed bastards had the guts to go anywhere near the Red. And if it weren't for Britt, their women would still be gettin' forked by the Injuns! For my money, they're the biggest goddamned bunch of ingrates I ever heard tell of."

"Cap'n, you might well be right. It's not for me to say." Bragg ducked his head, scuffing the powdery snow with the toe of his boot. "All I know is they're sayin' that horses are gonna be scarce as snake tits around here for a long time to come. And they figure any white man with a lick of sense could've made a better deal for the hostages."

"Jesus Christ! Any man that thinks like that is nothin' but a double-distilled sonovabitch. There's not one man in that bunch that could've crossed the Red without losing his hair. And knowin' the Comanch, they'd have cut his tallywhacker off and crammed it down his throat like a stuffed goose. Britt, am I right or not?"

"I can't rightly say, Cap'n. I know it was just pure luck that I was able to pull it off. And if the Indians didn't love horses so much, they might've fried me to a crisp anyway. What they would've done to a white man probably wouldn't be pretty to watch.

"You're goddamn right it wouldn't!" Barry gave the three white men a withering look, and his lip curled in a vicious snarl. "I guess you and those scissorbill heroes out there aren't aware that Britt had to fight a Comanche brave as part of the bargain. He told me all about it while you were out fetchin' them horses. Wasn't really much, you understand. Just had a friendly little tug-of-war over a pit full of rattlesnakes."

The men were thunderstruck, almost as if the officer's revelation defied comprehension. Their mouths popped open with astonishment, and they gaped at Britt as if some curious black deity had suddenly materialized before their eyes. Except for a muttered oath from Fitzpatrick, they stared wordlessly at the black man, their faces a stunned caricature of awe and supreme respect.

"C'mon! I thought we had this settled before you left to get them horses, but I see now it's time for a little ass-kickin'." Before they could recover their wits, the grizzly officer struck out across the parade ground, and the four men hurried along to keep pace. Never slackening his stride, Barry marched toward the milling horse herd and came to a halt before the mounted settlers. Where they had been grumbling among themselves only moments before, they now fell silent, sensing that the commander's surly disposition had somehow darkened during their brief absence from the fort.

"I understand some of you big-talkin' heroes still aren't satisfied with the way this exchange has worked out," Barry roared angrily. "Well, you'd better listen close to what I've got to say, 'cause I'm gonna say it once, and there ain't a sonovabitch among you that'll ever get to hear it a second time.

"Britt Johnson was seriously thinkin' of leaving the settlement because of the shitty way you people have acted since he got back. 'Course, if it had been up to you swizzleguts, your women and kids would still be north of the Red, and you could go right on feelin' sorry for yourselves. But instead of thanking him, you get up on your high-horse and act like you been robbed. Well, Bragg and Fitzpatrick and Johnson have got the whole story of what he went through to save your kinfolks. And if you've got any decency left at all, you'll go to the trouble to find out how he damn near got killed just to pull this deal off."

Barry turned and regarded the black man with a

speculative gaze for a moment, then glared back at the
settlers. "I think I've talked Britt into staying here. Leastways, I hope so. It's a damn cinch this settlement needs a
man with a little starch in his backbone. But irregardless
of what he decides, there's one thing I want to make
clear. If any of you *good citizens* try givin' him a hard
way to go, I'm gonna lay you out colder'n a well digger's
ass. And the way I feel right now, I'd purely welcome the
chance to give you a sample of what I've got in mind."

Tom Fitzpatrick stepped forward, shoulder to shoulder
with the burly captain. His eyes glinted fiercely, and
his ruddy face had gone almost ashen with wrath. "By
Jesus, I second that motion! And if there's anything left
over when the cap'n gets through, I'll give you boys a
taste of the best knuckle sandwich this side of St. Louis."

"All right, I think we understand one another," Barry
said, fixing the settlers with a malignant stare. "Now you
men just hold those horses right here till I tell you different. It's not that I don't trust you, you understand. But I
think we'll just let Britt and his friends drive the herd on
up to those Injuns."

Dismissing the settlers with a contemptuous look, he
turned and motioned for Britt to follow. Silently they
walked toward headquarters, trailed closely by Allan and
Tom. After a moment the black man glanced at Barry
uncertainly.

"Cap'n, I want to thank you for what you done, but I'm
not real sure—"

"Son, let me tell you something. Just one last piece of
advice and then you decide what you want to do. There's
generally three secrets in every man's life, whether he's
black, white, or candystriped. *What you tell others. What
you tell yourself. And the truth.* Most men play it so
close to the vest they never even get a look at the truth.
But if a man's able to handle it, he's pretty certain of
finding out that what's true for him is the best road to
travel. Course, most times it's a damn sight easier taking
the right trail than it is ownin' up to the truth."

Britt stopped dead in his tracks. The white man's
words had eviscerated his soul as neatly as a surgeon's
scalpel, and he was appalled by the sudden truth he saw
laid bare. Buck Barry's features twisted in a wolfish grin,
and he walked on, leaving the black man to stare after
him through the icy caress of the snowflakes.

7

Running Dog stood alone at the edge of the hill, watching the silent fort. Within him stirred a deep uneasiness. While there was no sun to measure the time, he knew that a reasonable hour for the exchange had long since come and gone. Already the Comanches suspected a trap and were talking among themselves of returning north, lest the white-eyes again trick them in some devious manner. Though the Kiowa braves trusted his judgment, they were still alarmed by the prolonged waiting and might easily be swayed by the Comanches' fears. Should the warriors become disgruntled or decide the tejanos were planning some underhanded scheme, he very likely would be unable to prevent the wholesale slaughter of the captives.

Something strange was going on inside that fort, and even he was growing skeptical that the white-eyes would honor their word. *Waugh!* But was that indeed so strange, for had not the tejanos fouled their honor with broken promises more times than a wise man could count.

Still, they had gathered the horses, for with his own eyes he had seen them driven through the gate. But if the white-eyes intended to complete the exchange, why were they taking so long? *Why indeed?* It was a good question, one which a leader worthy of his warriors' trust should be asking himself. And at the moment he had no reasonable answer.

The snow flurries had not slackened since dawn, and as he gazed across the white stillness, Running Dog's concern was as much for Britt as the worsening situation. *What fate had befallen Black Fox at the hands of the white-eyes?*

Certainly when he came with assurance of the exchange earlier that morning, there was much he had left unsaid. Even a *pawsa* could see that the black man was troubled beyond measure. It was in his eyes, his dispirited manner, and even more apparent in his open reluctance to return to the stockade. Clearly something was gnawing on Black Fox's vitals, and whatever the cause, it was to be found in that fort.

Perhaps the tejanos had berated him for trading so

many of their horses. But how could men, even white-eyes, covet horses more than their own women and children? Still, one never knew. The white devils' greed and lust for possession was a thing that could not be disputed. Many snows had passed since the tejanos came to this land, and the True People had good reason to know of their hunger for what belonged to others. Had not this very land upon which he stood once been the home of their fathers before them? And their fathers' fathers? But still the white-eyes had driven them into the wilderness.

His anger flared briefly, remembering again the countless indignities his people had endured while being driven from their sacred lands. But there were more immediate matters to be considered, and his thoughts turned once more to Britt's curious manner.

Somehow, in ways which defied understanding, Running Dog sensed that the black man was struggling with a bitter inner conflict. He couldn't have explained how he knew, nor for that matter, did he fully comprehend it himself. It was a thing of the spirit, an instinct or sudden truth that revealed itself inside a man's being. Most often it occurred among men who stood as brothers. There was some spiritual communion that passed between them, and without speaking one man suddenly found himself possessed of the thoughts of his brother.

And as sure as he believed that *Tai-me* saw every frail imperfection in a man's being, the Kiowa knew that Black Fox was trapped in an obscure limbo between the True People and the white-eyes.

Abruptly his reverie was broken as the gates of the fort swung open. Nerves taut, squinting through the falling snow, Running Dog saw Black Fox and two tejanos drive the horses from the stockade. With the black man on point they hazed the herd across the flats and brought them to a milling halt at the base of the hill.

Alerted by the commotion, both the warriors and the hostages joined Running Dog on the edge of the forward slope. In the distance they could see that the settlers had now crowded through the gate and were staring anxiously toward the hill.

Britt motioned for Allan and Tom to remain with the herd, then sent his chestnut plunging through the snow-drifts covering the steep slope. Moments later he reined to a halt before Running Dog and dismounted.

"*Hao*, brother." Britt's smile seemed forced, his voice strained. "I bring you a herd of fine horses for the True People."

"Black Fox is a man of his word. But it must be said that there is doubt among us concerning the white-eyes." Nodding toward the men huddled outside the fort, the Kiowa's meaning was clear. "Must we guard against the tejanos after the exchange, or will we be allowed to depart in peace?"

Glancing back at the knot of settlers, Britt's eyes seemed hollow and worn. "Have no fear, brother. The white-eyes' courage has been spent in loud talk and empty threats."

Running Dog regarded the black man for a moment, somehow filled with regret that his suspicions had been confirmed. "It was no less than we expected. *Waugh!* Let us cease this talk of men without honor and have done with our business. How is this exchange to be conducted?"

Without a word Britt turned and signaled with a sweeping motion of his arm. Allan and Tom immediately began popping their lariats, hazing the horses up the snowy hillside. Once they had the herd halfway up the slope, the two men reined about and returned to the base of the hill.

Leaping to their mounts, the warriors plunged down the slope, circling the herd with shrill, yipping cries. The waiting had ended, and the white-eyes' horses were theirs at last! Now they could return to their warm lodges and their waiting women and spend the winter basking in the esteem of their brothers. *For were they not the chosen few among the True People, the ones selected to perform this ultimate humiliation on the tejanos!*

Britt and Running Dog watched silently as the braves drove the horses over the hilltop and milled them on the reverse slope. Then the black man glanced at the hushed, shivering captives and back at Running Dog. The Kiowa nodded solemnly.

"All right, ladies," Britt said. "You're free, and your menfolks are waitin'. There's nothin' holding you here anymore."

The women looked at one another as if they couldn't believe their ordeal had finally ended. Then their voices lifted in a spontaneous clamor of relief and joy as they realized they were free at last. Jerking their children along behind them, the women broke into an awkward, shambling run down the slope. Screaming the names of their men, they fell repeatedly in the deep snow, only to rise and begin lurching once more toward the fort they had never again expected to see.

A hoarse roar from the settlers split the air, and they began running across the flats. Waving, shouting jubilantly, they raced over the snow-covered ground toward their women and children. Within moments the two groups converged on one another, and the blustery day was filled with the cries and screams of families reunited. Tears streamed down the faces of both men and women as they wildly embraced one another. Scooping their children up between them, they danced and whirled through the snow in a mad, abandoned fit of pure joy. Even the militiamen were caught up in the spirit of the moment, and the crowd quickly became a frenzied mob, surging back toward the fort in a swirling crush of tumultuous shouting.

From the hilltop Britt watched impassively. Beside him Running Dog looked on with detached amusement, as if he were observing a pack of hungry dogs chasing after the same bone. Mary and the children stood off to one side, staring intently at Britt. Seemingly oblivious to the exuberant mob on the flats below, they waited uncertainly to see where the black man would lead them.

Looking around, Britt's eyes had a wary, defeated cast to them. After a moment he nodded to Mary, indicating the fort with a jerk of his head. Silently she gathered the children and descended the hill.

The two men stood alone, each gripped with the same thoughts, yet unwilling to hear them put into words. The raw wind made their faces tingle with the icy snowflakes, and they stared grimly as the last of the settlers disappeared into the fort.

"It comes to me that Black Fox has made his choice." The Kiowa's remark brought Britt's head around. "Yet I wonder if the path he chooses will be one a warrior can follow."

"A man must be many things it seems." Britt's eyes returned to Mary and the children, watching silently as they trudged through the gate. "And not always can he take the path that he alone would choose."

Running Dog nodded, observing the direction of the

black man's gaze. "Brother, you are a man who pursues things that were not meant to be. Among the white-eyes you have suffered much in the past, and it will be so again. Today you have done them a great service, and for this they are thankful. But the tejanos' friendship is like the winter snow; it melts away when the sun once more appears."

"What you say is true. No man has better reason to believe that it will happen just so." Remembering the settlers' anger that morning, he now felt compromised and disgusted with himself. "But each man had an obligation to something greater than his own small cravings. Do not we all bear the responsibility of easing the way for those who follow?"

"Perhaps. But only the *puhaket,* the gifted ones, can say what the future holds. You and I, we are simply mere men and must do what seems best at the moment." Running Dog paused, turning to look at the warriors who waited for him on the backside of the hill.

"For the Kiowa there is only one road." He made the sign of death, one palm erasing life from the other. "Even if the tomorrows of our children are rubbed out, we must fight the white-eyes."

"Maybe what is to come will be better than we think." Britt's words had the ring of hope, but his voice lacked conviction. "Perhaps one day we will all walk this land as brothers, without hate or war."

"On that day will the sun rise from the west, and the mouse attack the bear." The Kiowa's face was grim, and for a long moment he stared sadly around the bleak hilltop. "What a strange place for Black Fox to die."

"Am I to die, brother?"

"No, not you. The man lives on, but the soul of Black Fox is no more. When I return to the mountains, I will carry with me the name and his spirit. And over the campfires we will often speak of that great warrior who chose to remain a tejano *Negrito.*"

"Running Dog's words sound bitter, and for that I am sad."

"No, it is I who am saddened. For even though you will remain as my brother, I must kill you, should we meet again."

Britt's throat tightened, and without shame he felt a mist form over his eyes. "What you said this morning about there being no halfway things in this life. Must that also include two men who have learned to walk as brothers?"

"Are we gods, that we can hold ourselves above our own people? I think not. So it is that any man who follows the path of the white-eyes is an enemy." His voice broke, and he was unable to look at the black man. "Even a brother."

Then the Kiowa's mouth curled in a tight smile, and he clasped Britt's shoulder. *"Walk boldly among the tejano dogs, Black Fox.* Do not let them break you. I carry your spirit in my heart. But I will make sacrifices to *Tai-me* in the hope that we shall never meet again."

Without another word Running Dog bounded onto his pony and rode to join the waiting warriors. Never looking back, he led the party north, toward the Red and the True People.

Britt watched until the small band was swallowed from sight by the gusting flurries. Then he turned and walked slowly toward the fort.

CHAPTER SEVEN

1

Spring came early to Fort Belknap. Warm March winds and a bright Plains sun had melted the winter snows, and the stockade once again became a beehive of activity. Each morning wagons loaded with settlers rumbled through the front gate, churning along a river trail that had been reduced to an axle-deep quagmire of mud and slush. The heavily laden wagons gouged deep ruts in the soft earth, and in the beginning the daily trips to and from the homesteads had been agonizingly slow. But as the month progressed and the sun grew hotter, the Brazos trail had hardened to the flinty surface of uncut granite. Shortly, even the sloughy Plains had baked out firm, and as one day faded into another, the wagons lumbered over the jolting trail with ever greater speed. But more than one man crawled into bed each night with an aching spine, dreaming fondly of a time when the bone-rattling trip had been made astride a light-stepping cow pony.

The settlement was still desperately short of mounts, and every saddle horse in the community had been pressed into service pulling wagons. Even then the settlers had to share the teams, and only after a week of argument and shouting did Buck Barry grudgingly agree to loan them some of the government mounts. Slowly trees were felled and snaked back to the homesteads, awaiting the day when each family had accumulated sufficient logs for a cabin raising. The settlers' idle winter spent in the fort was now to cost them dearly. For if cabins were to be erected and fields plowed in time to make a crop, it would require a herculean effort on the part of every man, woman and child.

But there were some, like the Johnsons and Tom Fitzpatrick, who had worked through the winter to be ready for spring. And on a bright, cloudless morning in late March, Britt whistled cheerily as he set out for another day on Elm Creek.

Perched atop a rattling wagon held together with spit and rawhide, the black man reined his team away from the stables and headed toward the front gate. Watching the chestnut strain into the traces saddened him, for the spirited gelding had served him well, and he hated to see it reduced to a common work horse. Still, everyone was in the same predicament and doubtless shared his feelings about their own prized mounts. Maybe even more so, since he was the one responsible for trading nearly every horse in the settlement to the Indians. But that had all been settled, neatly and with a gratifying sense of finality, and it was a thought that rarely troubled him these days.

Rounding the corner of the headquarters building, he heard his name called and turned to see Buck Barry leaning against the door jamb of the orderly room. Reining the team to a halt, he returned the greeting and waited as Barry ambled toward the wagon with the peculiar shuffling gait of broad-beamed men and large, surly bears. Since returning to the fort, Britt had grown quite attached to the militia commander, which gave him charter membership among a singularly small group of settlers. Strangely enough, Barry had also gone out of his way to cultivate the black man's trust and genuinely seemed to enjoy the friendship that had ensued over the past two months.

At first he had thought the officer's warm manner stemmed from the fact that he alone was responsible for Britt's decision to remain with the settlement. But after pondering the matter at some length, he concluded it was just as likely that Barry sought his company simply as another means of antagonizing the settlers. While hardly a cynic, Britt was aware that men offered their hand in friendship for a variety of reasons, not all of which were apparent on the surface. Yet there was something guileless and earnest about the burly soldier's nature, and Britt had long since resolved to follow Barry's lead. Whatever his motives, the black man liked him, and for the moment that was enough.

"Mornin', Britt. Where's your pardners?" Barry hawked, cleared his throat, and spat a wad of early morning phlegm on the crusted earth.

"Oh, they'll be along shortly," Britt said, glancing back at the barracks. "Probably havin' a last cup of coffee."

"Figures," Barry snorted. "Lay up on their dusty butts till the faithful ole darkey gets the team hitched."

"Now, Cap'n, what makes you say a thing like that?" The black man smiled and shook his head humorously. "You know as well as I do that we take turns with the team every morning. Sometimes you put me in mind of a man back home that used to tie cats' tails together just to see 'em fight."

"Well, seein' as how cats are sorta in short supply around here, I just have to make do with what's at hand."

"Damned if I don't believe you, Cap'n. I never saw a man so all-fired set on knockin' people's heads together."

"Christ, man, it gets boring around here!" Barry snapped with mock disgust. " 'Specially since you and your sidekicks trimmed Ledbetter's wick." A malicious gleam flickered in his eyes. "That was just naturally a stemwinder. Damned if it wasn't. You boys pulled it off slicker'n greased owlshit."

Britt grinned, still curiously amazed after all these months that a man of Barry's enormous physical power would remain so taken with such a minor incident. Thinking back, it all seemed so meaningless and insignificant now.

After the elation of being reunited with their families had passed, the settlers again started grumbling about their lost horses. Gathered outside the barracks one evening after supper, they pretended not to notice that Britt was standing on the fringe of the crowd along with Allan and Tom. The first flush of again having someone to warm their beds had worn off, and they were dismally bored with the inactivity of the fort. While they vaguely remembered Captain Barry's warning that the subject of their horses was a closed issue, they needed something to relieve the tedium. And at the moment Allan's pet coon seemed the most handy topic.

Then Sam Ledbetter made the untimely mistake of referring to Britt as "that ignorant nigger." Before anyone had time to catch their breath, Tom Fitzpatrick jumped Ledbetter, and both men went down in a thrashing tangle of fists and hoarse grunts. When the dust settled, Ledbetter was out cold, and his aroused cronies started closing in on Fitzpatrick. Shouldering their way through the crowd, Britt and Allan stood back to back with Tom, fully prepared to take on the entire settlement if it came to that. But the homesteaders suddenly found the odds not to their liking, and the moment had passed with nothing more deadly than an exchange of insults and hollow threats.   —

Still groggy from the beating, Ledbetter was hauled away by his friends, and the crowd wandered off to lick their wounded pride. Since then life in the fort had become a little more pleasant for Britt, and much as everyone expected, there was no further discussion of the horses. Not within hearing of Tom Fitzpatrick, at any rate.

Buck Barry had roared with laughter upon hearing of the brazen stand-off and in the next instant began huffing like a sore-tailed bear because he had missed out on the action. Watching him now, Britt could see the glint in Barry's eyes and knew that the militiaman was still miffed over having lost the chance to crack a few skulls.

"Cap'n, what you oughta do is get yourself a bulldog. Then you could sic him on the settlers' hounds every mornin' and have enough fights going to keep things from gettin' dull."

Barry chuckled, but then the smile faded, and he grew thoughtful for a moment. "By God, Britt, that's not a bad idea, even if you were joshin'. If those bastards in Austin keep me posted here much longer, I believe I might just do that." Puzzling over how in the hell he could get a bulldog transported halfway across Texas, the officer glanced up to find Britt observing him with a wry smile. "Well, goddammit, it is a good idea! Now quit your smirkin' and tell me what's happening out on Elm Creek."

"Just pluggin' along day by day, Cap'n. With three of us workin', things are moving steady. Cabins should be finished in a couple of weeks, and I'd say we've got about half the cattle corraled already. Few more days of warm weather, and the ground oughta be about ripe for plowin', so takin' things as they come, I'd say we're sittin' pretty good."

"Hell, it's better'n good. You boys are showin' the rest of these lardasses what it's all about. Maybe when they see what a little honest sweat can do, they'll get up off their haunches and start humpin' it too. Leastways, they'd better, if they want to eat next winter." Barry suddenly stopped, as if a forgotten thought had crossed his mind. When he resumed, his tone was more serious. "Say, that reminds me of something I been meanin' to ask you. Someone's gonna have to make a trip to Weatherford for supplies damn soon, and I was kinda hopin' you boys would volunteer for the job. Since you're way ahead of the others, it wouldn't set you back too much, and I'd sure feel easier knowin' it was in good hands."

"Well, it's all right by me, Cap'n. Course, I'll have to talk it over with Allan and Tom. But I got an idea they wouldn't mind turnin' the wolf loose. It's been a long time since they bellied up to a real bar."

"That's the ticket. Talk it over with them today and lemme know tonight. Way I've got it figured, someone's got to leave here within the week." Abruptly his thick brow knotted in a frown, and his face clouded over. "Say, there's something else I meant to tell you about. Not that it's what you'd rightly call good news. Folks have been tryin' to keep it hush-hush, but I got wind of it last night. Seems like Miz Claiborne is in a family way. Rumor is she's about four months gone, which means Ike Claiborne is gonna be jigglin' a half-breed on his knee come next fall. Course, knowin' Ike, he's not above stickin' the little bastard in a towsack and droppin' him in the river."

Britt's eyes narrowed, and he studied Barry intently for a long moment. "Cap'n, I'd purely appreciate it if you'd pass along word that Mary and me would be real proud to have that baby if the Claibornes don't want it." He turned, lifting the reins, and then paused. When his gaze swung around again, it had gone cold as ice. "Just so there won't be no misunderstandin', you might let the right parties know that if that baby ends up in a sack, he's gonna have a lot of company on the trip downstream."

Clucking to the team, Britt popped the reins across

their rumps and drove off toward the gate. Thoroughly
baffled, Barry stared after him in astonishment, wondering how in the name of God a white man could ever hope
to understand what went on inside a nigger's head.

2

Brooks and stream overflowed their banks in a wild ram-
page of rushing water as the snows melted in the craggy
fastness of the Wichita Mountains. The Snow Thaws Moon
had come and gone, and still the angry waters cascaded
down from the foreboding granite palisades. Seated in
his lodge, Santana could hear the roaring turbulence of a
brook which bordered the village, and he idly wondered
when the waters would once again return to their clear,
sparkling beauty. It had been a hard winter, ravaging the
mountains time and again with violent storms, and food
was growing scarce in the camp.

The True People were meat eaters, and many moons
had passed since they last tasted fresh venison or buffalo
liver generously sprinkled with gall. Even thinking of it
made his mouth water, and the husky chief resolved that
within the week he would have the Dog Soldiers organize
the first spring hunt. But for the moment there were more
weighty matters to consider. Reluctantly he wrested his
thoughts from savory visions of a hump roast growing
crisp and succulent over a slow fire.

Little Buffalo would arrive sometime today, and the
village was bustling with excitement and anticipation of
this great event. For the first time in memory one of the
haughty Comanche warlords was lowering himself to visit
a Kiowa camp, and speculation was rife as to the purpose
of this unprecedented honor. Only three days past,
messengers had galloped in from the north to announce
that Little Buffalo was even then departing the Canadian
and would reach the mountain stronghold two suns hence.
While the runners had no knowledge of what lay behind
the Comanche chieftain's visit, they did know that a matter of great consequence was afoot. Surely it must be so,
they had answered Santana's brusque questioning, because
Little Buffalo had sat in counsel with Ten Bears and the
tribal elders almost constantly for the past fortnight.

While curious and thoroughly puzzled as to this strange

turn of events, the elation Santana felt at this moment stemmed from another source entirely. Unlike the Bud Moon of one snow past, there was no contemptuous summons for the Kiowas to appear on the Canadian at an appointed time. Instead, the Comanche dog was coming *here* to parley. And in that simple fact lay a kernel of truth ripe with possibilities.

The arrogant Comanches would never lower themselves in this manner unless they wanted something badly and were willing to pay a stiff price to get it. Something had happened throughout the winter to humble the Comanches, and whatever it was, Santana smelled a situation in which an ambitious man might further his own cause greatly. Though his scheme to humiliate Little Buffalo at the hands of the tejano *Negrito* had surpassed even his wildest expectations, he found it difficult to believe that this alone would prompt such civilized behavior from the barbarian. No, there was something unseen here, a thing yet to be revealed, and he was determined to make the Comanche dog squirm a little while the full truth was being extracted.

Suddenly there was a great clamor from the northern edge of the camp, and within moments the villager's shouts became mingled with the thud of many hooves. Rising slowly, Santana carefully straightened his robe and adjusted the ceremonial headpiece he wore. Waiting until the horsemen and swarming Kiowas came to a halt outside, he drew himself erect and stepped through the lodge entrance with an air of regal hauteur. Before him were some thirty mounted braves, the warlord's personal janissaries, and leading them, seated astride the spotted *ehkasunaro*, was Little Buffalo. Head erect, Santana smiled.

"*Hao,* brother." Little Buffalo broke the strained silence, aware even as he did so that the Kiowa had deftly maneuvered him into a subordinate position.

"*Hao, to-yop-ke.*" Santana smiled crookedly, allowing the merest trace of insolence to creep into his voice. "My lodge is yours. Dismount and let us serve you. While the Kiowa food is humble, I have no doubt that the *to-yop-ke's* words will add spice to the meal."

Little Buffalo's eyes flared briefly, but without a word he slid from the pinto and entered the lodge. After seating themselves around the fire, they spoke obliquely of the winter and the spring thaw, while munching on pemmican and stewed jerky. Santana had not even bothered to kill a dog for the occasion, and the significance of this social oversight was not lost on Little Buffalo. Finally, with the meal finished and the nonsense of the ceremonial pipe out of the way, the two old antagonists got down to business.

Fixing Santana with a stony gaze, the *to-yop-ke* launched into the reason for his presence in a Kiowa lodge. "Brother, the war between the white-eyes grows broader each day. From the east we receive word that there are many battles, each more deadly than any the True People have ever witnessed. With every new battle more of the accursed ones are rubbed out, and there is reason to hope that they might exterminate one another in this strange war they pursue. And while they fight among themselves, they have no time for concern with the lands stolen from our fathers. So it is that the True People are once again handed the opportunity of driving the tejanos from our sacred hunting ground for all time."

"These words you speak are somehow familiar to my ears. Perhaps it is because I heard them even more eloquently stated on the Canadian only a short time ago." The Kiowa's tone was sardonic, laced with derision, and his eyes held firm under Little Buffalo's murderous glare. "Tell me, great *to-yop-ke,* do you *also* receive word from the Brazos?"

The Comanche's copper features blanched, and he struggled to hold his temper in check. Only after a long moment of deathly silence was he able to resume in a composed manner. "You pose a question which has clearly been answered by your own scouts. The tejanos are even now rebuilding their log lodges, and before the snow flies again, all will be as it was before."

"But what of our raid on the Brazos? Ten Bears and the Comanche counsel led us to believe that this great raid would rid us of the white-eyes throughout the tomorrows of our children." Santana's words dripped with scorn, and his tight grin was that of a wolf with its adversary at bay.

"Do not push me too far, Kiowa," Little Buffalo grated. "What the counsel said then is even more true now, and only a *pawsa* would fail to see that we must mount a raid of even greater magnitude in the days to come."

Santana shook his head sadly, as if listening to the tantrums of a small child. "Save your threats for those who would wilt before a strong wind, brother. Even the Comanche *to-yop-ke* would be ill-advised to test Santana's medicine."

Returning Little Buffalo's glowering look, the Kiowa chief contemptuously spat into the fire. "Now let us speak reasonably, with the wisdom our warriors have a right to expect from their leaders. The Brazos raid was an act of foolishness, a salve for the vanity of the Comanche. We burned the tejanos' lodges to the ground and stripped them of their horses, and by your own words all of this has accomplished nothing. Would you mount another great raid so that we might sit here at the next Bud Moon and repeat these same hollow words?"

The *to-yop-ke* stared blankly at Santana with the look of one who has discovered too late that great schemes do not make great men. "I wish only to see the white-eyes rubbed out, and for this reason alone have I come seeking the Kiowas' support."

"Brother, you are a great warrior, and for this I honor you. But do not mock me with deceit. You lower yourself to enter a Kiowa village because the Brazos raid was a failure. And for no other reason! You knew that if you again summoned the Kiowa to the Canadian, you would still be waiting when *Tai-me* called on us all to cross over to the other life."

Little Buffalo remained quiet, unable to refute the Kiowa's devastating logic, and a tense stillness settled over the lodge. Watching him, Santana found that victory had about it the taste of ashes, a bitter, unsavory taste. Rather than gloating, as he had long dreamt of doing, he was curiously filled with compassion for this proud warrior who had been humbled by the shifting winds of fate.

"Hear my words, Little Buffalo. For I too live only to see the tejanos destroyed. But great raids with hundreds of warriors riding under one shield are not the way to save the tomorrows of the True People. Instead, we must strike in small bands in a *hundred different places* on the same day. The tejanos must never know a moment's peace, always fearful of when or where we will strike next. What they build we will burn, and when they rebuild it, we will burn it again. Soon their terror will mount, for we will be as their shadow, waiting only until their backs are turned to strike where least expected. And only in this way, my brother, will you and I live to see the white-eyes rubbed out."

The *to-yop-ke* nodded, staring blankly into the fire, as if the answer somehow lay secreted in the flames. When he spoke, his voice was muted, and his eyes seemed focused on far-away things. "Ten Bears counsels that we no longer fight the white-eyes. His visions reveal that they are as leaves on the trees, and even the strongest medicine known to the True People could never rub out all of them."

"Ten Bears is old and feeble, like a woman," the Kiowa spat. "We must fight to survive, or else the accursed ones will take *all*. Even this wilderness where we now sit is not beneath their greed!"

"What you say is true, brother. And while it pains me to admit it, your words have about them more wisdom than any I have heard on the Canadian." Little Buffalo paused, reflecting for a moment. When he spoke, his voice was firm but resigned. "I will return to the Comanche and counsel them to adopt the cunning of the Kiowa leader."

"Now you begin to touch on the secret, brother. Once you grasp *that,* you will indeed be the *to-yop-ke!*" The Comanche's baffled frown brought the wolfish grin back to Santana's face. "Cunning, brother. Cunning! The kind of cunning the tejano *Negrito* used when he rode alone through the True People's nation. Why else do you suppose I named him Black Fox?"

"Yes, I see your point. The *Negrito* was all you say and more. He was a warrior, like few among us, and before this is over we may wish we had more like him riding at our side."

"Do not trouble yourself with what might be, brother. A power greater than you and I or all the peoples on this earth long ago laid out what would come to pass. Black Fox followed the road that was ordained for him, just as the True People must take the path that has been clear from the start. We were born to live free, as men should, and if a warrior must cross over defending that freedom, then it is a good day to die."

Past differences forgotten, their old animosities cleansed in the harsh glare of truth, the two warriors hunched closer to the fire and began planning for the Leaf Moon raids on the tejanos. Outside, the gentle spring winds whis-

pered in from the south, and the rushing mountain waters
glistened beneath the calm brilliance of a prairie sky.

3

False dawn spread across the land as stars slowly faded
from view overhead. Two wagons stood silhouetted in the
dim light near the front gate, and the jangle of the teams'
harnesses seemed muffled by the damp morning stillness.
Seven men were gathered alongside the lead wagon, and
four hipshot saddle horses stood ground, reined nearby.

Nearly a fortnight had passed since Buck Barry first
mentioned the trip to Weatherford, and supplies in the
fort commissary were running dangerously low. After a
tally of the remaining provisions and a few moments of
deliberation, Barry had sent for Britt the night before and
informed him that the trip could be delayed no longer.
Anxious to see the cabins completed before undertaking
such an extended journey, Britt had put off day by day as
the work progressed on Elm Creek. But the commander's
gruff tone left no room for argument, and after a hurried
conference it was decided that Britt and Tom would leave
for Weatherford at sunrise. Since Allan was more skilled
at carpentry, he was to remain behind and hopefully
would have the cabin interiors finished by the time they
returned.

Now the first shafts of light were spilling over the eastern horizon, and the supply party was about to depart.
Britt and Tom were to drive the wagons, accompanied by
four militiamen, and there was a stir of excitement in the
air. The two homesteaders hadn't been in a real town in
close to two years, and while Weatherford was hardly a
metropolis, the prospect of visiting the bustling Plains community had left them slightly dazzled. For the soldiers the
trip was even more heady. Bored with a year's isolation
in the fort, they looked on the whole affair as something
akin to a Roman holiday, and at the moment they were
the envy of every militiaman in the compound.

With his great shaggy head framed against the distant
sunrise, Buck Barry looked from face to face as he studied
the six men intently. "Boys, I don't have to tell you how
important this mission is to everyone in the fort. We've got
to have enough supplies to carry us over till the first crop,

and we're dependin' on you to get back here with them wagons loaded to the gunnels."

"Cap'n, you jest rest easy." Digging his buddy in the ribs with his elbow, one of the militiamen winked and grinned broadly. "With us along there ain't nothin' gonna go wrong, and we'll be back here quicker'n a cricket dancin' acrost a hot stove."

"Lemme tell you squirrelheads something," Barry rumbled. "I tapped you four to go along 'cause I felt you was the least likely to desert. And don't think you've got me fooled! You swizzleguts are gonna try and drink Weatherford dry in one night, and I knew it before I even picked you. But if you give these men any trouble, I'm givin' them permission to clean your plow right on the spot. Understood?"

The soldiers suddenly became very interested in their boot tops and sheepishly ducked their heads. Barry glared at them for a moment longer, then turned to the two settlers. "Tom, you make sure them storekeepers understand that my requisitions are the same as gold in Austin, and if they give you any argument, be sure and telegraph the governor just like I told you. But even if you have to load them wagons at the point of a gun, I want you back here pronto. Now how long do you think it's gonna take for you to get there and back?"

"Well, Cap'n, I can't rightly say." Fitzpatrick was still the cocky, fiery-tempered Irishman, but over the past year he sobered considerably. Frowning he concentrated on the problem for a moment. "Near as I recollect, it's about seventy miles as the crow flies. Course, we'd do best to follow the Brazos down and cut east at Mineral Wells, so that adds considerable. With any luck at all, though, I calculate we'd make it back in seven, maybe eight days."

"How about it, Britt?" Barry looked at the black man with a trace of skepticism in his eye. "That sound anywhere close to you?"

"Cap'n, since you asked, I'd have to say it don't." Britt glanced at the Irishman with a faint smile, trying to soften his discord. "Gettin' there shouldn't take more'n four days. But these cow ponies aren't built for pullin' heavy loads, and I figure we're gonna have to give 'em a breather every now and then comin' back. Way I see it, you shouldn't look for us back in less than ten days. Course, like Tom says, with luck we might just beat that."

"No, by God, you're right!" Tom nodded in agreement, slightly nettled that these same thoughts hadn't occurred to him. Grinning at the black man, he shook his head with disgust. "Jesus, as many wagons as I've hitched around, you'd think I'd know that saddle horses ain't got the grit of a work team."

"Well, boys, I've never set much store in luck," Barry said, "so I'm gonna top you both and figure twelve days. Besides, it appears to me you forgot to allow time to shop around for horses. You know, next to gettin' those supplies, horses is the thing this settlement is gonna need the most."

Britt and Tom exchanged a quick glance, then turned back as the officer resumed. "Now there's one other thing I want to caution you about." Casting a dark scowl over his shoulder, he froze the four militiamen in their tracks. "And you meatheads better pay particular attention to this. We all know the Injuns are on the loose again, so you're gonna have to be mighty careful. It's been near on a week since Fort Richardson sent word that they're raidin' heavy over that way, and if a man's smart, he's got to figure they've drifted south by now. Lookin' at it dead center, that means there might just be more'n one war party between you and Weatherford."

"Damned if there's any way to figure an Injun!" Fitzpatrick grunted. "Last year they rode through here with half the redsticks God ever created, and now they're back to raidin' with small bunches again. Just goes to show that there ain't nothin' dumber than a stinkin' Injun!"

"Irish, you're ridin' with a man that has good reason to disagree with you on that score." Barry regarded Britt's silent nod of confirmation. "And when it comes to fightin', I'd be the last man to ever underestimate a Comanche."

"Don't forget the Kiowa," Britt added. "Nobody ever saw them carryin' water for the Comanches."

"Damned right!" Barry snorted. "They're both dangerous as hell. And smart. Appears to me like they reared back and looked the situation over and saw real quick that the raid last year just didn't get the job done. Unless I'm way wide of the mark, I'd say we're in for a summer of more goddamn raids than you ever heard tell of. They're gonna hit quick and often, and before a man's got time to thumb the hammer back, they're gonna be off down the road, burnin' some other poor bastard to the ground."

"Well, goddammit, let 'em come!" Tom growled. "I got a few scores to settle with the sonsabitches. There ain't nothin' that'd please me more than to lay my sights down on some of that red hide."

"Trouble is, most of that red hide shoots back." Britt smiled, but his tone was far from amused. "Somehow, I just wish we could get all this fightin' done with so we could start in with the livin'.'"

"Amen to that!" Barry agreed forcefully. "But standin' around gabbin' like a bunch of hens at a church social isn't gonna solve it. Time's awastin', boys! Let's get this show on the road and see how fast you can make it back here with that grub."

Without another word the militiamen mounted hurriedly, glad to be out from under the critical eye of their churlish commander. Britt and Tom scrambled aboard their wagons, and Barry signaled for the gates to be opened. Walking forward to Britt's wagon, the officer extended a ham-sized fist and gave the black man's hand a crunching squeeze.

"Britt, bring 'em back safe. There's a lot of people dependin' on this food. And I don't have to tell you that it won't hurt none to have folks beholden to you for takin' on another risky job they should be doing themselves."

The black man nodded solemnly, filled with pride that Barry would entrust him with this vital undertaking. Then it dawned on him, and he felt like a fool for not having seen it from the start. This great bear of a man had purposely selected him so that the settlers would be even more in his debt! Suddenly he saw the burly officer in a whole new light, and with it came the pleasant awareness that his life was slowly being embraced by the respect and dignity he had always sought. *Yessir, for a nigger in a white man's world he was doing very well indeed!* Grinning widely, he gripped Barry's hand with renewed zest.

"Cap'n, you just set your mind to rest. We'll be back before you even know it." Popping the reins, he sent the horses lurching into the traces. The wagon creaked and groaned as it gained motion, and his laughing voice drifted back over the compound. "Hey, Cap'n! You remember that bulldog we was discussin'? Well, keep a sharp lookout. 'Cause if Weatherford's got anything that even looks like a bulldog, he's gonna be sittin' right here on this seat when we get back!"

Barry's broad jaw twisted in a huge smile as he watched the wagon disappear through the gate. *A bulldog!* Goddamn, if anybody could figure a way to get a bulldog, it was that big black buck with his flashing grin!

Over the distant horizon a flaming orange ball slowly crept skyward as the sentry swung the gates shut. Startled by a shrill, discordant sound he stared open-mouthed as Captain Buck Barry strode across the parade ground, whistling at the top of his lungs.

4

The wagons rumbled across the vast, rolling Plains, moving steadily in a southeasterly direction. For two days they had followed a trail roughly paralleling the Brazos, and gradually the contours of the land had become more defined, lending shape and substance to the earth even from a distance. Buffalo clover and bluebonnets were beginning to bud farther south, and already the prairie grasses were growing lush and green beneath the warm spring sun. They had made good time, pushing the horses at a ground-consuming pace from sunrise to dusk with only a short break for a cold meal at noon.

Thinking about it, Britt saw no reason to revise his original estimate. He still felt confident they would reach Weatherford sometime before sundown on the fourth day. While the horses remained sullen and balky at being hitched to the rattling wagons each morning, they quickly settled into the task and actually moved along at a faster clip than a work team could have sustained. Watching their corded flanks as they strained up a small knoll, Britt silently wished that the caravan's escort was as willing and eager as the horses.

The four militiamen rode bunched like a covey of quail far to the side of the wagons. Unsure of themselves on the open Plains, they preferred to let Britt set the course, even though a blind man could hardly have strayed from the rushing waters of the Brazos. While Britt and Tom were covered with grit from the shuffling hooves of the horses, the soldiers craftily remained upwind, free from the dust and grime of the trail. Glancing at them from the corner of his eye, the black man decided they looked like four schoolboys out on a summer lark. Clowning around with

one another, laughing uproariously at an endless string of
ribald jokes, they seemed concerned with nothing more
than enjoying their respite from Fort Belknap. And getting
to the fleshpots in Weatherford as fast as possible.

Though Britt had only a slight grasp of military tactics,
he was painfully familiar with the ways of Indians, and
with each passing mile his concern had grown. Instead of
riding together, the four men should be scouting ahead
and to the flanks, with one of their number always posted
as rear guard. As it was, they could be ambushed without
warning at any time, with never a chance to corral the
wagons and use them as a barricade. Bunched together,
the militiamen provided a highly tempting target, and in
the event the caravan was bushwhacked, Britt had no
doubt they would go under with the first volley of rifle fire.

Last night he had subtly broached the subject with
Tom, keenly aware that the soldiers would only sullen up
if the suggestion came from a black man. But when Fitzpatrick attempted to discuss it with them that morning,
they jokingly assured him there was nothing to worry
about. *They'd been fightin' Comanches all their lives,
and there was nothin' an Injun respected more than seein'
a bunch of white men formed and ready to fight as a unit!*
Glancing at Britt, Tom had shrugged his shoulders in a
gesture of futility. Short of knocking their heads together,
there was nothing more the Irishman could do, and the
situation remained unchanged.

But Britt was far from content to let it lay, and as the
day progressed, he alternately studied and discarded various means of forcing the militiamen to take their escort
duties a bit more seriously. Mulling the matter over shortly
after their midday break, his concentration was abruptly
shattered as a rider topped a distant hogback and galloped
toward them. Jerking the team to a halt, he grabbed his
rifle and shouted a warning to the four outriders.

Instantly they came alert, nervously milling their
mounts as they attempted to form a line and bring their
weapons to bear. Closing on them at a rapid pace, the
horseman began waving his hat frantically, and within a
matter of moments it became clear that he wore the makeshift garb of the state militia. Britt lowered his rifle and
watched with growing apprehension as the soldier reached
the bottomland near the river and pounded toward them.
No man in his right mind pushed a horse that hard on the

Plains. Not unless he carried bad news or was running from Comanches. Then the rider was upon them, wrenching his horse on its haunches as he came to a halt in a swirling cloud of dust.

"Howdydo, cousins," he greeted them, clapping the battered hat back on his head. "You boys wouldn't by any chance be from Fort Belknap, would ya?"

"Well now, ain't you the smart one!" cracked one of the militiamen. "Friend, we're not only from Fort Belknap, we're doin' our damnedest to get shed of it as fast as these nags'll travel."

"Do tell!" The rider's face twisted in a limpid smirk, and he stared at them for a moment. "I don't recollect hearin' Belknap was that bad. Matter of fact, when you hear what I got to say, you might just get to figurin' it's a regular little oasis."

"Mister, I don't mean to cut you short," Britt spoke up. "But we're a mite pushed for time, and we've got a long ways to go."

"Sambo, I don't remember sayin' nothin' to you. Or maybe you're the *boss* of this outfit." Turning back to the militiamen, he winked. "How about it, cousins? Is Sambo here ramroddin' your desperate little expedition?"

"Soldier, this outfit ain't got no boss." Dismounting from the wagon, Fitzpatrick walked forward, and his pugnacious manner wiped the smirk from the rider's mouth. "Now if you got something to say, spit it out. Otherwise, gig that runt you're ridin' in the ass and be on about your business."

"Mister, if I was you, I'd be more careful about who I started badmouthin'. It just so happens I'm on official business, carryin' dispatches from Fort Richardson to the commander at Fort Belknap."

"Well goody-two-shoes for you," Fitzpatrick replied caustically. "Now that you've impressed us, why don't you just pony up the good news, and we'll be on our way."

"Good news! Sodbuster, you're in for a real surprise." The courier patted the pouch strapped to his belt and snickered. "You know what's in here? Just a little scrap of paper sayin' some Yankee general name of Grant has whupped the shit out of the Confederates at a place called Shiloh. That's all!"

There was a moment of stunned silence from the supply party as they digested the courier's announcement. Then the militiamen began mumbling among themselves uncertain as to how this defeat would affect their status at Fort Belknap. But the war was like some distant impersonal calamity, a tragedy from history that had befallen those unfortunate enough to be in the wrong place at the wrong time. Like an earthquake or a tornado. And besides, who the hell ever heard of a place called Shiloh? Still, the news was sobering, and for a terrible instant the war suddenly seemed much too close for comfort.

"Say, you boys wouldn't have any drinkin' whiskey, would ya?" The rider's nasal twang now seemed like the grating of an iron file. "Cousins, I'm here to tell ya I haven't swallowed anything 'cept spit since yesterday mornin'."

Still absorbed with their own thoughts, the others seemed disinclined to answer, and Britt finally spoke up. "No, we been drinkin' river water for two days. Captain Barry sent us to Weatherford to get supplies."

"Just my luck," the courier grumbled. Glancing around the solemn faces, he suddenly brightened. "Hell, boys, don't let it get you down. It's only a war. And it ain't over yet. Not by a damn sight!" Then his squinched, ferret eyes took on a superior look, and his tone was that of a gossipy old crone. "But I'll let you in on a little secret, cousins. Hard times is comin'. The tide's turned, and 'fore long there's gonna be lots of rebs swearin' they never heard tell of Dixie or the bonny blue flag.'"

"What about Indians?" Britt inquired quietly. "We heard they've been raidin' pretty heavy over around Fort Richardson."

"Goddamn, Sambo, don't you talk to me about Injuns. I seen enough of 'em to last me two lifetimes. They been burnin' and scalpin' over our way like there ain't no tomorrow. And everything I seen since I left the fort says real plain they're movin' south and west 'bout as fast as them stump-legged ponies they ride will carry 'em."

"Comanche or Kiowa?" Britt asked.

"Hell, who knows." The courier spit and sent a skittish glance around the skyline as if the subject had somehow touched an exposed nerve. "Bastards all look alike to me. Never could tell one from another."

"Seems like I've heard some folks say that about niggers." Britt's voice was sardonic, and there wasn't a hint of a smile on his face.

"Yeah, well, I'll tell you how it is, Sambo." The courier's eyes flicked nervously around the group, and he somehow had the feeling it was time to move on. "Between here and Weatherford you might see a shitpot full of Injuns, and on the other hand, you might not see nothin'. But if I was you, I'd sleep awful light.". He paused for a moment, then his thin, weasel face broke out in a crooked grin. "Well, cousins, guess I better shag it. All them folks at Belknap must be pinin' away for a bit of *good news,* and we sure don't wanna keep 'em waitin'.".

Lifting his hat in mock salute, he swatted his horse across the flanks and galloped west along the river trail. Silently they watched until he disappeared over a rise, and the air suddenly seemed strained, fraught with some unseen danger. The militiamen's levity had vanished as abruptly as the courier, and the four men looked at one another with a tense wariness that had not been present before. Britt clucked to the team and headed the wagon once more in a southeasterly direction. Grinning to himself, he felt a twitch of perverse amusement as he observed the militiamen separate and take up scouting positions at the four points of the compass.

5

Dusk had fallen as the supply party prepared to make camp for the night in a grove of cottonwoods along the Brazos. The militiamen were still edgy, nervously peering over their shoulders and jumping at the slightest sound from the deepening twilight. Their jocular banter of the last two days had dwindled to a strained watchfulness, as if they had suddenly decided that this escort detail wasn't just a simple lark after all. Britt suggested they make a cold camp, pointedly adding that a fire might easily attract the attention of any hostiles in the vicinity. The four soldiers merely grunted in agreement and continued scanning the darkening shadows for any sign of the dreaded Comanches.

When the horses had been picketed, they consumed a hasty supper of jerky and hardtack, foregoing even the small comfort of an afterdinner pipe. The flare of a sulphurhead might just be their undoing, and as they were each well aware, the scent of smoke carried far on the soft night breezes. Afterward, they spread their bedrolls near the wagons and settled down for a sleepless night. Staring into the inky stillness, filled with a sense of their own vulnerability, they wondered what, if anything, lurked beyond the fringe of darkness.

Britt had volunteered to stand the first watch, and after tossing fretfully in his blankets for a short time, Tom decided to keep him company. Seated on the ground, with their backs propped against a cottonwood, they listened to the unseen sounds of night and conversed in low tones.

"Did you notice how them soldier boys changed their tune?" Tom chuckled silently. "Damned if they ain't moppin' around like a bunch of shoat pigs that just paid a visit to the cuttin' pen."

"They got good reason," Britt observed quietly. "Indians don't like nothin' better than to leave a white man with a stump instead of a tallywhacker. Maybe if we can keep 'em scared, they'll guard these wagons like they should of from the start."

"What did you make of that courier? Reckon things are as bad as he painted 'em to be?"

"Wouldn't surprise me none if they was worse," Britt said with easy confidence. "Allan's daddy always said nobody but a fool would start a fight with them Northerners, and I got an idea we're gonna see that old man's words come true with a vengeance."

"Well, I ain't much for the tellin' the future, but it sure enough looks like he was right." Tom grew silent for a moment, pursuing some elusive thought. The rustling of the leaves overhead was distracting, but after a time the right words finally came to him. "Course, if the Yankees were to win, that'd shore make life easier for the colored folks. What I'm tryin' to say is that there wouldn't be no more slaves then. See what I mean? *Everybody'd be free.*"

"Yeah, they'd be free all right," Britt rasped. "But bein' free is one thing, and havin' white folks treat you like a human being is somethin' else again."

There was a long silence as Tom pondered the black man's words, and Britt sensed that he was tussling with some hidden conflict within himself. After a while the Irishman sighed heavily and stared off into the night. "You know, sometimes I get real stumped thinkin' about you and me. I was reared up in a neck of the woods where colored folks wasn't no more than a good mule, and a white man just naturally knew he was better'n the blacks. I mean, it was like the arithmetic you learned in school. Two and two made four, and there wasn't no way of disputin' a simple fact. That's the way things had always been, and there wasn't nothin' on God's green earth gonna change it."

He broke off and the silence deepened again as he struggled to find just the right words for the thoughts crowding his mind. "Now you come along and knock a hole in everything I was taught. I may be a thickheaded mick, like Captain Barry says, but I ain't no damn fool. Ever day I see ways you're smarter'n me. Like figurin' how long this trip would take. We both stood off and looked at the same thing, but you saw somethin' in it I didn't. It's like that two and two business. There just ain't no way of disputin' a simple fact. And to put the frostin' on the cake, I finally come around to seein' that you're the first *real* friend I ever had." He paused, mulling over the deeper implications of his words. "It sorta puts a man to thinkin'. Maybe lots of things we was taught ain't the way it really is. Leastways, it ain't the way it should be."

"Should be and *is* don't always turn out to be the same thing." Britt glanced at the Irishman and shook his head ruefully. "Maybe we're tryin' to do something that nature never meant to happen. Just for instance, have you ever noticed that animals only mix with their own kind? When did you ever see a buffalo chummin' around with deer or cows takin' up with horses?" Abruptly he snorted with disgust.

"Christ, that sounds like somethin' old Sam Ledbetter would say. It's a puzzle for a fact. When I stop and think about it, I'm not real sure I understand the way things should be either. But I do know that people are smarter'n animals, and damned if it don't seem like we oughta be able to figure out some way to live together."

They both pondered the problem for a moment, then the black man resumed on a brighter note. "You know, it's not like it's never been done before. Just look at us. I got you and Allan for friends and maybe even a few more. Stop and think what it'd be like if every nigger on this earth had two white men for friends. Why, in no time at all people'd forget about black and white and just get down to the business of livin' and let live."

"See, that's what I meant!" Tom's voice was filled with

mild awe. "Jesus, a notion like that wouldn't of come into my head if I'd live to be a hundred."

"Maybe a man's gotta spend his life with his face squashed down in the muck before he gets thoughts like that."

"Could be. I can't rightly say. But I'll tell you one thing, Britt. You're wrong about people. I've seen my share and more, and some of 'em are double wolf for guts and savvy. But most of 'em are just plain assholes."

Britt chuckled quietly. "You won't get no argument on that."

Tom smiled, suddenly filled with a sense of well-being, and glad that he had this soft-spoken black man as his friend. Then he thought back to the day Britt had returned his son to the fort, and with the thought came a nagging question that had bothered him ever since. Reluctant to pry, he regarded the dim outline of his friend's face for a moment, then blurted it out.

"You know, there's somethin' that's had me in a quandary ever since you come back to the fort. Now I know it's none of my business, and if you feel like it, just tell me to shut my damn-fool mouth. But it'd purely settle my mind if I was to know the answer." Faltering, he felt the black man's eyes even in the dark and fumbled for the right words. "Well, goddammit, there just ain't no other way to say it. Captain Barry the same as told us you was meanin' to join up with the Injuns, and I'd just like to know why you didn't."

Britt stared at him for a long while, almost as if he were searching for a way to explain something that he himself had never fully understood. Finally, just when Tom had decided that the black man didn't intend to answer, Britt spoke up in a voice that was somehow eerie and illusive, like a risen ghost from a man's distant past.

"I guess that's what I really meant when I was talkin' about how animals stick with their own kind. Right or wrong, the whites are travelin' the road I want my kids to take. Maybe it's like the sparrow tryin' to join up with the hawks, I don't know. The way things are today, the white folks think the black man's the wrong color to fit in, and maybe there's nothin' that'll ever change their minds. But a man's got to have faith, otherwise he's no different than things that never learned to walk on their hind legs. And somewhere along the line he's got to have enough belief

in his faith to make a start. I suppose that's what it all
boils down to. Faith and belief that people really can
change. Maybe not today or even next year but sometime.
Sometime soon."

Tom stared at him, dumbstruck. He knew all about
faith in the Good Book, and the kind of faith the fire and
brimstone preachers ranted about. But this was something
different. A faith in man's essential goodness. And that
was a thing he had never even considered, much less
credited to the shiftless, scheming blood-suckers he had
known all his life. Watching Britt, he hoped that things
could change, that men somehow could rise above the
hateful ways they had been taught. But just in the event
they couldn't, he silently resolved to beat the shit out of
anyone who even looked like they were going to give the
black man a hard time.

6

Early in the afternoon, with the sun directly overhead,
the supply detail halted at a tree-fringed clearing to water
the animals and wolf down a quick meal. This was their
third day on the trail, and without voicing it, each man
felt the urgency of reaching Weatherford as rapidly as
possible. Their chance meeting with the courier had occurred only yesterday, but his words lingered on. The
warning was clear, and it had brought home the highly
dangerous nature of a mission they had undertaken so
lightly. Roving across the countryside were bands of hostiles who would like nothing better than to catch six men
exposed and helpless on the open Plains. Captain Barry's
terse warning had now become very real and threatening,
and not a man among them doubted the menace they
faced. While the likelihood of stumbling across a war
party in this vast land was remote, many a man had sacrificed his life needlessly by scorning the capricious bitch
called fate.

And right now their only thought was to reach the sanctuary of an organized settlement, just as fast as their
horses could be pushed.

With any luck they should hit Mineral Wells tonight,
and by the following evening sight Weatherford. But they
still faced close to forty miles of exposed prairie, and since

dawn there had been few smiles and even less conversation among the six men.

The day had been unseasonably warm, and the four militiamen appeared drowsy and somewhat fatigued. The tension curdled in their guts, along with a sleepless night, had drained their spirits and left them sapped of energy. Dismounting, they led their horses to the riverbank, then began splashing their own faces with the cool, invigorating waters of the Brazos.

Britt and Tom drove the wagons directly to the water's edge and let the horses begin swizzling greedily. They had no intention of unhitching the teams and allowing them to graze as they had done the last few days. This was to be a brief stop, limited to the essentials of watering and a few mouthfuls of food, and afterward they would again take to the trail with the utmost speed.

Britt jumped from the wagon and walked a few paces upstream. Kneeling, he dipped his hands in the rushing stream and brought them up to his parched lips. Sloshing the water around in his mouth, he felt the dust and grit loosen its hold on his throat and spat with an immense feeling of relief. Tom had hunkered down beside him and was noisily sloshing water over his entire head. Spewing and sputtering like a red-thatched whale, he then leaned forward and thrust his face into the cooling waters. Watching him, it occurred to Britt that the Irishman was really an overgrown boy, taking his pleasures from the simple things of life, as carefree as a yearling colt in a field of clover. Maybe they hadn't hit it off at first, but Tom had become a good friend, as good as any Britt had. And the black man somehow felt deeply grateful that this thickheaded mick had come over to his camp at last.

Suddenly Britt tensed, alert to some unseen danger. Instinctively wary and somewhat puzzled as to the cause, he glanced around the shaded glen. Something wasn't right, but as his eyes darted around the clearing, everything appeared calm and still. Maybe too still. Then the horses spooked, their eyes wide with fright. Rearing away from the water, they scrambled backward, jackknifing the wagons wheel to wheel in a splintering crash.

Springing toward the horses, the black man caught a glint of movement from the corner of his eye and halted in midstride. Looking downstream he saw one of the militiamen lurch forward with an arrow protruding from his chest. Grunting with pain, the soldier grasped the shaft with both hands, staring in horror as the blood gushed down over his arms. Then he pitched face down in the water and floated off with the current.

Stunned by the suddenness of the attack, the men seemed frozen in their tracks as they watched the soldier die. Before they could react, the trees on the opposite side of the stream exploded with gunfire and a shower of arrows. The horses screamed and reared, digging furiously with their hooves as they whirled up the slight incline leading to the bank. Desperately the militiamen fought to control their mounts, clutching the reins tightly in a vain effort to stop the horses from stampeding. Clawing pistols from their holsters, the soldiers jerked at the reins while firing blindly at the trees across the river. But the plunging horses spoiled their aim, and the slugs harmlessly kicked up geysers of water in midstream.

While the militiamen cursed their horses and thumbed off shots at an unseen enemy, Britt and Tom sprinted forward in a running crouch and dove headlong under the nearest wagon. Though terrified and still fighting at the traces, the two teams were unable to move as the rear wheels of both wagons were now locked in a grinding embrace. Slithering on their bellies, the men crawled to a position between the wagons and jerked their six-guns. Peering through the spokes of the wheels, their gaze swept back to the riverbank just in time to see the soldiers play out the final act in futile courage.

Realizing too late that they couldn't save both themselves and their mounts, the three militiamen released the horses and began backing toward the wagons. Britt and Tom watched helplessly as the men advanced step by step, firing bravely as they moved in a huddled bunch across the open ground. Then the opposite treeline erupted in a fusillade of rifle fire and gleaming feathered shafts, raking the clearing with an invisible hail of death. The three men spun backward, their clothes pocked by the dusty spurts of lead, arrows jutting cruelly from their torn bodies. As if a giant scythe had swept over a field of wheat, the men fell before the bloody storm and pitched to the ground.

Britt stared at the shattered bodies in an agonized trance, unable to believe that four men had been brought to death in only a matter of moments. Somehow it didn't

seem real, as if he were merely a spectator at some grim
ritual that would abruptly end with a burst of applause.
Every muscle in his body strained as he waited for the
men to rise, willed them to stand again. But their lifeless
forms lay unmoving, crumpled in the impersonal savagery of death, and he knew then that it was absolute.
Blinking, his senses slowly returned and he became aware
of Tom's hoarse muttering beside him.

The Irishman's eyes were wild with rage, bulging from
their sockets, shot through with red, swollen veins. From
his throat came a dry, deathlike rattle as his lips moved
soundlessly, and his face was contorted with the horror
of a man who has looked into the pits of hell and come
away demented. Leaping to his feet, he scrambled from
the ground, clawing his way up the side of the wagon,
screaming with crazed, maddened fury.

*"You murderin' sonsabitches! Come on out and fight
like men! Where are you? Stand up and fight, you yellow
bastards!"*

Startled by the Irishman's frenzied actions, Britt
moved too late to drag him from atop the wagon. The
crack of a single rifle shot split the air, and Tom staggered, mortally wounded. Slowly he fell away from the
wheel and dropped between the wagons in a sodden
lump.

Britt grabbed his shirt and dragged him underneath
the wagon, searching frantically for some sign of life. The
Irishman's breathing was labored and shallow, and a
dark, crimson blotch covered his chest. Working feverishly, the black man ripped his shirt open and stared
sickenly as a small, neat hole beneath the breastbone
pumped a bright fountain of blood. Tearing a strip from
the shirt, he jammed it against the wound, trying desperately to staunch the bubbling hole. But even as he
did so, he knew that Tom was dying. Numb with grief, he
stared on helplessly as the Irishman's life spurted out beneath his hand.

Then Tom's eyes slowly opened and focused on the
black man with glazed brightness. His arm raised ever
so gradually, as if he had all the time in the world, and
his rough, thorny hand clasped Britt gently around the
neck. "I wish I'd been born a nigger. Couldn't we've had
fun?"

He chuckled, as though the thought pleased him greatly,

and a thin trickle of blood seeped from his lips. Then he closed his eyes and died.

Britt stared vacantly at his dead friend, overcome with a shuddering sense of loss. Tears streamed down his face, and his breath came in great, sobbing gasps, as if a steel band was constricting ever tighter around his chest. The pallor of death had settled over the Irishman's features, but his mouth was frozen in a gentle smile, and Britt unconsciously found himself returning the smile. Tom had greeted death with the same cocky, devilishness with which he had faced life, and the black man somehow felt proud that he had passed over with his swaggering spirit intact. Still, his own life was diminished beyond measure by his comrade's abrupt end, and a sour bile swelled in his throat as he once again heard the Irishman's jaunty words. *Couldn't we've had fun?*

Bit by bit, Britt's mind emerged from the brutal funk of his despair, and he slowly became aware that a deep, unnatural stillness had settled over the clearing. There was something abnormal and strangely eerie about the silence, as though the ghosts of the dead had taken with them every creature and sound from the grove of cottonwoods. Crawling forward to the front of the wagon, he cautiously scanned the riverbank. Then his eyes were drawn to the opposite shore, and he sucked in his breath with the wheezing gasp of a man who had been kicked in the pit of the stomach.

Crowding the far bank, eleven Kiowas sat mounted on ponies, their war paint and garishly decorated shields glistening in the bright spring sun. Motionless, they waited in the deepening silence, staring with grim, patient eyes at the wagons. Britt's startled gaze darted from face to face, recognizing each in turn as warriors from Santana's village. Then he grunted with shock as his eyes locked incredulously on the stern, tight-lipped visage he remembered so well. *Running Dog!*

Cursing beneath his breath, he damned the gods, *Tai-me* and Jehovah alike, for amusing themselves with a deadly little game between mere mortals. Wherever they sat in judgment, it must be a festive day indeed, for what better sport than to pit brother against brother in the ultimate test? How very fickle they were with men's lives, lookiing on with detached smiles as they snuffed out a man like a mindless child squashing a beetle. *What a joke! A filthy, rotten, bastardly joke that could have only one end.*

Crawling from beneath the wagon, Britt stepped a few paces into the clearing, vaguely aware that he still clutched the Colt in his right hand. Holstering the pistol, he faced the Kiowas and waited for some sign of how this thing was to be done. Their features were cold, remote, as if they were observing a white-eye who by some quirk of fate happened to be black. Their manner made it clear that no quarter would be granted, and Britt smiled thinly in admiration. They were the Kiowa, the True People, and he really hadn't expected any less.

Then the black man raised his arm in salute. *"Hao*, Running Dog! It appears that *Tai-me* sees fit to bring us together one last time."

The Kiowa regarded him stoically, but beneath the dull sheen of his eyes there was an infinite sadness. Within him coursed the bittersweet sense of pride and dismal sorrow. How fine and brave Black Fox looked standing there! Straight and tall, alone but unafraid, flaunting his courage as a warrior should when he crossed over. Somewhere on the other side they would meet again, and *Tai-me* in his wisdom would at last allow all men to walk side by side in peace.

"Make your fight, brother," Running Dog ordered. "It is a good day to die!"

Understandingly, Britt nodded, certain now that Running Dog had instructed the other warriors on how it was to be. The Kiowa meant for Britt to kill him so that they might cross over together. And only after the black man's shot had struck home were the remaining warriors to open fire.

Drawing his Colt, Britt raised the pistol and sighted on Running Dog. Then with an imperceptible movement of his wrist he lowered the sights and fired. The slug kicked up a spurt of sand at the hooves of Running Dog's pony, and in that same instant came the whispered twang of a bow string.

The black man lurched backward, his chest pierced by the feathered shaft, and slowly sank to his knees. Running Dog looked on without expression, more proud than ever that Black Fox had ridden with him as a brother. Yet while he was unwilling to be the instrument of the black man's death, he was equally unable to halt the inevitable.

Gritting his teeth, Britt fought against the swirling darkness of pain and willed himself to stand erect. Thrusting the Colt to arm's length, he steadied himself and fired blindly into space. With the report of the pistol a rifle exploded on the opposite bank, and a puff of dust leaped from his shirt front. He staggered, releasing his grip on the gun, and like a giant tree torn from its roots, toppled to the earth.

Silence once more settled over the clearing, and the Kiowa braves watched impassively to see if Black Fox would rise again. But it was over, and there was no need for further waiting. Running Dog gave the signal, and the warriors kneed their ponies into the water, whooping shrill war cries of victory as they splashed across the river. Leaping from the ponies, they swarmed around Tom and the fallen soldiers, their scalping knives glinting in the shining rays of the sun.

Running Dog slid to the ground and stood for a moment looking down on Britt. Kneeling, he jerked the arrow free and gathered the black man in his arms. Struggling under the weight, he carried the body to the riverbank, near a clump of trees. Lowering the great frame gently, he propped the black man against a towering cottonwood. Working swiftly, he tugged and pulled until he had the body sitting in an upright position, carefully arranging it so that it wouldn't fall over. Walking back to the wagon, he collected Britt's rifle and returned to the tree. Checking to make sure the gun was loaded, he placed it across the black man's lap, then stood back to observe his handiwork.

Approaching, one of the braves grinned broadly, displaying a curly, burnished gold scalp. Running Dog ignored the gory trophy, and sensing his mood, the warrior's grin vanished. Looking at the body, he studied it solemnly for a moment, then glanced back at Running Dog. Nodding his approval, he grunted with deep respect. "Only the earth endures forever, brother. Black Fox died a good death."

"*Waugh!* He was a warrior!" Running Dog grated. "And there are not many of us left."

Having bestowed the final epitaph on his friend, Running Dog abruptly strode to his pony and mounted. This was the signal for the braves to have done with scalping and plunder, and within moments he led the war party back across the stream. Halting on the opposite bank, he wheeled his pony and stared back at the body for a moment. Then his arm raised in salute, and his voice boomed proudly across the glen. *"Hao, Black Fox!"*

The sun rippled fleetingly on the shining water, and the man called Britt Johnson gazed peacefully upon the tranquil solitude of the cottonwood grove.

Black Fox had crossed over at last.

ZANE GREY'S
GREAT WESTERNS

_____ 80451 ARIZONA AMES $1.50

_____ 81434 BOULDER DAM $1.50

_____ 81326 FORLORN RIVER $1.50

_____ 81017 KNIGHTS OF THE RANGE $1.50

_____ 81136 LIGHT OF WESTERN STARS $1.50

_____ 81321 LONE STAR RANGER $1.50

_____ 81325 LOST PUEBLO $1.50

_____ 81275 MAN OF THE FOREST $1.50

_____ 80454 MYSTERIOUS RIDER $1.50

_____ 80453 RAINBOW TRAIL $1.50

_____ 81374 ROBBERS' ROOST $1.50

Available at bookstores everywhere, or order direct from publisher.   ZGA

ZANE GREY'S

GREAT WESTERNS

_____ 81228 SHADOW ON THE TRAIL $1.50

_____ 80522 SUNSET PASS $1.50

_____ 81322 TRAIL DRIVER $1.50

_____ 80701 TO THE LAST MAN $1.50

_____ 80447 TWIN SOMBREROS $1.50

_____ 80456 U.P. TRAIL $1.50

_____ 80450 VALLEY OF WILD HORSES $1.50

_____ 80728 WEST OF THE PECOS $1.50

_____ 80523 WESTERN UNION $1.50

_____ 81323 WILDERNESS TREK $1.50

_____ 80317 WILDFIRE! $1.50

Available at bookstores everywhere, or order direct from publisher.   ZGB

POCKET BOOKS
Department ZG B
1230 Avenue of the Americas
New York, N.Y. 10020

Please send me the books I have checked above. I am enclosing
$ _____ (please add 50¢ to cover postage and handling). Send check
or money order—no cash or C.O.D.'s please.

NAME_____

ADDRESS_____

CITY_____STATE/ZIP_____

ZG B

POCKET BOOKS